T0155071

Other books in this collection:

Falling In Love... Again
When Love Goes Bad
Losing It For Love

FORBIDDEN
LOVE

TALES OF RISKY CHOICES, IRRESISTIBLE PASSION AND TEMPTATION

The timeless love stories from
True Romance and True Love live on.

Edited by Barbara Weller,
Cynthia Cleveland and Nancy Cushing-Jones

A BROADLIT BOOK

BroadLit

June 2012

Published by

BroadLit ®
14011 Ventura Blvd.
Suite 206 E
Sherman Oaks, CA 91423

ISBN 978-0-9855404-8-7

Produced in the United States of America.

*This collection is dedicated to all of you who are
looking for true love or have already found it.*

FORBIDDEN
LOVE

TALES OF RISKY CHOICES, IRRESISTIBLE PASSION AND TEMPTATION

Table Of Contents

Introduction 13

FROM ONE-NIGHT STAND—TO INDECENT OBSESSION
He tasted my body once—and he'll stop at nothing for more 15

I MARRIED MY SPERM DONOR DAD 43

INNOCENCE LOST: *Too young to save myself* 61

MY HIGH SCHOOL AFFAIR 77
Will We Live Happily Ever After?

I'M STANDING BY MY RAPIST HUSBAND 99
Even his prison sentence cannot dim the light of our love

I'M A GOOD GIRL GONE BAD 119
I couldn't keep my panties on, and now I pay the price every single day

THE TRUTH HURTS! 137
Why do I destroy the people I love most?

WE SAW A MURDER AND DID NOTHING 161
It changed our affair forever

NAUGHTY ORGASMS WITH MY EX 175
They're getting me in hot water!

HIS MISTRESS IS BI– AND SO AM I! 197

KISS, DON'T TELL 217
Keeping my affair from him was the right thing to do

MOM'S BOYFRIEND TOOK MY VIRGINITY 239
I dangled my goods in his face so he'd make me feel like a woman

Introduction

No one is immune to the temptation of forbidden love.

Many of us merely dip our baby toe into this realm -- perhaps by Googling the names of old lovers to see what they look like now, years later, while our spouse watches television in another room. Or we spy on an alluring married co-worker by studying his Facebook page to learn as much as we can about him. Or we create detailed fantasies about someone who is definitely off-limits for one reason or another.

However, the sexually adventurous characters in these tantalizing stories have plunged much deeper into the web of forbidden love, making the rest of us look like pikers. Why have sex with just your husband when you can also have it with his best friend – or even his mistress? You'll read about preachers who provide solace of the sexual kind and babysitters who look after more than just your children. Some of the sexual partners in these stories are illicit soul-mates – and some are selfish psychos. Who knew there was so much forbidden love to be had?

But what pushes someone from merely thinking about forbidden love to actually engaging in it? Boredom or loneliness, of course. Sometimes it's motivated by a desire for revenge or by a streak of rebellion or a bout of feeling really low. Most often, though, a palpable carnal chemistry that ultimately proves irresistible can overwhelm even the most prudent among us with a breathtaking swiftness.

This much is true about forbidden love: It is never boring. Unlike true love, it ultimately forces you to face the question: Is it worth it? And while forbidden love almost always comes with an expiration date, there are exquisitely rare occasions where it actually morphs into true love.

The stories in this collection let us venture deeply into the libidinous world of forbidden love – all while never leaving the comfort of our own lives. Sit back and succumb to its pleasures.

FROM ONE-NIGHT STAND—TO INDECENT OBSESSION
He tasted my body once—
and he'll stop at nothing for more

I don't even remember what I was feeling when I drove to work that Thursday morning. A little depressed, probably. Bored with reading romance novels, where wonderful, exciting things happened to everyone but me.

Most of all I was lonely. I missed Frank, and I was frightened. With each passing day, I felt us growing further and further apart, and it seemed that there was nothing I could do to stop the process.

What would life be like without him? In just two months, we'd be married five years. I couldn't even remember what it'd been like before we met.

Unlike my best friend, Angela, I hadn't fallen in love during my teenage years. I'd gone to college first and completed my Associate's degree. My feet were firmly planted on the ground when Frank Connor moved into the apartment across the hall from mine.

We started out speaking when we met in the hallway, and slowly worked our way up to borrowing things from each other. Over that first year, our friendship grew into love, and the following spring, we were married in a small ceremony at my family's church.

Frank and I honeymooned at a romantic little cottage overlooking a secluded, mountain lake. He was tender and loving, and my wedding night was everything I'd ever dreamed it might be.

I woke early that first morning and slipped quietly out of bed to sit, wrapped in a warm robe on the window seat, and watch my husband sleep. His dark hair was mussed, and I reached over to trace with my fingertips the tiny lines at the corners of his eyes, etched there from years of working hard at the outdoor jobs he loved. His broad shoulders were relaxed, one hand curled on the pillow; his lips were parted slightly in sleep.

My heart ached with love. I knew beyond any shadow of a doubt that I'd found my partner for life.

"What happened to us, Frank?" I murmured as I wove my way through the traffic, driving to the offices of the Steadman Insurance Company, where I worked. "When did you stop caring?"

Our first year together, we could hardly wait to come home to each other in the evenings. We grew comfortable together; I dreamed about buying a house and starting a family. But Frank wanted to wait.

Then, during our second year of marriage, Frank received a promotion at work with a sizable salary increase. Unfortunately, his new position required that he spend a lot of time out of town, traveling on business.

"We're building a foundation, Mariska," he said. "Let's make certain that our future is secure, and then build our lives on that."

As impossible as it seemed now, three more years had slipped past. Frank had become totally involved in his work, and he never even mentioned children anymore. Pride wouldn't let me beg him.

I kept quiet about other things, too. Like the way Frank never noticed when I had my hair highlighted, or bought a sexy new nightgown. I felt as though I held second place in his life, and I grew lonelier with each passing day.

Still, as low as my spirits were, I felt something in the office atmosphere that morning, as soon as I walked onto the floor.

"What's up?" I asked Angela. She'd been my best friend ever since I'd come to work here, right out of college.

"I don't know all the details yet," she said, pouring me a cup of coffee, "but rumor has it that we're getting a hot, new salesman from

Chicago. He's single, with a penchant for fine wine and sports cars!"

About ten that morning, Jared Beacon strolled through the claims department with Mr. Steadman, himself. Jared was tall, dark, handsome, and tanned, with a demeanor that exuded self-confidence. The room practically throbbed with the collective heartbeats of single women as he passed through—and a few married ones, as well, I suspect.

Still, Jared was all business, listening attentively to Mr. Steadman's introduction to the company. But just as he started to get on the elevator to go back to the executive suite, something totally unexpected happened. Jared turned and our eyes met.

Time after time in those romance novels I'd read, the meeting between the hero and heroine had been described as "electric." Sparks flew, bodies tingled, or lightning bolts split the atmosphere. Well, it had never been that way with Frank, so I'd always believed this was just a device used by the authors to make their stories more titillating.

But when Jared Beacon looked at me that day, I experienced everything I'd ever read about. Sparks, tingles, and lightning bolts shot though me, one right after the other.

I caught my breath and forced my eyes back to the work on my desk. Surely, I'd been mistaken. Even if I weren't, the man surely wouldn't play any part in my life. My job held no prestige, and my looks were not stunning, by any means. Jared Beacon had simply provided me with a few moments of excitement. A stirring of emotions long dormant. Nothing more.

Which goes to show just how mistaken we can be.

The following morning, I stepped into the elevator and pushed the button for my floor. At the last second, a man's hand grabbed the closing doors, causing them to spring back open.

"Hello," Jared said. He stood there, smiling. As his eyes took in my every feature, I could feel a flush spreading over my face.

Finally, he stepped into the elevator and allowed the doors to close behind him.

"I haven't had the pleasure," he said.

"I . . . I'm Mariska Connor." My words came out in a hoarse whisper.

To my horror, it occurred to me that Jared might think I was trying to sound sexy. I cleared my throat quickly to dispel that illusion.

"Jared Beacon," he said, extending his hand.

"Yes, I know." I spoke too quickly, and my face flamed anew. What was wrong with me? I hadn't acted so immaturely since high school!

Halfway to our floor, Jared reached over and stopped the elevator. My eyes widened in surprise.

"You can't do that," I said.

Jared smiled. "I already did. But don't worry—it's only for a minute. I'd just like to ask a favor."

"A favor? Of me?"

"Yes. Are you free for lunch? My treat?"

I was both flattered and curious all at once. "Well, yes—I mean—I—I suppose I could," I stammered awkwardly, blushing a deep, miserable shade of crimson red. "But—where—"

Jared returned the elevator to motion; it hummed as it whirred back into gear. "Meet me outside by the fountain at noon sharp."

As we walked onto my floor, I felt Jared's hand briefly touch my back as he passed me by. That simple gesture left me with a warm feeling which lasted half the morning.

"So? How did it taste?" Angela asked.

I looked at her blankly. "What?"

"You look like the cat that swallowed the canary. What's going on? Give."

I laughed, glancing around to make certain that we were alone in the break room. "Actually," I told her, "I don't *know* what's going on. Jared Beacon has asked me to lunch."

"*What?*" Angela shrieked.

I nodded anxiously. "He says he wants to ask me a favor."

Angela's eyes narrowed. "What *kind* of favor?"

I shook my head. "I don't have a clue. I *swear*. But I'm *dying* to find out. Anyway, can you cover for me—just in case I'm late getting back?"

"No problem," she said. "But you have to *promise* not to keep any secrets from me!"

I laughed. "I promise," I told her, raising my hand in a scout's oath.

As I rode the elevator downstairs at noon, I wondered why Jared hadn't asked Angela out instead of me. Angela's husband had walked out on her two years earlier. She had a dark, haunting beauty about her, and if Jared was looking for a date, the two sons she was raising alone shouldn't have been any more of an obstacle to him than my husband would present.

Jared had parked his little red sports car by the curb out front. I got in, and as we sped away, I leaned my head back for a moment against the soft headrest and breathed in the aromas of new leather and aftershave. Angela and I usually ate in the company lunchroom, and it felt wonderful just to get out of the building for a change.

"Where are we going?" I asked, glancing at my watch.

"Maria's," Jared said. "Do you know the place?"

Did I ever! Maria's was one of the finest restaurants in our area. Frank had taken me there once, on our anniversary.

"Yes," I told him, "but I only have an hour."

"They're expecting us. I've taken the liberty of selecting the wine in advance. I hope you don't mind."

At Maria's, a hostess in period costume led us through the dimly lit interior to a table beneath a spiral staircase. Rich woods polished to a high sheen reflected the glow of candlelight; original prints of horses and carriages hung on the walls.

"Jared," I said as soon as we were seated, "I—I can't help feeling as though you've made some kind of mistake. I'm—"

"Married," he finished for me. "Actually, that's one of the reasons I decided to go through with this. Very few people are available for platonic, male/female relationships nowadays."

I can't say whether I was pleased or disappointed. Before I had time to consider it, though, Jared went on.

"May I be honest with you, Mariska?"

I nodded.

"When I saw you yesterday, I felt . . . something." He spread both of his hands out in front of me, palms upward. "Do you know anything about soul mates?"

"I—I've heard the term. . . ."

"Once in a lifetime, if we're lucky, we find people we've known since time began. I happen to believe that this is true for you and me."

I'd never met anyone so direct; it left me speechless.

"Mariska, let's just put that aside for now. What matters right now is that I'm new in town, and all the women I've met so far are only hoping to rope and tie me. You, on the other hand, are off-limits, so I can relax with you, enjoy your company. Will you show me around? Will you be my friend?"

I began to relax. "Oh, of course I will, Jared. But you didn't have to buy me an expensive lunch to ask that question."

Jared relaxed, too. The tension was finally broken, and our relationship began that day.

During that first month, Jared took me out four times. I kept my guard up, just in case. In spite of my original attraction to him, I didn't intend to allow anything to develop with him, or with any other man, for that matter.

When Frank came home one weekend, I told him about meeting Jared, and about the times we'd gone out together. Maybe I was hoping that Frank would be jealous, but I knew in my heart that he trusted me completely, just as I trusted him.

"I know you're lonely, Mariska," he said. "But it won't be for much longer. If everything goes as planned, I'll be transferred here permanently within the year, and we'll finally be able to settle down and live normal lives at last."

The problem was, I'd heard this promise before. Frank always made it sincerely, but then the executives would ask him to take on another assignment, and Frank would cave in to their wishes, eager as he was to establish himself with the company. He couldn't seem to realize, as I did, that they were simply using him, giving him assignments that no one else would take.

When Frank left again that Monday morning, he promised faithfully to come home for our fifth wedding anniversary at the end of the month.

"It's special to me, Frank," I told him. "It's a milestone; it means more than all the others."

Frank renewed his promise, and I spent days making plans. I even rented a suite at a hotel, as a sort of second honeymoon retreat. I also made reservations at one of the finer restaurants in town, one that had a rooftop ballroom. I figured we'd dance and dine in style.

I carefully chose Frank's gift, and spent days choosing a dress and all the accessories that went with it. On the afternoon of our anniversary, I had my hair done up in a style that would show off the necklace Frank had given me as an anniversary gift the previous year.

His flight was due in at three. That was cutting it close, but it was the best Frank could offer, and I took it. When the hour came, I was walking around the apartment in my robe, nervously wringing my hands and looking at the clock. Frank wouldn't forget. He just couldn't!

By four o'clock, when the phone rang, I was frantic.

"Oh, Frank," I cried, when I heard his voice, "I was so worried that you wouldn't make it. But you still have time. Was your flight delayed?"

There was dead silence for a few seconds, and then Frank said, "Mariska, something's come up."

My heart sank right through the floor. "Oh, no," I whispered.

"Honey, I can't tell you how sorry I am, but just hear me out. Okay?"

There had been a storm, which had resulted in damage to the structure that Frank was overseeing. He'd be delayed at least twenty-four hours.

"I'm not canceling on you," he said, laughing nervously. "I'm just asking you for a slight delay. Reschedule our reservations, Mariska. And then—"

I didn't hear any more. I lowered the receiver into my lap, and I sat there gripping it, rocking back and forth while tears streamed down my cheeks. How much longer would my husband put everything else ahead of me and our plans together?

After we'd ended the conversation, I sat there, sobbing out my grief and despair. It was more than a canceled engagement. To me, it seemed like absolute proof that Frank didn't love me anymore.

The phone rang again then, and my heart leaped with the wild hope that Frank had changed his mind. He would somehow get a flight out and come home, after all.

But it wasn't Frank.

"Mariska? Is that you?"

My heart sank. "Yes, Jared."

"You sound as though you've been crying."

I completely lost control and started weeping uncontrollably at his words.

"Hang on, honey." Jared said. "I'll be there in a minute."

The next thing I knew, I was in Jared's arms, sobbing out my disappointment, and my anger at Frank. Jared held me until I'd finished, and then he took me by the shoulders and gave me a little shake to get my attention.

"Here's what you're going to do," he said. "You're going to go and get dressed, and wash your face, and put on your makeup. No way am I letting you waste those reservations."

"But—"

"Go!" Jared said, turning me toward the bedroom. "If I have to, I'll dress you myself."

I was beyond thinking rationally, but I felt instinctively that Jared was right. If I stayed home, I'd cry the entire evening, and tomorrow, my head would ache, and what would I gain from all that misery?

Jared's plan offered me the chance to divert my attention before I let this thing grow to impossible proportions in my mind. And although I'd never been a spiteful person, it also offered me the opportunity to "get even" with Frank.

How can I describe that evening? Absolutely everything about it was perfect, except for the glaring fact that Frank wasn't there. Jared and I dined and danced, and I didn't even have to worry about the bill, because he insisted on paying it. If only my heart wasn't breaking, it would've been a night to remember for the rest of my life.

Jared ordered a bottle of wine, and kept encouraging me to drink more of it. I obliged, because I found it numbed the pain. When the evening ended, Jared drove me home and helped me up the stairs. For the first time in my life, I was drunk.

Once inside, I sank onto the sofa and pressed my fingertips to my temples, in an effort to focus. I felt very, *very* strange.

Jared handed me something and said, "Drink this. It'll help."

I didn't question him. I turned up the glass and emptied it, and then I felt as though I simply floated away.

The next thing I knew, it was morning, and I was so sick that I wanted to die. My head pounded and I barely made it to the bathroom, where I was violently ill. When that was finished, I wet a washcloth with cold water, but I couldn't make it back to the bed. I sat beside the toilet and tried to think why on earth anyone would ever get drunk a second time, if this was the result.

When I heard noises coming from the bedroom, I thought that Frank had come home, as promised.

"Frank?" I called weakly. "I'm in here."

"Hi," Jared said, sticking his head around the door and smiling in at me.

"Jared?" I struggled to sit upright, and managed to focus at last. "What . . . how did you get in?"

"I didn't leave," he said, laughing. "Sweetheart, don't you remember?"

Jared reached down and lifted me from the floor. To my utter amazement, I realized that I was wearing a nightgown—only, I had no memory of putting it on. He carried me to the bed and put me there, but I scrambled to a sitting position and grabbed a blanket to cover myself.

"Sweet baby," Jared said soothingly, as he reached out to touch me.

I pulled away.

"Mariska, it's all right. Don't you understand? You needed me. I was there. What happened was beautiful, and we should treasure it always."

The room swam before my eyes. I grabbed the side of the bed to steady myself.

"Wh-what do you mean?" I whispered. "What are you talking about?"

"You and I have a special relationship, Mariska. It isn't like you were unfaithful, because I came first in your life, remember? We're soul mates. We've known each other since time began. You just didn't understand how wonderful that is until last night."

With each beat of my heart, I felt as though someone had crashed a hammer into my skull. I wanted to scream, but what would that accomplish? I needed time alone—time to think.

"Please, Jared—go now," I said, my voice sounding hollow.

"I understand, sweetheart." He smiled as he got up from the bed, then reached down and cupped my cheek in his palm. When I shuddered involuntarily, he gave a soft, indulgent laugh.

"We'll talk later," he said.

Talk? I thought. *About what?* But I didn't want to prolong his stay by asking.

"Oh, Frank," I cried aloud when the door had closed behind Jared. "Oh, Frank, what have I done?"

The next hours were agony. Frank came home, just as he'd promised, all ready and eager to celebrate our anniversary. It'd taken me all that time to recover, physically, from the sickness I felt that night. If I ever recovered emotionally, it would be a miracle.

"I know we can't get dinner reservations so soon at the same restaurant," Frank said, happily making plans, "but it isn't the only nice place around. How about going to Maria's? Then we can go dancing later."

Jared's invitation to Maria's, six weeks earlier, had started this whole thing, and I never wanted to go there again as long as I lived.

I had to tell Frank what had happened, but I'd had only a few hours to prepare. And what on earth could I say? How could I ever break this terrible news to him?

The answer was, I couldn't.

Not yet.

Maybe not ever.

In the end, I asked Frank if we could postpone our celebration a little longer. He noticed my appearance then, seemingly for the first time, and immediately became convinced that I had the flu. I certainly *looked* like I was standing at death's door. My eyes were puffy and swollen from crying, and they had dark circles underneath.

"I'm sorry, honey," Frank said gently. "I was just so excited, I didn't notice at first. But I have something that'll make you feel better. I'd planned to surprise you over dinner, but I'm not going to wait."

"Surprise me?" I repeated numbly.

Frank nodded eagerly. "Honey, it's finally happened! I've been transferred back to town. All I have to do now is help my replacement settle in. One more week, and I'm home to stay!"

A sudden surge of joy made my heart skip a beat. My prayers had finally been answered.

And then I remembered Jared—and I could have died with shame.

Would Frank even want me back, after what had happened?

Jared called once that weekend. I hung up the phone. I knew I'd have to have a final conversation with him, eventually, but I simply wasn't up to it just yet.

Frank left on an early flight Monday morning. I had to have someone to talk to, so I called Angela and asked her to meet me in the coffee shop on the ground floor of our building before work that morning.

Angela was sympathetic, but puzzled.

"I know you, Mariska," she said. "This isn't something you would ever do. Not even if you *were* drunk."

"Do you think Frank will ever understand?" I asked.

"You'd be a fool to tell him. Just start all over and consider it a lesson well learned."

Was that possible? Could I live with the guilt, if I didn't make a full confession? Well, I had four days to think it over. At the end of that time, Frank would be home to stay.

When I arrived at my desk that morning after the coffee shop, I found a dozen roses waiting for me. My fingers trembled as I opened the enclosed card.

In celebration of starting our new life together, it read.

I smiled, and clasped the card to my heart, tears rolling down my cheeks. Frank did love me. Maybe Angela was right. If I could just put that horrible night out of my mind, Frank and I could really and truly start our life together anew.

I placed the card where I could see it, and for half the morning, I pretended that nothing had ever happened between Jared and me. Frank and I would buy a home; I would leave my job, have a baby, and be a full-time mother, at least until our children were in school. And then—

"Hello, sweetheart."

I felt his arms go around me as I turned. Before I could stop him, his lips came down on mine, right there in front of the whole office.

"Jared, no!" I said, pushing him away. When he released me, I reacted automatically, scrubbing my mouth the way a child does when trying to wipe away a kiss.

Jared drew back, shocked and angry.

My anger matched his own. Even if we had been intimate, what gave him the right to approach me in public? Surely, he would be more considerate than to advertise it to coworkers.

"What's the matter with you?" he demanded through clenched teeth.

"Jared, I realize we have to talk, but not here."

"You're right," he said, giving me a forced smile. "You're absolutely right. I'll meet you in the parking lot after work. We'll take a long drive together."

My heart thudded weakly against my chest. I couldn't take the chance of going out with him again, and in fact, the very thought repulsed me.

"No," I said, but he ignored me, turning to walk away. At the last minute, he turned back and smiled.

"I see the flowers arrived."

My phone light had been blinking persistently, and now the backup ring started. But I couldn't have answered it if I'd tried.

Jared had sent the flowers. Not Frank. I grabbed the card and ripped it in shreds, but those words echoed in my mind throughout the long afternoon.

Not Frank.

Not Frank.

Not Frank.

True to his word, Jared waited for me in the parking lot after work. He'd pulled his little red car alongside my more economical model, and he was leaning up against it, his long legs outstretched, glancing impatiently at his watch from time to time.

My head pounded. My heart ached. I'd made a complete mess of my life and I was not in any mood to argue with this man a minute longer.

Jared had not risen to the rank of top salesman without an ability to read expressions and produce appropriate responses. As he unfolded his arms and pushed away from the car, his expression softened.

"I'm sorry, Mariska. We've been on the wrong foot all day, and I don't want that. Frank's gone now, and we can make our plans."

"How did you know that Frank left?" I asked. As a matter of fact, Jared shouldn't even have known about Frank's arrival.

But he didn't answer me. He opened his car door and gestured for me to climb inside.

"Jared, I'm not going anywhere with you. Maybe it would be best if you phoned me, after I've gone home."

His sharp eyes narrowed. "What are you saying, Mariska?"

Tears, always close to the surface now, welled in my eyes again. "I'm so sorry," I told him. "I—I must've given you the impression that I hop into bed with every man who comes along. But that—it isn't the case, Jared. I was drunk, and I was terribly hurt that night. But I love Frank. I—"

I broke off with a cry of pain as Jared grabbed my arm and practically threw me inside his car. He slammed the door shut then and walked quickly around to the driver's side.

I'd ridden in his car a dozen times by then, but it still took me a few seconds to locate the tricky door latch. Unfortunately, he'd climbed in beside me by that time, and he reached across suddenly and grabbed my arm with brutal force.

"Stay where you are," he ordered, starting the engine and jerking the car into gear. I managed to get the door open, but the rapid acceleration jerked it shut on me.

"Please, Jared—let me out. I can't go with you—it—it isn't right!"

"What kind of woman are you?" Jared shouted suddenly, muscles working in his jaw. "One moment we're planning our lives together, and the next, you don't even want to talk to me!"

Those words sobered me. "Wh-what do you mean, planning our

lives together?"

Jared raced down the street, defying the speed limits, and reached the ramp to the interstate.

"I'm talking about your divorce," he snapped. "I'm talking about our marriage. What the hell do you *think* I'm talking about?"

Suddenly, he pulled a small box from his pocket, jerked it open, and flung it into my lap. I looked down and saw that he'd bought me a ring in a lovely setting, with one of the most stunning diamonds I'd ever seen.

"Oh, Jared," I said, collapsing in despair. "This is all such a mess!"

We rode in silence for the next ten miles. At one point, Jared reached across and took my hand; I didn't try to pull away. He would have to stop eventually, and when he did, I would try to make him understand.

An hour or so later, we parked in a secluded cove by a lake, and Jared turned to take me into his arms.

"No," I told him firmly, drawing a line that I intended to keep in place.

"No?" he repeated.

His habit of throwing back my words at me suddenly infuriated me. "No," I said stubbornly. "Jared, I'm not responsible for what I might've said or done that night when I was drunk. I have no intention whatsoever of ever divorcing Frank. I had no real intention of sleeping with you, let alone having an affair. It's over, Jared. We can't even be friends after what's happened between us. I'm sorry. I'm sorry for everything."

I had braced myself for anger. I'd even wondered if Jared might hit me. No man had ever done that to me before, but if he was hurt deeply enough, I knew that he might very well lash out, and lash out brutally. Clearly, Jared was very unstable.

So why hadn't I seen this coming? Though, try as I might, I couldn't recall any prior evidence of Jared's growing attachment to me. Everything had always been perfectly platonic between us, right up until the night of my anniversary dinner.

To my surprise, Jared simply reached across and cupped my chin in his hand, turning my face gently toward him. If he'd tried to kiss me, I would've resisted. But he didn't. After caressing me, he simply put the ring back into his pocket and started the engine.

"You've seen the ring, so the surprise is ruined. But this isn't the right time to put it on your finger, anyway. We'll go out Wednesday evening. I've made reservations already, at Maria's. That's where it all started, darling. And at that time, we'll be officially engaged."

I didn't say a word. All the way back to town, I prayed that if God would only let me get safely home, I would never, ever, for the rest of my life, let anything like this ever happen again.

My prayer was answered. Jared delivered me back to the office parking lot, where I picked up my car. He kissed me good-bye then, and while I didn't respond, neither did I resist, for fear of inciting him all over again.

Once home, I closed the door behind me and locked it. Then I sank down onto the carpet with my back to the door and hugged my knees, rocking back and forth as I wept.

Eventually dragging myself to my feet, I went to the bathroom and found a bottle of medication that my dentist had given me months earlier, when I'd had dental work done. Tomorrow, I'd call in sick and take off the rest of the week. Somehow, I would figure out how to fix the mess I'd gotten myself into. Tonight, though, I had to have some rest.

The phone rang just as I was climbing in between the sheets.

"Hello?" I said, expecting to hear Frank's voice.

"I just wanted to tell you good night, darling," Jared said.

I hung up without answering. Ten minutes later, the medication took effect, and I drifted into blessed oblivion.

I woke the following morning at the usual time from long habit, and got up and made coffee. When I'd forced down some toast and orange juice to settle my queasy stomach, I called Angela, explained my plans, and asked her to arrange for my sick leave. When that was done, I crawled back into bed.

The phone rang about mid-morning. Frank wouldn't be calling in the middle of the day, and Angela knew that I'd intended to sleep.

Therefore, it could only be Jared, who would've missed me at work by now.

I unplugged the phone and slept until sundown, when I awoke feeling rested at last. I made soup for dinner and called Angela. She sounded awfully upset when she answered.

"Mariska, did you throw out Jared's flowers?"

"Not exactly. I had them sent to the hospital, with instructions to give them to a patient who would benefit most. Why?"

"Jared stopped by to ask where you were, and he got upset when he noticed that they weren't on your desk. He said he knew you hadn't taken them home last night. Mariska, something's seriously wrong with that guy."

I felt a band tighten around my head. "He'll get over it," I told her, trying hard to sound glib. "If I don't see him for a while, he'll realize there's nothing between us."

"I sure hope so," Angela said. But she sounded about as convinced as I felt.

I left the phone plugged in that night, because I knew that Frank would call. When it rang, I counted to ten and picked up the receiver.

"I'm on my way up," Jared said, by way of greeting.

"No—"

A click, followed by a dial tone, made it clear that further protests would be useless. I quickly checked to make certain that the door was locked, and just to be on the safe side, I slid the deadbolt into place.

No sooner was that done than the doorknob turned, making me jump and clamp my hand over my mouth to keep from crying out.

"Mariska?" Jared said, from a distance of less than three feet away. "Open the door, Mariska."

His voice sounded angry and demanding, and though it was impossible, I felt as though he could actually see me through the door.

I slipped into the bedroom and dialed Angela, but she must've gone out, because she didn't answer. I thought of calling the police, but what would I tell them? That a man I'd had sex with wanted to come and see me again? That should entertain the men at the precinct for a while.

When I gathered my courage and went back into the living room, padding across the carpet in bare feet, there were no more sounds coming from the hallway. It was dark in the apartment now, but a side window opened onto the street, and I went cautiously over and looked out and down onto the cars parked below at the curb.

"Oh, no," I moaned, seeing the distinctive top of Jared's little car, three stories below. He was still someplace near the building!

I turned—and practically ran into a dark form that had come up behind me. I'd have screamed, if Jared hadn't clamped his hand across my mouth to prevent it. With his other arm, he jerked me roughly against him, laughing.

"It's okay, sweetheart. I didn't mean to startle you."

"How did you get in here?" I cried when he released me.

"I woke you when I called, didn't I, precious? You didn't understand when I told you that I was coming up. You'd have let me in if you'd understood me, wouldn't you?"

Suddenly, it seemed like a good idea to agree with him. I managed a nod. Then I backed slowly away until I felt the door behind me, but there was no way I could release the deadbolt and the lock, and still have time to escape before Jared grabbed me again.

"We're soul mates, Mariska. Remember? Nothing can ever come between us."

Jared rambled on and I kept quiet, desperately trying to think of an escape.

"Did you file for divorce yet?" he asked. "Has Frank moved his things out of the apartment?"

Frustration made me forget my resolve to humor this madman. "I'm not going to divorce Frank, Jared," I told him firmly. "I've told you that already. Jared, you have to understand that I'm married to the man I love. The reason I was so disappointed, and hurt, the night of our anniversary, is because I love him so much."

I'm not sure what would've happened if Jared had actually comprehended what I was saying. But he twisted my words around and applied them to himself.

Had the man been insane all along, and I'd been too stupid to notice? Or can insanity strike instantly? I only knew I wouldn't be safe unless Jared was out of my apartment and out of my life for good. I forced myself to try and remain calm. To think.

"Jared, I have to get some rest. Frank will be here any minute and I need to talk to him." Frank wasn't due home for three more days, but the last part of that sentence certainly wasn't a lie.

"Did you come in the back door?" I asked, knowing that was the only plausible answer to his presence. Apparently, he'd had keys made, probably the night he spent with me. "Let me walk you out," I said, trying to keep my voice light.

At that moment, the phone rang. I sprang to answer it, grateful for any outside contact.

"Mariska, did you just call? I was out jogging, and when I came in, I found your number on my call return."

Angela's voice had never sounded sweeter. "Frank!" I said loudly. "Where are you?"

I hesitated a moment, and tried not to think about what must be going through Angela's mind.

"Downstairs?" I managed a laugh. "I just can't get used to cellular phones! Okay, I'll see you in two minutes."

I hung up and turned to Jared. It wasn't necessary any longer to mask the panic I'd felt since I'd found him in my apartment. It came through in my voice as I urged him toward the kitchen.

"Frank's on his way up in the elevator," I said. "Let me show you out. You don't need to be here when I break the news to him."

Jared looked a bit confused, but he headed toward the back door, nevertheless.

"You'll get him out tonight?" he asked.

"I don't have time to discuss it right now. He's almost here."

We'd reached the back door, which opened onto a tiny landing with a steep flight of stairs descending to the alley below. It didn't have a bolt, but I could nail it shut if I had to.

"Go," I urged him. "Frank will be at the front door any minute now. I have to let him in."

Jared frowned, but he bent to kiss me quickly, and then went out.

"Call me when he's gone," he said. "I'll move my things in tomorrow."

I didn't reply. I closed the door and jumped toward the kitchen phone, my hands shaking so hard that I had to dial three times before I got Angela's number right.

"Can I come over?" I asked the moment I heard her voice. "Angela, you were right. Jared Beacon is insane!"

Angela didn't ask questions. She simply told me to throw some things into a bag and get out of the apartment as quickly as possible. "I'll call the cab myself, and if you aren't here in twenty minutes, I'm calling the police."

I stayed with Angela that night, grateful for her hospitality and her support. When we arrived at work together the next morning, I called a locksmith and arranged for him to meet me at my apartment that afternoon. I told him to bring along everything he would need to keep someone from breaking in.

At ten o'clock that morning, Jared stepped off the elevator and strode over to my desk. Angela left her station immediately and came over to provide me with moral support.

"You lied to me, Mariska," Jared said at once, his voice bitter and bruised. "I trusted you, and you lied. Frank didn't come home last night. I phoned and you didn't answer, so I went back, and you weren't there. I waited for you all night long."

The thought of this man waiting for me in my apartment, literally lying in wait, made me physically ill. But I didn't have time to indulge myself at the moment. This would probably be the best chance I would ever have to finally get through to this sick man.

"Jared, I've told you all along that I have absolutely no intention of ever divorcing Frank. You have to understand that."

Finally, he did. I saw his eyes register the information, and then something happened which I would never have expected. Jared completely lost control.

He began shouting curses as he picked up whatever was in reach and threw it. The telephone bounced off the wall. He grabbed a stand with a fax machine and roared with rage as he flung it aside.

Angela and I took refuge in the women's rest room. Jared came after us, screaming what he would do to me for destroying his life.

Security arrived, and two guards barely kept him from breaking open the restroom door. Finally, city police officers were summoned, and the four men managed to subdue him.

Mr. Steadman talked to me in his office, then allowed me to wait there while he went down to the police station to find out from Jared what was going on.

I don't suppose I'll ever know for certain what passed between the two men. I do know that Jared possessed exceptional persuasive skills.

When Mr. Steadman came back, he said, "Mariska, I'm disappointed in you. You've been with our company for six years and I would never have expected such behavior on your part."

My nerves had settled down by then, leaving me numb inside. "Mr. Steadman, I'm prepared to accept blame for my part in all of this, but I'm not about to confess to something I haven't done."

Mr. Steadman waved a hand in the air to stop me. "I don't want to hear a confession," he said abruptly. "I simply want things to return to normal as quickly as possible."

"Has Jared been . . . transferred?" I asked, choosing that word at the last minute, because asking if he'd been fired presumed a little too much.

"Of course not," Mr. Steadman said, his steel gray eyes riveting mine. "Jared Beacon is one of the best salesmen I've ever employed and I'm not about to lose him over a tawdry affair with some. . . ."

His voice trailed off before he spoke the words. I swallowed hard and waited, knowing I might very well need to keep this job after I'd told Frank what had happened. And I would tell him. At long last, I'd made up my mind.

"I'm putting you on suspension, Mariska. If you can manage to remind yourself that you're a married woman and stop harassing Jared, I'll keep you on. But I absolutely refuse to tolerate any further misconduct from you. Is that understood?"

Arguing would have cost me my job. Tears welled in my eyes as I nodded meekly and left the room.

Jared was waiting for me at my apartment when I arrived home that night. At least he'd had sense enough not to confront me in the office parking lot.

I speeded up and drove past. Jared pulled out and followed me, and the only safe place I could think to go was the police station, six blocks away. Minutes later, when I swung over to the curb out front, Jared sped off.

I went inside, and when a sergeant on duty had heard my story, he shook his head in sympathy.

"The world's full of kooks," he said. "Unfortunately, our state doesn't have a law which will protect you, unless he's done some real physical harm."

"Then . . . what can I do?"

The man shrugged. "Short of hiring a bodyguard, I'd say just watch your back. Get some good locks installed and be aware of your surroundings at all times. Sounds like the guy's getting out of control. Maybe someone else'll trigger him, and he'll get himself arrested. Or maybe he'll find another girlfriend and leave you alone."

He checked through some files on a nearby desk, then looked up at me. "They ran him through this morning, as a matter of fact. He comes up clean. Your boss stood up for him so they let him go."

I left the station feeling like the weight of the world rested on my shoulders. It was bad enough when I realized I had no choice but to tell Frank. Now, who could predict what Jared was going to do next?

Jared's car was nowhere to be seen when I reached my apartment the second time. Still, I went cautiously into the lobby, ready to scream at the top of my lungs if he stepped out of the shadows.

He didn't. But it would be several days later before I learned why.

I wanted to spend the night with Angela again, but I refused to place her in danger. And I had no place else to go.

I don't think I breathed until I was inside my apartment with the door locked. I'd missed the locksmith, so I had to rely on bracing the doors with chairs, as I'd done before.

The light on the answering machine was blinking, and I hit the play button, expecting to hear Frank's voice.

It was Jared.

"You'll pay," he said. "If you think the police will help you, you're crazy. They're all my friends now."

He rambled on until his time ran out. A lot of it made no sense at all, but other things were perfectly clear. Jared blamed me for everything that had happened. He was furious because I'd disposed of the flowers he'd sent.

At first, I sat on the sofa, arms locked around me, and rocked back and forth in terror and despair. The man truly was insane.

Then suddenly, it dawned on me that the answering machine tape was all I needed for proof of that fact. Gradually, I began to relax. When the phone rang, I answered it, and finally, I heard Frank's voice on the other end of the line.

My relief was so great that I started to cry. At that point, I wanted nothing in the world so much as to tell him what had happened, and find out if he could ever forgive me. After that, I would try to put my life back together.

"Honey, what's wrong?"

"Almost everything," I said, weeping openly. "When are you coming home?"

"That's the reason I called—to tell you that I'm catching a flight out tonight. Our days apart are over, Mariska. I'm coming home to stay."

My heart ached, and I know the pain came through in my voice when I answered him. "If only that could be true. Frank, but—I've done a terrible thing. You may not ever be able to forgive me."

There was a slight pause, and I knew he was trying to digest this information. To think what I could possibly have done that would be too awful for him to forgive.

"We'll talk about it when I get there," Frank said gently. "I love you, Mariska. I doubt you could do anything to ever change that."

"Oh, Frank—I love you more than life itself. If you can ever forgive me, I swear to you that I'll never again give you any reason to doubt that love."

We hung up, and I went to pace the floor, going over and over the things I would say. In the end, I gave up. I would not shade the truth; I would simply state the cold, hard facts and pray that Frank could be as generous and loving as he'd sounded on the phone.

I'll never know what might have happened. I passed the remainder of that evening doing chores around the apartment to occupy my mind and keep myself from going completely insane with worry. Over and over, I checked the doors and looked for Jared's car down on the street below.

Then I got a blanket and lay down on the sofa to wait for Frank's arrival. He'd said he was leaving at ten tonight, and his flight would take three hours. Including the forty-minute ride from the airport, he should arrive just before two in the morning.

To my surprise, I eventually drifted off to sleep, and when I jerked suddenly awake again, I had no idea how much time had gone by.

What had woke me? Had Frank tried the door and found it bolted? Was he going around to the back, or had he called out to me from the hallway?

I got up and looked at the clock. It was one-forty-five, so I was certain that Frank had arrived. I called his name from beside the front door, and when he didn't answer, I started through to the kitchen to remove the barricade I'd placed in front of the door there.

But I could see through the little pane in the door that Frank wasn't outside, and when I heard a popping sound from the front hallway, I ran back to the door there.

"Frank?" I called loudly.

"Open up."

His voice was muffled, but I had no reason to doubt his identity. I fumbled with the bolts and pulled the door back.

Then I screamed in terror.

Jared was standing there with a gun in his hand.

Frank's still form lay on the floor of the hall behind him.

I tried to slam the door shut, but Jared caught it. As he pushed his way inside, I screamed for all I was worth. Then he caught me by the shoulders and shoved me out of the way. Turning, he closed and bolted the door behind us.

Under normal circumstances, Jared could've overpowered me with one hand. He was six feet tall and muscular from his regular workouts at the gym. He outweighed me by at least eighty pounds.

But these were not normal circumstances. As I backed through the apartment, still screaming, I grabbed every item in my path and used it as a weapon.

Amazingly enough, I was still coherent, and instinct told me not to go to the bedroom. I went to the kitchen, instead.

There, I slid my hand along the counter, still not turning my back on Jared. I felt the wooden block that held the steak knives, and I grabbed one of those and held it in front of me.

Jared looked as though he were in some kind of trance. He advanced on me steadily as I waved the knife in his face and warned him of what I'd do.

His smile didn't fade, even when I slashed out at him, cutting his hand, which he'd raised to take hold of me. Blood spurted, and still he came at me.

I lashed out again and again. I'd backed around the counter by then, and I felt behind me with one hand and managed to knock over the chair I'd placed under the back doorknob.

I'd never have managed to get outside, though. The few seconds it would've taken to open the door and step through would've given Jared the opportunity he needed.

That didn't prove necessary, though. I heard voices shouting suddenly, and noises that meant that someone was kicking open the front door.

"In here!" I screamed, slipping out of Jared's grasp.

I didn't elude him for long. Jared lunged and came down on top of me just as the policemen appeared in the kitchen doorway. His fingers closed around my throat—

And the rest is a blur.

I woke up on a stretcher, with men and women in pale blue uniforms standing over me. My throat ached, and I fought to breathe.

"Everything's fine," a young woman assured me. "Calm down and you can breathe more easily."

I did as instructed, and found that she was right. "Frank?" I managed to get the word out, and of course, she misunderstood.

"The police took him away. They had to pry his fingers off your throat and they thought he'd slashed you because of all the blood. But it was his blood, wasn't it? You did a good job of defending yourself."

I was shaking my head furiously. "Not him. Frank. My husband."

"Oh," she said, and then her smile faded. "I can't tell you his condition. He was shot, I'm afraid. They've transported him to the hospital."

I was fighting to get up then. The pain in my throat disappeared as I forgot my own injury to concentrate on Frank.

In the end, I convinced them that I could ride to the hospital in a car. On the way, I learned that a neighbor had called the police for me when he heard the gunshot and my screams.

Frank was in surgery when I arrived at the hospital. After my examination, which determined only severe bruising, I was allowed to go into his room and wait for him to return from Recovery.

I expected the worst. After all, the past two weeks had been a living nightmare; I'd lost all hope of ever really waking from it.

Instead, Frank smiled at me before he was even moved from the stretcher. The doctor came along right behind him, wearing an even bigger smile.

"I'm sorry I didn't manage to talk to you sooner," he said, "but it's been a wild night in the emergency room. Frank's wound is not by any means critical. He'll recover with no ill effects."

Frank confirmed that news. He was a bit groggy from the anesthesia, but he'd already started to make jokes, trying to calm me down.

It was immediately clear that Frank thought we'd been the victims of a random robbery; he was elated that we'd survived. I wrestled with my conscience, wanting to postpone the truth at least until morning. In the end, though, I decided I couldn't bear this agony alone any longer.

I told Frank everything. I emphasized over and over how I'd never meant for anything like this to happen, and that I loved him and no one else.

He was silent until I'd finished. Then he said, "Mariska, we've both been through a lot tonight. I don't want to say anything while my mind is clouded. Can we talk tomorrow?"

My part was done, and I felt a relief so great that I practically collapsed with fatigue. The nurse who came in to check Frank's vital signs noticed my condition, and she insisted that I go home.

Frank was right when he said we'd been through a lot that night, but it wasn't over. A police lieutenant called early the next morning and insisted that I come down to the station.

"Do I have to?" I asked. "I want to see my husband—"

"There's something you need to see," he told me. "I think you'll be happier when that's done."

I went down to the station—and reeled in shock when Lieutenant Adamo explained what he wanted to show me.

It was a videotape, of my night with Jared Beacon.

"He—he taped it?" The words came out in a hoarse whisper. I felt weak with shock, positively sick with shame.

"Mrs. Connor, please trust me—I wouldn't ask you to look at something like this without a reason. And you don't have to view it, if you feel that you can't. But the fact is, nothing happened that night. This tape is absolute proof. Jared gave you too much sedative, and you passed out. The tape runs six hours, right up to the time when you awoke vomiting the following morning. You slept like a baby the whole night through, in spite of his efforts to wake you."

My tortured mind registered one word. "Sedative?" I asked.

Lieutenant Adamo nodded. "He gives it to all his victims. The man has a library full of these tapes, and most of the women were not as lucky as you were. Jared Beacon's a rapist, but not the usual kind. He insists on his victims 'cooperating,' and he achieves that by drugging them."

"Nothing happened?"

"I give you my word. You're welcome to view the entire tape if you like. You can watch yourself sleep while Beacon paces the floor and waits, occasionally shaking you good and hard, or slapping your cheeks."

My relief was almost overpowering. I viewed the tape then, and except for the part where Jared undressed me and put me into a nightgown, there was little to cause real horror. In fact, Jared's efforts to wake me would've been almost comical, had he not caused me so much pain and misery.

I felt almost giddy with relief as I drove back to the hospital.

"Frank," I began, as soon as I walked into his room.

"No," he said. "Let me talk first."

"But—"

Frank reached out and put a hand over my lips. "This is as much my fault as yours," he began. "I wish it hadn't happened, but we'll get past it, honey. We'll recover—"

"Frank, it didn't happen," I said, ready to shake him if he wouldn't let me finish. "Frank, he's a rapist. He drugged me, but it didn't work. Nothing happened. It's all on tape. The police say you can watch the whole thing if you want to."

Frank looked confused. I couldn't blame him.

"I don't get to forgive you?" he asked at last.

I went into this arms then, careful not to touch the bandage on his shoulder.

"Yes," I said, "you do. Forgive me for being impatient, Frank, and for letting another man get close enough to put me into that position. But I'm not an adulteress. Before I passed out, I fought him off. It's all on the videotape."

Frank had to stay one more night, and then I took him home. Our lives together truly did start that day. Frank forgave me; I hadn't thought it was possible to love him more, but I do.

Lieutenant Adamo eventually turned over the videotape, and I insisted that Frank watch it, in case he ever had any doubts. After that, we burned it in a little private ceremony in our backyard.

It turned out that Jared had a long record of assault, but he hadn't shown up on the police computer because he'd changed his name. Due to Mr. Steadman's support, he wasn't even fingerprinted that day down at the station.

Thankfully, though, Jared didn't get off easily this time. For one thing, the shooting added substantially to his offense. Records showed that he'd purchased the gun when I returned home that night, which explained why he hadn't been waiting for me when I arrived. As it stands, judges seem to be taking less lenient attitudes toward repeat offenders, and Jared got twenty years. They tell us he will have to serve at least seven of them.

Mr. Steadman apologized to me personally, and asked me to stay on at the company. But Frank and I want to try an old-fashioned lifestyle for a change, so I left to keep house and plan our family. Mr. Steadman tells me that I will always have a job with him, should I ever decide to return to the workforce.

That won't be for a few years, though. The only work I do these days is to travel around our state, speaking to various groups about the passage of an anti-stalking law.

Frank and I moved out of the apartment, into a home we bought in the suburbs. Our first child is due in three months, and we plan to have at least one more.

At long last, I'm living out my dreams. THE END

I MARRIED MY SPERM DONOR DAD

My mom and I were very close, despite the vast number of years between our ages. She'd waited a long time to have me because her career as a pediatrician had been very important to her. In fact, when she finally realized her biological clock was ticking at warp speed and she still hadn't found Mr. Right, she conceived me without the luxury of marrying my father.

I never knew who my father was. Every time I asked Mom, she'd just shrug and shake her head. She said it didn't matter because he'd never be a part of my life.

Naturally, I assumed he was someone she'd had an affair with. She didn't confirm or deny it, so there was no reason to believe otherwise.

Mom was wonderful to me. Although she had a very demanding career, she made sure all my needs were met. I never doubted her love for me, either. We had many wonderful times together, something a lot of my friends couldn't say.

I went through high school studying hard, with the goal of following in my mom's footsteps when I was finished. My aptitude for the sciences was extremely high, and Mom told me I should use this in making a career decision. So I decided early on that I wanted to be a pediatrician. She told me I could join her practice and we'd be the best children's doctors in town. I had no doubt she was right.

I made it through college with flying colors and then I attended the same medical school as Mom. My grades remained so high, I managed to get scholarships for the majority of my tuition. Mom supplemented the rest. I didn't have to work, which made it much easier for me than some of the students who had to take out loans and take on part-time jobs to finance their education.

After all my classes were completed, I did my residency at the local hospital in the emergency room. This was where I met Dave, an emergency room doctor and the head of the department.

This man was incredible. He was quite a bit older than I was, but he acted like most men my age. He'd been married and had one child, according to the gossip mill. But his wife had decided she didn't like being married to an emergency room physician because of the demanding hours and being on call twenty-four hours a day.

What I liked about him was his high energy and enthusiasm for his work. He believed nothing was out of the realm of possibility, even when people came in with limbs practically severed or hearts that had stopped long enough to declare them dead. We worked on people until there was absolutely no hope for recovery.

Dave also had the philosophy that once we did everything we possibly could to take care of our patients, if they died or didn't get better, then it wasn't meant to be. "Once you've done all that's humanly possible," he told me, "it's in God's hands. Sometimes they're better off not recovering."

At times, that attitude was hard to take. But when I saw him in action, I knew that if a miracle could be worked, Dave would be the one to do it. He took full responsibility for his department, too.

I'll never forget when we had a brand new nurse on our team. She'd started crying over having lost a patient several minutes earlier. I was sad, too, but we'd done everything in our power to save the woman, who'd suffered head trauma in a car crash. This nurse was walking around in a blue funk, and she couldn't seem to stop the tears.

Finally, I pulled her over to the side and told her that she did a wonderful job trying to save the woman, but that there were times you had to let go. She told me she couldn't. Then I reminded her of all the lives she'd saved and that we couldn't play God when the end was inevitable. The nurse offered a shaky smile, then thanked me.

After she walked away, I thought about the words I'd said. I was amazed when I realized I sounded just like Dave. I'd taken on his philosophy and made it my own.

With a grin, I went to the cafeteria for my coffee break. One of the doctors from the next shift had taken over when the emergency room slowed down. I was exhausted from a very busy morning.

I spotted Dave sitting over in the corner of the cafeteria all by himself. This was unusual. Dave is one of those people who almost always has a crowd sitting around him. He's a positive person, and he always has wonderful stories to tell, drawing people to him like a magnet.

"Hi, Claudia," he said as he motioned to the chair next to him. "Have a seat."

I sat down and fixed my coffee. Neither of us said anything at first, but it was a comfortable silence. Dave and I had known each other professionally for several months, so we were pretty much at ease with each other.

Finally, he started nodding his head and smiling at me. "What?" I said.

He chuckled. "I heard what you told the nurse. That was very nice of you, letting her know how much we appreciate what she's doing."

"You would have done the same thing," I told him. "We have a tendency to expect way too much of ourselves. I tend to agree with your philosophy on medical care."

Our eyes met. "Good," he said. "That 'philosophy', as you call it, has kept me going for many years. I love what I do. It's great to save lives, but I also know I'm not a super-hero."

Actually, Dave was a super-hero in my book, but I didn't say that to his face. I just smiled back at him.

A warmth came over me as he and I made small talk. We had so much in common, and I was completely myself with him. Over the next several months we had coffee together almost every day we were both on duty during the same shift.

One day, after I'd had a particularly rough shift, Dave sought me out at the nurse's station.

"I have two tickets to a new show that's playing at the Community Theater this weekend. Would you like to join me?"

I swallowed hard. Was Dave asking me out on a date? Because I'd been so busy with medical school, I hadn't gone out with men much.

Slowly, I nodded. "Yes, I'd like that."

"Good. I'll pick you up at seven. After the show we can go someplace nice for dinner."

After he walked away, I felt like I was on Cloud Nine. For the first time in my life, I had a crush on a man. Mom had always told me it would take a very special kind of guy to get my attention and hold it for any amount of time. I knew now that I'd found that guy.

Dave was quite a bit older than me, but he certainly didn't look it. He had golden brown hair that he kept short. His eyes were sort of a greenish golden. He was slightly under six feet tall, which seemed perfect next to my five-foot-six height. I looked up to him, but he didn't seem like a giant, which I liked.

His easy laughter was infectious. Everyone smiled within seconds of being around him. He loved people, and they loved him back. Kids were drawn to him like little magnets.

One afternoon, after he'd stitched up a little boy's chin, I watched as Dave magically pulled a toy Matchbox car from his pocket. He held it out and asked if the boy had lost it. The boy said he hadn't, so the doctor told him to take it home and make sure he didn't lose it. The child left with a smile on his face, in spite of the pain he must have felt from a really nasty fall.

The boy's mother obviously adored Dave, who seemed oblivious to his own charm. She stuttered and stammered all over the place as she backed out of his office.

The nurses in the emergency room all placed bets as to when Dave would ever meet a woman who could have the same effect on him that he had on nearly every person he made contact with. I laughed about this. He was the kind of man who would never get caught unless he wanted to.

Well, Friday night finally rolled around. We'd both been working the late shift the evening before, so we were getting ready to go home when the sun came up.

"See you at seven?" he said as he backed toward the door.

"Sure. Do you know where I live?"

He winked, sending shivers up my arm. "Of course I do, Claudia.

I've had your phone number and address for months."

I didn't think anyone had heard us until I turned around after he'd gone. The eyes of the nurse standing behind me were open so wide, I thought they might fall out of her head.

"This is so cool, Dr. Sims." A slow grin spread across her face.

"What's so cool?"

"You and Dr. Wichert are going out."

"Oh, that." I tried to act nonchalant. "We're just going to a play. He got two tickets and didn't want to waste them, so I agreed to go."

"Uh huh."

I knew that news of my date with Dave would be all over the hospital by the time I came in to work my next shift. But that was okay. I really liked Dave. I just hoped he wouldn't be too upset over it.

And he wasn't. In fact, when he picked me up for our date, he told me he'd heard everyone was speculating on our relationship. I pulled back and looked at him very carefully.

"Are you okay with that?"

He belted out a hearty laugh. "I'm fine with it, Claudia. If you promise you won't tell anyone, I'm terribly flattered that anyone would think you'd be interested in an old man like me."

Before I could think, I said, "Oh, but you're not an old man."

Dave smiled and reached for my hand. "I'm almost old enough to be your father."

My feelings said otherwise. Dave was warm, sensitive, and caring, not to mention the hottest-looking guy I'd ever seen. The fact that we were both interested in almost the exact same things didn't hurt a bit.

We laughed our heads off during the play, which was a romantic comedy. Then we went to a nice little Italian restaurant in the heart of town for a late dinner. Over a bottle of Chianti, we talked and discovered that we loved all the same foods, music, sports, and almost everything else you can possibly imagine.

I'm not saying it was love at first sight because I'd known Dave for quite a while. But on our first date, I had the feeling he just might be "the one" for me.

It was awful that the night ever had to end, but it did. We had to be at work the next night.

"Get some rest, Claudia, honey." Dave reached out and gently touched the tip of my nose.

I started to nod, then he leaned over and kissed me. It started out being a gentle lip-to-lip touch, but then we sort of melted into each other's arms.

Being a doctor, I never thought I'd be able to feel such a physical attraction to another human being. I'd seen every part of a person exposed, and I couldn't imagine the thrill of feeling a man's touch. This was a whole new experience for me.

Finally, he pulled away and told me he looked forward to seeing me again. I laughed.

"You'll see me in just a few hours."

"That's not what I'm talking about, and you know it. I want to be with you, just the two of us, alone, so we can talk and really get to know each other even better."

He wanted the exact same thing I wanted. I smiled back at him, not saying a word, and when he got to his car, I turned and went inside. I was in love.

Somehow my body quit buzzing long enough for me to go to sleep. I dreamed of Dave and me holding onto each other. It was as though there was no one else in the world but us. I loved being with him more than anything else in the world.

When it was time to go to work, I wondered how we'd act around each other. I'd never been involved with someone I worked with. Actually, I'd never been involved with anyone before. I'd have to let him take the lead.

The first thing Dave did when I arrived at the hospital was lean over and kiss me on the cheek. "Ready to go to work?" he whispered, ignoring all the gawking nurses and hospital staff.

I nodded and grinned as I turned toward the nurses' station where I needed to look over the charts. Everyone watched me, but I forced myself to maintain my cool. It was hard because I wanted to jump up, run, and kick up my heels to let everyone know I was in love.

We had two serious car crashes come in during the first few hours. Then we took a break together, letting the other two doctors take over. They knew where we'd be if they needed us.

Over coffee, Dave started telling me about an idea he had for our next date. The feeling was exhilarating, knowing he'd taken for granted that we'd be going out again. I loved the thought of being part of a couple, as long as *he* was the other part.

The last half of our shift was pretty quiet. We had a woman in who thought she was having a heart attack, then some man came in because he thought he'd taken the wrong medication. He said he'd tried to take his medicine without getting his reading glasses. His wife was frantic with worry. Fortunately, all he'd taken was a laxative, and Dave told him he'd better get home before it started working.

When the shift was over, Dave said he needed to stick around because he had some administrative work to do. "How much longer will you be working here, Claudia?" he asked.

Dave knew I was a pediatrician and that my plans were to join my mother's practice as soon as I was able to. He said he liked that about me.

"Only a few more months," I told him. "Until the end of May."

"Good," he said. "I think it'll be better for both of us if we're not working together."

I left the hospital smiling from ear to ear. Dave wanted us to keep seeing each other. Now I knew what those high school and college girls had been talking about when they described that heady feeling of being in love.

Not only did I get tingles when I was with Dave, but my respect for him grew the longer I was with him. The depth of his caring nature reached far beyond anything most people saw. He took a week off every summer and went to a Third World country to help the poorest of the poor. He administered immunization shots, set broken bones, and gave food to people who were starving to death. He made me want to join him.

"You should, Claudia," he told me. "We can do it together. I know it's just a little thing compared to how large the problem is, but I feel like if we can help a few people, then at least we've done something."

Never in my life had I met such a kind, intelligent, caring man. His dreams became my dreams.

Dave took me to dinner to celebrate the end of my residency. Finally, I'd become a partner in my mother's practice. And now, he told me he wanted to meet her.

Mom said she'd love to meet the man who'd managed to sweep her daughter off her feet. We all got together at one of the best restaurants in town for a second celebration dinner.

My mom obviously approved of my choice in men—I could tell from the moment she first laid eyes on him. She saw that same sparkle I'd seen from the very beginning. I felt like I was on top of the world.

"I'd been hoping you'd meet someone closer to your own age, Claudia," she said. "But he's so young at heart, it doesn't really matter. You have my blessing."

"There's only one thing that would make this whole thing perfect," I told her.

"What's that, sweetie?"

"If Dave could have met my dad. I wish I knew what happened."

Mom sighed and looked away. "That's not possible, Claudia. Please don't keep bringing that up."

I had no idea at the time what bugged her about my asking what was surely a natural question. But I did notice a strange expression that crossed her face every time I did. I dropped the subject but decided to discuss it with Dave.

He was very attentive when I told him the mystery of my father. I explained how I'd never even seen him, and my mother never told me a single thing.

"Do you think that maybe he was a one-night stand?" Dave asked. "That would probably embarrass your mother enough to make her clam up about him."

I shook my head. "I don't think that's it. Mom's not the type to lose her head over some guy just because she has the hots for him."

"Have you ever met any uncles or other men she can't explain?" he asked. "Think back to when you were little."

"No, I don't remember any uncles. My mom only has one sister, and she lives up in Maine with her husband and two cats."

"Is it possible he could have been killed?" Dave asked. "Or maybe very sick with some disease she doesn't want to discuss?"

"No. I asked her about that, and she said she has no idea where my father is, but she wasn't widowed or left behind."

Dave agreed with me. "Yes, this is very strange."

I let out a loud sigh. "I just wish I knew."

He took my hand and kissed the back of it. "One of these days, we'll figure it out. Together."

The way Dave put emphasis on the word "together" made me feel like everything would be just fine. He'd see to it that I learned about my father. I had no doubt about that. Dave could do anything.

I didn't tell my mother what Dave said, but I did let her know he was one of those people who seemed able to do just about anything. She smiled.

"Sounds like someone else I know," she said with a twinkle in her eye.

"Who?"

"You."

I've always been one of those can-do types of people. When someone said something couldn't be done, I made it my goal to prove them wrong. I almost always succeeded. When people moaned and groaned about things not going right, I smiled and got through whatever it was. I wasn't the type to let anything get me down, which was what got me through medical school. And it certainly helped me in the emergency room.

"I really admire you, Claudia," my mother said. "Nothing seems to rattle you. Maybe you and Dave are meant to be together. Certainly seems that way."

Her words were like the icing on the cake. I had my mother's approval to forge ahead in the relationship with the man I knew I'd love for the rest of my life.

Dave and I were literally inseparable from then on. We worked different hours, now that I was in business with my mom, but he stopped by when he had a chance, and I waited for him in the hospital cafeteria when he worked late. By then, we'd professed our love for each other, and it was only a matter of time before I knew we'd get married.

He'd been married before, but it had only lasted a year. However, that had been long enough for him to produce one daughter, who was now five years old. I still hadn't met her, but I had no doubt she'd be wonderful since she was Dave's daughter.

It was a really pretty summer afternoon when Dave finally proposed. He totally caught me off guard.

We'd just come back from a picnic where a bunch of people from the hospital had gotten together for one last summer fling. I had on shorts and a T-shirt, and Dave was wearing a muscle shirt that looked better on him than it would have on most guys half his age. He kept looking at me with a strange expression all day, and I wondered what was going on.

Then, when we got to his car, he turned to me and said he loved me with all his heart. I laughed out loud. "I love you, too, Dave."

"Then will you accept this?" He pulled a black velvet box from beneath the seat of his car.

The ring was simple elegance, a solitaire marquis-cut stone set in a plain band. Suddenly, I was speechless. All I could do was nod.

Since he'd been married before and I didn't like the idea of a huge wedding, we had a small ceremony with just my mom, his parents, and a few friends from the hospital.

"I wish my daughter could be here," he told me. "But she won't be back into town for several more weeks, and I didn't want to wait that long."

I hugged my new husband. "That's okay, Dave. We'll meet soon."

One of the first things he wanted to do now was for us to get together with his daughter when she came back. "I just hope you and Ashley get along," he said often.

"Of course we will," I assured him.

In spite of what I said, I was very nervous about meeting Ashley. After he thought about it some more, he told me he had no doubt she and I would hit it off. Now it was my turn to worry. Sure, I was around kids all day, but this was different.

I knew her mother—Dave's ex-wife—would be with her when we met. I didn't want to make a bad impression on any of these people since I knew they'd be in my life now.

Dave suggested that I might be more comfortable meeting them if we brought my mother along with us. I hugged him and told him he was the most wonderful man in the world for making that offer, and that yes, I did want my mom with me. She had an amazing ability to see when the conversation was falling apart, and she could pick up and run with it, if needed.

We all met at a nice restaurant on the edge of town. Dave, my mom, and I were there first.

Mom reached out and patted me on the hand. "Everything will be just fine, Claudia," she told me. "The little girl will love you."

"I certainly hope so."

Ashley and her mom, Delia, were late. When they walked in, I stood up, shook Delia's hand, smiled at the cute little girl, and sat back down.

I didn't notice my mother's reaction at first, but when I glanced over at her, I saw that her face had turned a sickly shade of gray.

"What's wrong, Mom?" I whispered.

"Oh, my God," she said, covering her mouth with her hand.

The whole evening, my mom didn't say two words. Dave noticed, too. He leaned over and whispered, "Is something wrong with your mom?"

I shrugged. "Obviously."

Delia was a very pleasant and attractive woman, but I could see why she and Dave hadn't stayed married. She wasn't interested in any of the same things; in fact, she seemed rather shallow. But I still liked her. And the little girl was absolutely precious, and very smart, too.

After Delia and Ashley left, I let out a sigh of relief. Dave turned to me and grinned.

"See? It wasn't so bad, was it?"

I shook my head. "No, in fact, I really liked both of them." Turning to my mom, I said, "Mom, are you okay?"

She just sat there, staring at the opposite wall, still not saying a word. Dave offered to drive her home, but she looked absolutely horrified at the very idea.

"I can drive myself home," she snapped.

It was so unlike Mom to behave like that. I had no idea what had gotten into her, but obviously, something had surely happened.

After trying unsuccessfully to pry it out of her, I stood up and said I really needed to get back to my condo to pick up some more things to take to the house where Dave and I lived. I was scheduled for appointments very early in the morning, and I needed my rest, so I wanted to get going.

Dave drove me home to the condo. He was as befuddled as I was.

"Do you have any idea what might have happened?" he asked.

"No idea whatsoever."

"Maybe you can discuss this when the two of you are alone." He pulled up to a traffic light and stopped when it turned red. "It was almost like she saw a ghost or something."

"Yeah, I know. It's really weird."

All night, I thought about Ashley and Delia. I had to admit, Ashley looked awfully familiar. I kept thinking she must have looked like one of the many patients I'd inherited from the doctor in my mom's office who'd just retired.

My mom showed up to work the next day in a strange state. Her hair, usually neat, looked uncombed and her clothes were rumpled.

I pulled her to the side. "Mom, what's the matter?"

She didn't say a word. She just slowly pulled a picture from the pocket of her lab coat and handed it to me.

I glanced at the picture and smiled. *Where had she gotten such a great picture of Dave's little girl?* I wondered. *Maybe Delia had dropped it on the floor?*

We were so busy, I didn't have a chance to ask her about it until it was time to lock the doors to the office. When I did, she leveled me with a cold stare.

"Claudia, that's a picture of you when you were a little girl," she said in a monotone.

"You're kidding!" I looked at it again. "I could swear it looks exactly like Ashley."

Mom shuddered, grabbed the picture, and went straight to her car. I was left standing there all by myself, wondering why she was still acting like this. Something obviously bugged her about Ashley and me resembling each other. For the life of me, I couldn't figure out what in the world it could be.

I didn't say anything to Dave about it because I didn't want him to think something was wrong with my mom. And I especially didn't want him to think she didn't like his daughter. Mom wasn't like that. She loved all children.

Several days went by, and I had almost forgotten about Mom's reaction, when Dave called me at home. He told me he'd gotten the strangest phone call from my mother.

"She said we need to meet so we can discuss something that happened years ago," he said.

"What does she want to discuss?" I asked.

"Beats me. But she gave me strict instructions to come alone. She doesn't want you there."

"Okay," I said. "I don't mind if you and my mom get together. Just don't say anything bad about me."

"There's nothing bad to say, Claudia."

It hadn't taken Dave and me long to fall into a comfortable routine centered around our work hours. Because I'd worked with him in the emergency room, I knew what he had to deal with. One of the big advantages we had over most couples was that we understood each other's work. It was demanding, and that was the way it always would be.

Since Dave wasn't coming home for dinner that night, I fixed myself a salad and ate in front of the television, something I rarely did. But it was nice having a little time to myself. Since Dave and I had gotten married, we spent all our time in bed when we weren't eating or working. That thought made me smile. My husband was what teenage girls call a "hottie," and I was very fulfilled.

I thought Dave would be home by midnight, since he was only scheduled to work until nine. I figured he'd meet with Mom for a couple of hours, then he'd come on home. But when one o'clock rolled around and he still wasn't home, I got worried.

As much as I hated to bug him, I dialed his cell phone number. But he didn't answer it. His voicemail clicked in, letting me know he wasn't available and that he'd call me back when he was. I hung up and frowned. What was going on?

Finally, I went to bed alone, something I hadn't done since I'd gotten married. Whatever Mom had to discuss with Dave must have been really earth-shattering. I wondered why she didn't want me there. It wasn't anywhere near time for my birthday. I couldn't imagine any secrets she might want to tell him that she wouldn't share with me first.

When I heard the door open sometime after two o'clock, I sat up in bed. *Well, it's about time*, I thought.

"Dave," I called, "I'm in bed, honey. Come on back."

He came to the door and just stood there, leaning against the frame. Since the only light was the hall light behind him, all I saw was his silhouette. But he looked haggard.

"What's wrong, Dave?" I asked.

"You don't know the half of it," he muttered. Then he turned and walked away.

I jumped up out of bed and ran after him. "You're right, Dave, I don't know any of it. What in the world happened?"

Now that we were in the light, I saw that Dave had been crying. My big, strong, never-rattled husband looked like a miserable pile of bones.

Reaching out to touch his shoulder, I said, "Dave, please tell me. I'm your wife. Maybe I can help you with whatever the problem is."

He jerked away and glared at me. "You can't be my wife, Claudia."

"What?" All of a sudden, he looked like he was insane.

Sucking in a breath, Dave forced himself to gather a little strength. "You can't be my wife, Claudia, because you're my daughter."

"What are you talking about, Dave? Have you been drinking?"

He shook his head and walked into the kitchen. I followed him all the way in there and blocked the door when he tried to leave. "Oh, no, you don't, Dave. You're not going anywhere until you explain."

It took several hours for me to get it out of him. In fact, the sun had already started to rise when he finally broke down and told me what my mom had wanted. Now I wished I hadn't asked.

At first, Dave shook as he explained how he'd gone to a sperm bank and made a donation, back when he was in medical school. He'd needed a little money, and some of the other students had told him that was a great and painless way to make a few bucks.

My mother had been in her medical practice for a few years when the "mommy bug" bit her. She wanted a child, but she had no marriage prospects lined up. And being the sort of woman she was, she didn't want to have a one-night stand. She went to the sperm bank and was artificially inseminated.

Now, as he unraveled the story my mom had revealed to him, I began to see the whole picture. "But how do you know I'm your daughter?" I asked. "It could have been anyone."

"When your mom saw Ashley, she went straight home and dug out your pictures from when you were that age. She waited a few days, but after she thought it over, she decided she'd better call the sperm bank. They didn't want to tell her who the donor was, but after she told them how important knowing the information was, they finally relented." He licked his lips. "And they're sending the paperwork so we can be totally certain."

Now I was shaking. "It could be a mistake," I said. "Look at the odds of that happening."

"No, it's not a mistake," he said. "I should have seen something like this happening." With trembling hands, he started to reach for me, but then pulled back as if a snake had bitten him. "I've never been a big proponent of sperm banks, and this is the very reason why."

Dave shook all over and tensed when I reached out to touch his face. I quickly pulled my hand back.

"What are we going to do now, Dave?" I finally asked.

"I have no idea, but I do know I can't sleep with you anymore, Claudia."

His voice sounded very ragged and filled with angst. I ached inside, but he was right: we couldn't sleep together. That would be incest.

I called my mother at work the next day. She told me she'd cover for me at the office. She apologized to me, but I hung up on her. I didn't feel like listening to anything from her lying lips.

All this time, I thought I had a dad who'd either abandoned us or died. I never dreamed she'd gone to a sperm bank and taken a withdrawal. The very thought of that made me sick to my stomach.

I didn't go back to work for nearly a week, and when I did, my mom and I didn't even look at each other. I knew she was upset, but I was even more furious. How could she have done this to me?

Of course, given the circumstances, Dave and I couldn't remain married. We quickly got an annulment, which was no problem since I hadn't gotten pregnant, thank goodness.

Fortunately, I hadn't sold my condo yet. I took it off the market and moved right back into it, leaving Dave in the house. It was almost like we'd never even met. But my heart ached, and nothing seemed to fill the void.

Three months later, I knew I couldn't even stay in the same town with either Mom or Dave. So I started contacting medical practices all over the country where I'd heard someone was retiring. It took me a couple more months before I finally found what seemed like a good fit.

My mom didn't try to talk me out of the move. She knew it was something I had to do. But there were tears in her eyes as I drove away from her for the last time.

I didn't even bother to call Dave to say good-bye. It would have been too hard to talk to him, after all that had happened. I knew it was as hard for him as it was me, and it wasn't his fault. My mom should have told me years ago. After all, I wasn't a child anymore.

I've been in a small town several hours away from my old medical practice. It's okay, but I sure do miss my old condo that finally sold after I arrived. I took the money and bought a cottage near the business district in town, figuring I could walk to and from work for the exercise.

Looking back at my short marriage, I still shudder to think about the situation. I'd been married and making love with my biological father, something that is really disgusting, no matter who you were.

I doubt if I'll ever allow myself to fall in love again. However, if it ever happens—and that's a big *if*—I'll do a thorough investigation. My happiness is worth it. THE END

INNOCENCE LOST
Too young to save myself

I met Sean Potter when I was fourteen and he was . . . thirty-seven? Thirty-eight? It was the day he moved into the house across the street with his family. My girlfriend, Stacy Harris, my pesky kid sister, Melanie, and I stationed ourselves on the sidewalk. We relayed a running report to my grandmother—who professed to hate nosy neighbors—on what was coming out of the moving van.

"Go tell her a blue love seat, a blue couch, and two matching chairs."

Twelve-year-old Melanie flew inside where Granny was nursing a hangover.

She returned like a boomerang—"Granny wants to know what color the chairs are"—and flew back inside with the answer.

This went on for several hours. We'd catalogued just about the entire contents of the Potter household for Granny when an awesome red sports car pulled up to the curb. Stacy and I dissolved into giggles and blushes when the handsome driver rolled down his window to introduce himself.

"Hey, Barbie dolls!" he called to us. We were just too naïve to recognize the difference between a smile and a leer.

Sean had a way about him that could have lured a nun. We were soon bantering back and forth. Stacy and I felt terribly sophisticated, yet at the same time, embarrassed by the interest of such an attractive older man.

Years later, I would contact Sean Potter in an attempt to exorcise the demon of rage that possessed me. My psychiatrist called it "closure."

"I was only fourteen!" I protested. "How can you justify the way you exploited me?"

To my indignation, Sean replied, "You were a woman fully grown at fourteen."

"That's ridiculous!" I cried. "I was no more a woman at that age than Stacy was. Why me and not her?"

Sean shrugged, and suddenly I saw an animal, not a man—a predator who instinctually knew how to separate a weak one from the herd.

"That first day we met, we were just talking. It was no big deal, but Stacy's mother didn't like it. She called Stacy in and raised holy hell with her about approaching a stranger's car. Remember?" he asked.

I remembered. He'd made some kind of derogatory remark about "apron strings" after Stacy left. I remember he eyed me up and down appreciatively as he commented that it was a relief to see there was no shortage of "babysitter talent" in the new neighborhood.

After years of psychiatrists, lawyers, and experts on sexual abuse, I still remember.

We had one of those families where the mother moves from man to man, with the children dropped along the way like excess baggage. How I envied Stacy's stable, orderly home and the overly protective parents she groused about. Her father, John Harris, was a minister and a pillar of the community.

Melanie and I had Granny and chaos. Granny did the best she could for us, but she was an alcoholic and needed care herself.

Mom was in and out of our lives—vivacious, scatter-brained, and quite frankly, dishonest. She made an unsteady living bilking insurance companies with false accident claims. She was constantly suing somebody. Work was a four-letter word to Mom, and eventually she ran afoul of the law and wound up in prison.

Was it any wonder I was crazy about the Potter family?

Brenda and Sean were adorable. With their two little boys, Colin and Nicky—and later, my special pet, baby Lindsey—they were every wholesome sitcom family I'd ever seen on television.

I started working for them almost immediately. With a new household to set up, pregnant Brenda needed help with the boys. After school and on weekends, I kept them occupied while she put together what I regarded as a showplace.

"House proud," Granny called Brenda. At the time, I thought the old lady was just jealous. Our small bungalow was always a mess. In hindsight, I see that Brenda's obsessive housekeeping was part of a very disturbed pattern.

No one was permitted to cross the Potters' threshold in shoes. Brenda provided disposable slippers to all her visitors. There were parts of the house the children were forbidden to enter. God help them if one of their toys strayed from its appointed place. Every shelf, from the pantry to the cellar, was arranged with mechanical precision.

Still, I really admired Brenda and hoped someday to emulate her style and taste. She was absolutely gorgeous. As exacting in her grooming as she was in her housekeeping, I can honestly say I never saw Brenda with a single golden hair out of place or her makeup less than perfect.

"You always get everything just right," I sighed that first Christmas season as I tasted Brenda's fancy cookies. The house was decorated like a holiday dream come true.

"Its a matter of discipline." Brenda smiled. "I've been called inflexible, but I achieve things. That's unforgivable to most people, because most people are slobs."

I wanted to sink through the floor, convinced she was referring to my family, and by extension, me. I thought if Brenda ever looked down from her pedestal and saw the way we lived, I'd just die.

Granny professed to hate Christmas, so if Melanie and I wanted a tree, we had to drag one home ourselves. That year, Stacy helped and the three of us had a hilarious time on Christmas Eve, getting a half-price, half-bald scotch pine through the snow.

"So tell me, how can you be around Antonio without drooling?" Stacy demanded.

"Antonio" was our code name for Sean Potter. We thought he was the spitting image of a movie star by that name. Stacy had a total crush on Sean and never stopped nagging me with questions about him.

"It's a matter of discipline," I replied.

"So how's the perfect marriage?" Stacy didn't need to elaborate.

We often speculated about the Potters' relationship. They seemed like such complete opposites. Devil-may-care Sean was a charmer, full of nervous energy, while Brenda was sedate and rather prudish. Stacy expressed her pet theory that they only stayed together for the children as we struggled with the tree.

"You might be right," I conceded, each word punctuated with a white puff in the frosty air. "Lately, he's been putting Brenda down a lot, making fun of her figure."

"Well, she is huge." Stacy was quick to defend Sean. "I mean, I know she's pregnant, but she didn't have to turn into an elephant."

I shrugged. "Some stuff he says is really funny, but other stuff makes me kind of uncomfortable. He complains about her to me. He says she's not very affectionate."

Stacy nodded with all the wisdom of her fourteen years. "She's going to lose him someday, you mark my words." I knew this was one of Stacy's fantasies—that Brenda would lose Sean to *her* someday.

"Aren't you thrilled that he's confiding in you? Amanda Reese, you are one lucky duck!" she exclaimed.

I admit I was tickled by Stacy's envy as we rolled the tree up to our porch steps.

Short, stubby little Granny opened the front door. Her breath was easily ninety proof, and she was weaving in a way that told me she was drunker than usual.

"Don't you bring that green son of a bitch in here!" She pointed to our tree. "We've got enough in here already. Your mother! In here already with some son of a bitch."

My holiday spirits fizzled like a punctured balloon. Melanie's small face fell. I'm sure we both had a premonition of disaster.

Inside, Mom swooped down on us in her usual frenzy. Her hair was a new color: a bright, shocking red that suited her. She was wearing a fluffy white peignoir; the big, floppy ruffles at the neck reminded me of a clown's collar.

"Oh, thank God I'm back with my family! I'm back with my family for Christmas!" she cried as she threw her arms around Stacy and slobbered kisses all over my friend's startled face.

"I've got a surprise," Mom squealed. "Wait until you see the surprise!" Bouncing like a puppy, she pushed us forward. "Meet your new daddy!"

The man in Granny's recliner had the monstrous, distorted physique of a body builder on steroids. His shaved head seemed grotesquely small on his massive shoulders, but it was his eyes—hateful little piggy eyes—that remain with me today.

My mother was over the moon with excitement. Every one-night stand was the love of her life. "Daddy Ben," she insisted we call this stranger, who beamed waves of hostility at us.

Stacy wisely went home. Granny was soon snoring on the couch. Melanie and I spent a grim evening watching Mom make a fool out of herself before we escaped to bed.

What happened between them I can only imagine, but around one in the morning, we awoke to terrifying screams as Daddy Ben slammed through the house with a hammer in his hands. He gouged our walls, smashed the furniture, even reduced our toilet to rubble, while Mom cowered in a closet and Granny cursed.

Melanie and I climbed out our bedroom window in bare feet. We jumped into the snow. I grabbed my sister's hand, and in a blind panic, we bolted across the street for help.

Out of the frying pan and into the fire.

Over the years, Brenda would come to refer to me as "a member of the family." How appropriate that the crazy Daddy Ben incident marked the start of the many confusing roles I would play in that family—little mother to the children, Brenda's sister-servant-therapist, Sean's surrogate wife.

Melanie, worried about Granny, returned to what was left of home as soon as the police escorted Daddy Ben to jail. I virtually moved in with the Potter family that night. Brenda had a difficult delivery on New Year's Day, and I was pleased to take over for her during the crisis, caring for the boys much as a young aunt would.

She was in the hospital for two weeks, and in a way, it was like playing house. Sean certainly encouraged me.

"What would we do without you, doll?" he said over and over.

"You're my little wifelet." His extravagant praise made me feel very grown-up and competent.

The night before Brenda was due to be discharged, I tucked the boys into bed and came out of their room to find Sean waiting on the stairs. He held up a bottle of champagne and two glasses.

"Celebration time," he announced, popping the cork.

My hands flew to my mouth in horror as the sparkling wine sprayed in a wide arc all over the stairwell.

"Sean! She'll go bonkers if that stains the carpet!"

He shrugged. "She *is* bonkers, doll. Come on downstairs and watch a video with me."

It was my first taste of champagne and my first "adult" movie, a silly soft-core porn comedy that we had fun ridiculing. We watched it by shimmering candlelight, and I felt the stirring of an appetite that I'd never known before.

During one sensuous scene, a nude actor was massaged by his on-screen lover, who wore a demi bra and garter belt. I would soon learn that Sean had a fetish for lacy undergarments.

Giggling, I looked away and inadvertently met his eyes. I realized with a shock that we were sharing the same thought.

My heart fluttered in my chest as I dismissed the erotic tension as one-sided, no more real than Stacy's fantasy. I couldn't believe that Sean, Mr. Cool, might find me attractive. I risked one timid move, childish, really: I meant to tickle his hand, but my touch turned into a caress.

Before I knew what was happening, I was in his arms, his lips pressed to mine. His hot, probing kisses thrilled me into submission.

"It's happening!" he cried deliriously at the moment of impact. "You want this. You want me, doll!"

And that was ultimately how he justified sex between us. In Sean's cunning mind, I led him astray. I was a teenage temptress, a lustful Lolita who made the first move on a vulnerable older man.

"If I'd refused you that night, you could have made accusations, cried rape," he blandly informed me when I tracked him down later as an adult.

So much for closure.

Brenda came home from the hospital pale and silent. She could barely get out of bed and needed help more than ever. I thought she was simply exhausted from the trauma of Lindsey's birth—what would a fourteen-year-old know about postpartum depression?

Feeling guilty, I was wildly conflicted over what had happened with her husband, and I fretted that we were somehow responsible for Brenda's suffering. *Impossible*, I assured myself. She couldn't know what we'd done on her immaculate ivory couch. I prayed that she'd never know. I was sure she'd just die if she found out.

I never wanted to have an affair with Sean; I wanted a family, a home, a place where I felt loved, protected, and appreciated. It was my hope that he could give me these things without hurting Brenda or the kids.

I was willing to do anything to please: I cut myself off from normal relationships with boys my own age, I distanced myself from Granny and Melanie, I endured Brenda's short temper and sharp tongue. I was Sean's little wifelet, with no will of my own.

Stacy knew something was amiss. It was scary how close she came to the truth when I turned down a trip to Florida with her family during spring recess because, "The Potters might have plans."

"You mean *Sean* might have plans," Stacy snapped, disappointment clouding her face. "I'm sick of the way you fawn all over him!"

My laugh was uneasy. "You should talk. I don't leave for school a half an hour early so I can see Antonio go to work."

"I haven't done that in ages, dear," she countered sarcastically. "I think he's a creep."

"Since when?"

"Since he turned my best friend into a junior Stepford wife!"

My face went hot with shame. For a hellish second, I thought she'd divined my secret.

"I don't know what you mean," I objected lamely. "I just work for Sean, that's all."

"Work? Ha! You don't have time for anything else. It's like you're obsessed. Brenda says jump and you ask how high—it's pathetic,"

Stacy sputtered angrily. "You act grateful, like they're doing you a favor. Can't you see how the two of them are using you?"

I went weak with relief. Stacy didn't know what was really going on. She wasn't implying anything illicit between me and Sean.

"You don't know squat," I said with contempt. "You're just jealous."

"Yeah? Well, my dad thinks there's something really strange about the Potters."

"Oh, yeah? Well, Sean calls your dad Elmer Fudd!"

That shut her up.

In truth, it was Brenda I fawned all over, not Sean, for it was Brenda who increasingly provided me with the support and guidance I craved. She called me her "best friend" and gave me advice about everything under the sun. She helped me with my homework, taught me how to cook, how to sew, how to apply makeup, how to dress. I simply shut my mind to how I was betraying her with Sean.

Stacy was right: I was obsessed. No matter how much work Brenda piled on me—laundry, cooking, and heavy cleaning, on top of child care—I was happy. I had no time for friends or after-school activities, but I didn't mind. I just wanted to be with Sean and Brenda.

"Full steam ahead" was Brenda's motto. She worked herself as hard as she worked me.

Of course, I can see now that the darkness that descended on her after Lindsey's birth never really lifted. Frantic busy work and over-scheduling herself was a way of pretending nothing was wrong. She volunteered her time like a maniac, running herself ragged with the PTA, the church, various civic groups.

"It's tough being married to superwoman," Sean would sigh. "She leaps tall buildings in a single bound, then locks herself in the bathroom and bawls all night."

Brenda cried on my shoulder all the time, as if I had nothing better to do than listen to how much she hated sex. She couldn't stand for Sean to touch her. She'd vent to me for hours about her problems, her weight, her marriage.

Then Sean would grill me: What was "Fat Stuff" bitching about now? I was caught in the middle, trying to balance on a tightrope between them. I was so ashamed when Brenda told me I was the only person she could trust.

Sean had a genius for finding time alone with me. Strangely enough, he was often aided and abetted by Brenda, another burden on my guilty conscience because it made me feel like a skunk to take advantage of her ignorance.

"Sean, you promised you'd go to the store with Amanda . . . "

"Sean, Amanda needs a ride to . . . "

"Sean, I've got a headache. Take Amanda . . . "

What we called our "road trips" gave her husband a chance to indulge his lingerie kink. He'd buy an assortment of wispy little things during our travels, and on the way home, we'd make a detour to the Pink Flamingo Motel, where I would model for him. "Play clothes" he called these silken bits that he always kept as souvenirs.

Looking back, I see that Sean certainly liked to take risks. I was a month shy of my sixteenth birthday when we were exposed, in a way we could never have been foreseen.

Sean and I had just stepped out of unit six at the Pink Flamingo when the door to unit five was opened by a woman who had shockingly red hair. How many mothers would be delighted to discover their teenage daughter leaving a motel room with a married man?

"Amanda!" Mom squealed, clapping her hands. "Oh, look, Daddy John, it's my older girl." She turned to the stunned man standing behind her.

Stacy's dad needed no introduction.

Mom insisted that we all sit down together and have a drink. She and Sean chatted like old friends, while a mortified Pastor Harris and I squirmed.

"Amanda, I can explain," Stacy's dad whispered urgently.

I couldn't raise my head to look him in the eye.

Sean was obviously enjoying Pastor Harris's humiliation. "So how long have you and Daddy John been an item?" Sean asked my mother with a sly wink.

Mom hooted. "People who live in glass houses, eh, Sean? Well, I guess you've got some explaining to do yourself, seeing as how

Amanda here is what you might call jailbait."

That wiped the grin off Sean's handsome face. Pastor Harris would only endure a scandal if his little lapse was made public, but Sean would be talking to the district attorney. I knew my mother, and I knew that dollar signs were dancing in her empty head.

It cost Sean plenty to keep Mom from going to the police. If only my mother had cared enough to double-cross Sean and turn him in. What a difference it would have made in my life. If only Pastor Harris would have intervened then. My self-esteem, always low, dipped lower. I began to function on emotional autopilot.

And Daddy John never did explain.

Every summer, the Potters rented a cottage on the lake for a two-week vacation. I was always included, and so was Melanie. It was a big deal for my little sister, so I was grateful to Sean and Brenda for their generosity.

Granny was frequently sick, so my sister had responsibilities far beyond her years. I helped out at home as much as I could, but Melanie was really devoted to Granny. I thought it was a good thing for her to get away from cleaning up after a drunk. At the lake, she could just be a kid for two weeks.

Melanie was fourteen, a lovable, strawberry-blonde pixie. I was sixteen and miserable. I realized how completely isolated I was from people my own age when a boy I met on the beach asked me out.

"I can't. I have to . . . like, baby-sit."

"Every second of the day?" he teased. "You don't get a break? What are you, a slave or something?"

"The Potters are really good people," I said stiffly. "They've helped me out a lot, but they don't own me."

He raised an eyebrow. "Does that mean you want to come down to the bonfire tonight or not?"

I didn't have an answer, so I just shrugged. What *did* I want? I was so confused. How could I tell him that evenings were reserved for moonlight swims with my middle-aged lover? What I accepted as normal behavior seemed bizarre when taken out of its context.

The boy's laugh was young and spirited as he dashed off down the beach towards a volleyball game.

"You're weird!" he called to me over his shoulder.

Tears stung my eyes, because that's how I felt—weird, like a freak. I had no life of my own. My attachment to the Potters was based on the illusion that they could somehow replace my own broken, neglectful family. I'd grown so dependent on them that I didn't know how to relate to other people outside our cozy threesome.

Determined to prove to myself that I didn't care if the Potters liked it or not, I joined the group at the bonfire that evening. I was welcomed—the boy who'd invited me flirted outrageously—but I couldn't enjoy myself there. I felt like a fraud among my peers.

Sean had raised hell about my going. "What do you want with a bunch of bums sitting around a fire?"

When I returned to the cottage, I found Brenda drinking iced tea outside, fanning herself languidly. It was a steamy night. Two-year-old Lindsey ran to me with her chubby arms outstretched.

"Mandy!" the toddler cried. That was the closest she could come to pronouncing my name. Her big brown eyes always melted my heart.

Things were awfully quiet. Not even the crickets were chirping.

"Where is everybody?" I asked.

"Boys are asleep," Brenda grunted.

"Where's Sean?"

"Went down for a swim."

Holding Lindsey on my hip, I was about to pull up a plastic lawn chair when Brenda added, "Melanie went with him."

My heart pounded. Alone with Sean meant only one thing to me.

"I suggested it," Brenda continued snippily, "since you had other plans for the evening."

Lindsey began to wail when I handed her to her mother. On trembling legs, I started down the wooded path to the water. There were no stars, so the moon was a pendant dangling in the sky. In the distance, far down the beach, I could see the bonfire still blazing.

Near the pier, there was one splash and then another. I hurried towards the sound.

"Relax." Sean's voice cut clearly through the darkness. "Just lay back and let yourself go, doll."

If he did to her what he did to me— "Melanie!" I screamed. She was just a baby!

"Amanda?" My sister swam noisily towards the pier. "What's the matter?"

My voice was shrill with panic. "Get away from him, Melanie."

"Sean's just teaching me to float, Amanda."

"I don't care! We have to go home."

Melanie pulled herself onto the pier. "Is something wrong with Granny?"

Sean was wading to the shore. I could make out his silhouette, a black figure moving against blackness.

"What's the matter, Amanda, jealous? Worried about a little competition?" he asked.

The bastard! I was so furious, I could have scratched his eyes out.

"You stay away from us, Sean. I mean it! I don't want anything to do with you ever again. I'll tell Brenda."

He gave a short, scornful laugh. "Go ahead."

Melanie tugged on my arm. "Amanda, what's wrong with Granny?" she repeated.

I waited until Sean's silhouette disappeared between the trees. "Nothing's wrong. We need to go home, that's all."

Melanie pestered me with questions as I hustled her off the beach. We hiked to a pizza parlor in the town where I knew there was a pay phone. I made a collect call to Stacy.

"Stacy, Melanie and I need to get home tonight. Tell your father to come get us. I can't think of anyone else with a car."

"Amanda, you're a hundred miles away. I can't ask my dad to—"

"Stacy, please. Just ask your father to come to the phone. I'll explain to him."

While Stacy put down the receiver, I could hear a conversation in the background.

She returned with, "Dad says he'll come get you, but it'll have to be tomorrow morning."

"Then put your mother on the phone," I barked. "I have something to tell her, something about people who live in glass houses!"

Pastor Harris got two speeding tickets—one on the way down to the lake, one on the way home with us—that night.

I made my mind up to have nothing further to do with the Potters. Their story was that I refused to obey a curfew they had set. Brenda told Granny that they were concerned about me hanging out with "a rough crowd" setting fires on the beach.

"That's a lie," I countered angrily. "What curfew? This is the first I've heard of any curfew. And I wasn't hanging out with anyone. I met a boy, that's all. The kids at the lake have a bonfire every night. The Potters want to control me, run my life. Sean thinks he owns me."

Of course, I sounded like a whiny, willful brat who ran away because she didn't like having limits set for her own good. The Potters came off as responsible, caring adults. Sean gambled on the fact that I couldn't bring myself to tell Granny the truth.

He set about wooing me back in the most romantic ways. He sent flowers. He wrote me a poem. He swore up and down on the telephone that I'd misinterpreted what was going on that night with Melanie.

When I didn't budge, he played his trump card. "The kids don't understand why you've abandoned them, Amanda. Lindsey asks for you all the time. 'Where Mandy? Where my Mandy?' She's the innocent party in all of this. Don't punish her."

Brenda begged me to come back to the fold. "You're like a sister to me, Amanda. Think of all we've shared. We can't allow a silly misunderstanding to come between us. Let's be friends again."

I missed Colin, Nicky, and my darling Lindsey as much as I missed Brenda's companionship.

I told Sean I would return on one condition: "You and I are through. I don't want you to touch me ever again. I'm not coming back for *you*." I willed myself to believe it. God help me, I still wanted him.

Things went back to "normal" for a brief time. I tried to avoid Sean. His longing looks and secret smiles would have broken down my resistance eventually.

The truth is supposed to set you free, but in my case, it set me on a long, painful journey to find myself.

I'd been in the Potters' bedroom on many occasions, of course, but I'd never had a reason to go inside Brenda's walk-in closet until she asked me to fetch a skirt she needed to hem. A pretty, flowered hatbox on the shelf caught my eye. As I was admiring it, I caught a stray whiff of my favorite perfume.

Brenda had once received this expensive perfume as a gift, which she then passed on to me. It was "too flowery" for her. Curious, I took the box down. What I found inside made me sick to my stomach.

Inside were Sean's "play clothes," the wispy silk and lace souvenirs he had kept from our motel romps. There was no way that Brenda, who organized every square inch of space in her house, could not be aware of the contents of this box. There was no way she could not know what these sexy items, still sweet with my scent, represented.

Stacy's words returned to haunt me: "Can't you see how the two of them are using you?" The *two* of them.

Brenda had known what Sean was up to all along. The knowledge made me reel. She'd not only accepted the affair, she'd actively encouraged it. I could only guess at her sick, selfish motives for keeping the evidence of her husband's adultery among her own belongings. Did she get some kind of vicarious thrill out of these souvenirs? Was it a form of masochism?

I threw the hat box against a wall and fled their house, never to return. Then I agonized for weeks. I couldn't eat or sleep; I refused to go to school. This time, the Potters kept a wary distance.

Stacy actually forced her way into my bedroom to see me. She threatened to have her father come to the house if I wouldn't talk to her.

"Don't, Stacy, please don't," I pleaded. "He'll just go to Sean, and Sean'll deny everything, and I'll die."

"Deny what, Amanda? I don't understand." My friend's smooth brow furrowed with concern.

Finally, what I'd been holding back for three long years spilled out. Stacy was shocked, then angry—at Sean for taking advantage of my innocence, at me for not confiding in her sooner.

We cried together and held each other. She made me promise to get help. I made her promise not to discuss what I'd told her with anyone.

Neither one of us could keep our promise. I continued to hide like a wounded animal. Stacy couldn't carry the weight of my secret alone. After much soul searching, she went to her father.

As I predicted, Pastor Harris went to Sean. A week later, there was a FOR SALE sign on the Potters' front lawn.

"I didn't give him a chance to deny anything," Stacy's father told me. "He thinks no one will believe you. I reminded him that I could corroborate your claim. That caught him completely off guard, because he was counting on me remaining silent to protect my reputation. I'm willing to go to the police with you, Amanda, if you intend to file charges."

I shook my head. "Oh, no, I couldn't go to the police. I don't want anyone to know. You don't know how clever he is, how he can twist things around. I'm so ashamed already."

"The worry is that he might repeat this behavior with another girl." Pastor Harris couldn't know how those words would one day come back to haunt me.

"I don't care. I just want to get on with my life," I insisted. "I just want to be free." Another girl could have him, with my blessing.

Freedom wasn't possible. The Potters were gone, but far from forgotten, when I started college. Try as I might to leave them behind, they went with me to my first job. They were with me in my dreams. They were beside me at Melanie's high school graduation, Granny's funeral, Stacy's wedding.

At twenty-five, I truly believed I was cursed. I had no chance at such ordinary passages of adult life as marriage and children, because of my memories.

At twenty-eight, I began psychotherapy.

"Let's pull up a chair for Sean and Brenda," is how Dr. Lowell often began our sessions.

Slowly, I began to focus my anger. I would rave and rant at the empty chairs until my voice was hoarse. Only then could I talk about how much I hated being a victim.

It was when I stopped being ashamed that my rage really came into its own and I was able to act. I considered making some kind of case against the Potters and consulted lawyers. Dr. Lowell suggested that I might find peace without going to war if I located Sean and confronted him about how destructive the affair had been to me.

I had a vague idea that the Potters had moved to Brenda's hometown on Long Island. Thanks to the Internet, I played detective and found their upscale address quickly.

I showed up on their doorstep unannounced. At first, Brenda actually tried to pretend she didn't have a clue what I was talking about. Sean, more handsome than ever, was unrepentant.

"You were just lucky I didn't go to the police," was my parting shot.

"Oh, please." Brenda waved her hand dismissively. "Nobody would have believed a little slut like you."

At that moment, I stopped merely *considering* a lawsuit. I was going to war. As ugly and difficult as it was going to be to go public, these depraved people were going to answer for what they did to me.

Outside, I was getting into my car to leave when someone tapped my shoulder. I turned around and found myself looking into a pair of big, brown eyes.

"Lindsey!" She was fourteen, another tall, gawky, timid girl—the ghost of what I had been at that age.

I smiled. "You don't remember me, do you? You used to call me—"

"Mandy. I remember you." Her eyes cut quickly towards the house and back. She grabbed my hand. "I believe you," she whispered urgently.

My blood went cold at the reflection of myself in her frightened brown eyes, and then she ran off . . . another woman fully grown.
THE END

MY HIGH SCHOOL AFFAIR
Will we live happily ever after?

When I met Josh, he was just as wild and fun-loving as I was. He was a senior and new to our school. I was a sophomore, attending some advanced classes. So at first, Josh didn't realize I was only fifteen.

Josh liked to cause a ruckus in class, which I thought was funny. Everybody liked him. He soon started hanging around with my group of friends.

"My parents divorced last year," I told him the first time we were alone, wandering around the shopping mall. "My mom's so serious all the time. I just hate going home. And we *never* have enough money."

"I know exactly what you mean," Josh said. "A few months ago, my dad took off with his newest fling. He's such a jerk. It just about killed my mom to have him cheat on her like that. We used to have a nice house, but now we live in a tiny condo. Mom cries all the time. I wish I never had to go home again."

So Josh and I started hanging out together all the time. We never went home if we could help it. My mom worked long hours, so it was easy to say I'd been home doing homework when I'd really been out somewhere with Josh. That made it convenient for me and Josh to start fooling around sexually.

After about a month, we were having sex. We were both virgins, so we weren't worried about catching any diseases from each other.

"But what if I get pregnant?" I asked after the third or forth time.

"We'll get married," Josh said, as if it was really that simple.

I started daydreaming about how great it would be if Josh and I were married. We could both leave our unhappy mothers behind and start a life of our own. We'd have our own apartment somewhere, Josh would find a job, and we wouldn't have any more problems.

On weekends, we'd hang around the shopping mall with friends from school and have a good time. We got into mischief and laughed a lot. We never meant anybody any harm; we were just trying to be happy for a little while. Life was too scary, and none of us wanted to face it. I don't know what made me think getting married would solve anything.

"You'd better get your grades up, Lauren," my mom said when she got my midterm report in the mail. "You'll never get into college this way."

"I'm not going to college," I muttered. "We don't have the money for that. Besides, it's a long way off. I don't even graduate for two and a half years." Two and a half years sounded like a long time in those days.

"It'll be here before you know it. Your father's going to pay your way through college—I'll see to it. I don't want you facing life with no education and no job skills. I'm thinking of your future, Lauren."

"*I'm* thinking about Saturday night," I said sarcastically.

"You'd better listen to me!" she yelled. "Life is very hard when things don't work out the way you expected."

"Tell me about it." I rolled my eyes. I felt guilty for talking to her like that, but life was so dismal in our house.

I ran for the door because I could feel a lecture coming on. I could hear Mom yelling my name after I went out, but by then, I was already halfway down the block.

When I got to Josh's place, he was doing chores. His mom seemed to think if she forced him to do loads of chores he'd realize that manual labor wasn't very much fun; he'd start studying harder, get better grades, and eventually make it to college. He already knew he wasn't going. He didn't have the grades, and he didn't seem to care.

"Wait for me out back," he told me at the door. "Mom's on a rampage today."

So I waited for him in the parking lot of his building. I didn't understand why our mothers couldn't be more cheerful. I knew they were going through painful times, but did they have to take it out on us?

Josh and I were so in love, we didn't care about anything. We lived for the moment. We lived for the scraps of happiness we could find together and the pleasure of making love when we got the chance.

I knew sex was risky, but it just didn't seem to matter somehow. If both our mothers had tried to do their best and wound up divorced anyway, who could say being "good" was a guarantee of anything?

I guess there wasn't anything that anybody could have done for us in those days. We were determined to find a way to get married, and *having* to get married seemed like a great idea. We just did what came naturally, wondering when our lives would start to change for the better.

Well, by Christmas, I hadn't had a period, so I was starting to get nervous and excited. Mom worked her long hours, oblivious of me and what was going on in my life. We were a million miles apart in those days.

I'd keep our house clean the way she wanted, and I'd study the classified ads for apartments. When I called a few places to check on the rent, it was a really big shock to discover what even an efficiency apartment cost per month.

"The cheapest place is a room over somebody's garage," I told Josh. "We're both going to have to work to make ends meet."

Maybe that's when I started to get a little tingle of fear inside. I wasn't old enough to work, and Josh's mother didn't want him to get a job. She wanted him to concentrate on his schoolwork.

And if it was hard for our mothers to make ends meet, what made Josh and me think we could do any better? At least both our mothers were high school graduates. I started to worry, but of course by then it was already too late.

I didn't wise up, though. I still hung out at the shopping mall every weekend with Josh, laughing like there was no tomorrow.

Deep down inside, I was getting very scared. I was starting to feel sick every morning and didn't feel like going to school. Soon I was going to have to tell Mom what we'd done. I knew she was going to cry; I dreaded that. I wondered if she would even *let* us get married. I wasn't of legal age to marry yet. What if—

I wouldn't let myself think about anything going wrong. I was pretending everything was fine when it wasn't. I figured as long as Josh stood by me, we'd be all right.

Well, I was able to convince Mom I just had a touch of the flu over Christmas break, so she didn't suspect I really had morning sickness. But when I still wasn't feeling well in January, she wanted to take me to the doctor.

"Maybe you have something more serious than the flu," she said, looking worried.

I knew she was worrying about paying the deductible on her health insurance. Suddenly, I wondered, *How are we going to pay for a hospital stay when I have the baby?* Jeez, it was so complicated being grown-up. I wanted to crawl in a hole somewhere and hide.

"I don't need to go to a doctor," I insisted. "I'll be fine soon."

"Well, if you're not better by next week, we're going to the doctor, and that's that. Your father could sue for custody if he thought I was neglecting you."

"I'm not a kid, Mom!"

"In a court of law, you're a minor in this state. I can't lose you, honey."

That's when it began to dawn on me that I was in the deep end of the swimming pool, and I was drowning and didn't even know it.

Well, I didn't feel better the next week. I didn't want to go to school at all by that point. Mom let me stay home for a couple of days. I felt better in the afternoon, and by evening I was fine.

"Are you faking, Lauren?" Mom finally asked. "Are you failing in school and don't want to admit it?"

I couldn't stand it anymore. I walked out and headed over to Josh's, leaving Mom to call after me. By the time I got to his house, my mom was already on the phone with his mom.

"I can't have your mother threatening me, Lauren," Josh's mom told me when I got to the door. "You can't come here every time you have a fight with your mother. Now go home and behave yourself. I have enough trouble in my life without this."

I wanted to yell, *You're going to have a lot more trouble pretty soon!*

I went home, reluctantly apologized, and sulked in my room all weekend. I started wondering what the baby was going to wear, where was it going to sleep, what it would eat, and whether it would be a girl or a boy.

On Monday, I cornered Josh in the hall at school. "We have to talk right now!"

He was always looking for an excuse to ditch school, so we sneaked out just before lunch and spent some time wandering the shopping mall, looking at wedding rings, baby clothes, and maternity clothes.

When we were together, it was like there was no tomorrow. I could believe everything was going to be all right for us, but deep down, I was getting really worried. I'd made a dumb mistake letting myself get pregnant at fifteen. If I couldn't work, how was I going to bring in enough money to help Josh pay the bills?

That afternoon, we ended up at the park, feeding the last of our burgers to the ducks.

"What are we going to do?" I asked Josh. "We need to get married pretty soon. I can hardly button my jeans anymore. This is really happening, Josh! I'm pregnant! I'm getting a little scared. You're going to stick by me, aren't you? You're not going to let your mom keep you from marrying me, are you?"

That was my real fear. I was pregnant, not Josh. In my experience, the guy could cut out anytime, just like my dad had done when he got tired of Mom and me. I wanted to cry and hang onto Josh, but I was afraid suddenly. Our love was strong enough for high school, but was it strong enough for real life?

"I think we'd better wait before we tell anybody," Josh said, looking very serious suddenly. "My mom's getting suspicious. She's warned me a couple of times about getting a girl in trouble.

"She's also been talking on the phone with my dad a lot lately. I don't know if they could make me go live with him or not. I mean, I don't want to. I can't stand the sight of that jerk and his bimbo. Being with Mom isn't so bad, really. If she would just stop jumping down my throat every day."

Then Josh started crying. Until that moment, I guess I had thought he was really grown-up the way a man should be. I thought everything would be all right just because he loved me. But Josh was just seventeen—and scared, same as me.

"What if I can't get a job, Lauren? What if I can't make enough money to support you and a baby? We've been stupid. We might not be able to get married right away. You might have to go on living with your mom so you'll be able to use her insurance for the hospital and doctor bills. My mom doesn't have health insurance at all."

"Oh, God," I whispered. "What are we going to do then?"

"We're going to keep quiet about this until it's too late."

"What do you mean, too late?" Suddenly, I couldn't breathe.

"Until it's too late for somebody to drag you off to an abortion clinic to get rid of it. We're not old enough to be doing what we've been doing—not in the eyes of the law, anyway."

"It's not fair!" I cried.

"When I say that to my mom, she just looks at me with this creepy anger in her eyes and says, 'That's life, kiddo.' I think she's glad I'm as miserable as she is."

For just a moment, I blamed our mothers for my pregnancy.

"Something will have to work out, Josh! My parents won't force me to get an abortion—they can't!"

"I don't know, Lauren. Sometimes I think my mom *wants* me to get into trouble so I'll see that she's right. Maybe she is, but couldn't she at least love me a little? I'm not like my dad! Even if we can't get married right away, Lauren, I want you to know I really love you. I'm not going to turn my back on you. As far as I'm concerned, we're married right now. Nothing's ever going to change that!"

I believed him.

Naturally, the school called Mom at work to tell her I was absent. I was sitting at home, thinking I'd fooled her, when she walked in that night. She looked tired and angry. She put her purse down and looked at me. I knew it was time to tell her, but I kept thinking about what Josh told me. We had to wait until it was "too late." *But how late is too late?*

Mom started in. "I know you skipped school today, and I want to know why. With everything we've been through together since your dad left, I can't understand why you would choose to hurt me this way."

I felt bad that I was hurting Mom, but I was angry, too. It was like I wasn't supposed have any feelings. Dad had hurt me, too, by leaving. But I was supposed to be good as gold.

"Well, you know, Mom, I just can't stand it anymore. How come Daddy gets to go off and do whatever he wants, and you have to do this stupid job you hate so much? And I have to be perfect. I've got feelings, too!"

I started crying. I knew it wasn't right to blame my dad, but in a way, I did feel like everything was his fault.

Mom and I talked for a long time that evening. She was actually afraid that she was at the root of my problems. She hugged me when we were done and went into the kitchen to make macaroni and cheese for dinner.

I started to feel really guilty. I realized I was going to make Mom's life a whole lot harder by having a baby, and there was no stopping it.

Being pregnant was like riding down a steep hill too fast on my bicycle and knowing I was going to crash into the tree at the bottom. I needed Mom's help, but I feared she was going to hate me forever.

In March, I rigged a loop of elastic to hook over the buttonhole of my jeans and left them half zipped. I had lots of baggy shirts, so I figured I could go quite a while before Mom noticed I was getting bigger around the middle.

When midterm grades came out again, Josh was grounded. My grades were a little better, actually, so Mom looked pleased for a change.

"Can't you study a little more so you don't get in trouble?" I asked Josh at school that week.

"I've got a lot on my mind, Lauren!" he snapped at me. "Don't you start in on me, too!"

It was the first time we'd ever had a fight. I got so scared, I didn't know what to do.

"Like *I* don't have anything on my mind?" I shot back. "*I'm* the one who can't button her jeans anymore. *I'm* the one who's going to have this baby, not you."

Suddenly, I understood why my mom and Josh's mom were so irritable all the time. They were left holding the bag, so to speak, same as me. Josh might make a million promises, but it was still going to be me in the labor room come August.

"If you're going to turn out to be just like my mom, we might as well break up right now!" Josh shouted.

"Oh, so now I have to be perfect all the time or you'll leave, right? Just like my dad? Just like yours?"

He stared at me. I saw the scared little boy in his eyes. I melted inside and softened my frown.

"I'm sorry, Josh."

He hung his head. "Me, too."

I guess we thought everything would be fine after that. What we didn't know was that somebody at school had overheard us talking.

We never could figure out if it was a teacher or a student, but that was the last time Josh and I were able to talk for a long, long time. In my fantasy, I envisioned a little trouble and a few tears when my mom found out I was pregnant. I didn't know the sky would fall, too.

Mom was waiting for me when I got home from school that day.

"Did you get off early?" I asked, trying to act cheery.

I should've known by her pale face and red eyes that something was wrong, but she cried a lot, so it wasn't unusual to see her like that. When she didn't say anything, I paused on the way to my room. A creepy feeling came over me. I looked back at her, and somehow I just knew that she knew.

"Sit down, Lauren," she said ominously.

I sat down, my heart pounding, trying not to cry. I wanted to be grown-up about it all, but suddenly I felt like a little kid. I longed to be comforted and protected from all the bad things I was certain were going to happen to me in the coming months.

I waited for the questions and accusations to begin, but Mom said nothing. She just kept looking at me.

Mom was my one and only defense against the world. Even though Josh said he'd stand by me, I had begun to realize I didn't really know him all that well. He couldn't even do his homework. What made me think he was going to be there when my labor pains started?

Then there was a knock at the door. "You can get that," Mom said, her voice shaking.

That's when I really got scared. Something big was going on. I couldn't believe it was all on account of me. It was just a baby, after all. It wasn't like I'd committed a murder.

When I opened the door and saw Daddy standing there, I didn't know what to say. It had been months since he'd been to our house. He had visitation rights, but he never seemed to have time for me. It seemed like he was always on a business trip.

"Hello, Lauren," he said seriously.

I wanted to throw myself into his arms, but he didn't look like he was glad to see me. Suddenly, I felt very ashamed about the news I was going to have to tell him.

I stepped back and let him into the living room. That's when I saw two more cars pulling up. I recognized one as Josh's mom's car. I'd never seen Josh's dad before, but I knew it was him getting out of the other car. He and Josh looked a lot alike.

And then I saw the police car. I started to feel sick to my stomach. I guess I staggered a little, because Daddy caught my arm and drew me back as Josh's parents came into the living room, followed by a policeman and a policewoman. Nobody was smiling.

"What is this?" I asked, my voice quivering. "Where's Josh?"

Suddenly I thought Josh had been in a terrible accident, and I went wild inside. My face must have reflected my thoughts because at that point the policewoman gave me a kinder look, although it was still not a smile.

"Josh has been arrested, Lauren," she said, introducing herself as Officer Amy Marlow.

She introduced everybody in the room, but I didn't hear a word. My head was spinning. I realized Daddy was helping me to the couch. Mom was crying already and so was Josh's mom, who was also giving me dirty looks.

"What's he done?" I asked.

"He's been arrested for statutory rape," Officer Marlow said gently.

I was stunned speechless. "Who did he rape?"

"*You*, Lauren. You're below the age of consent. Even if you thought it was all right to have sex with Josh, it wasn't legal. Josh is probably going to go to jail."

It was a wild, horrible night, there in my mom's living room. The officers tried to keep things calm, but it seemed like everyone was yelling all at once.

I just sat there crying like a lost two-year-old. I felt like my life was over. All Josh and I had been trying to do was have a little fun and find a little relief from the misery in our families, and we'd come to this.

I guess finally everybody started to notice that I was coming unglued because my dad ordered everybody out. He called the advisory nurse for the hospitalization plan Mom had and got permission to take me to the emergency room. He was leading me out to his car when I realized what was happening.

"You're not going to make me have an abortion!" I screamed. I started fighting Daddy, hitting him and yelling about how he'd abandoned us and didn't love us. I said all the things I had wanted to say when he moved out and left us alone.

"Lauren!" he yelled, trying to get my attention. He pulled me into his arms and held me until I calmed down. "Lauren, we're not going to do that. I thought you needed to see a doctor. You're hysterical!"

"Promise me," I whispered. "Promise you won't make me do something I don't want to do. Promise you'll help Josh. He didn't rape me! We made love. We just wanted to be happy!"

Right there in the middle of the sidewalk in front of the house, Daddy held me as tightly as he could and promised he would help us.

I did not know a family could cry as hard as we cried in the next few days. We talked and I explained. I tried to sleep while listening to Mom and Daddy talking—sometimes arguing—in the living room.

I felt trapped in a nightmare that didn't feel like it was ever going to stop. It was just going to keep on going until I had the baby, and then I'd have even more problems. I wanted to die. I didn't think I could go on.

As my family talked through everything, Josh came home on bail. He was permanently grounded, and his father wouldn't let him call me. So I had to imagine what Josh was thinking and feeling. He probably hated me. He probably wished he had never met me.

His life was ruined. If he went to jail, how would he ever get a good job afterward? If he was convicted of raping me, he would have to be registered as a sex offender for the rest of his life. I felt so overwhelmed by it all.

I couldn't bear it. My anguish for him was so intense, I began to worry I'd lose the baby. If I lost the baby, Josh would still go to jail. So I had to get my fear under control.

Mom took me to see an obstetrician. We went to a female doctor who was very gentle with me. She prescribed a mild antidepressant and counseling.

"You can go back to school anytime," she told me.

I just looked at her. "I can't!"

I don't know how I got through that next month. I prayed a lot, but it didn't seem to do any good. The counselor kept a close eye on me. The obstetrician said the baby and I were coming along nicely. She predicted my baby was due the first of August, a little earlier than I'd thought.

I kept asking to speak to Josh, but his mother refused all calls. There was all kinds of legal stuff going on. I had to give a statement to a judge. I didn't even get to see Josh that day.

Then the reporters started coming around. They put an article in the local newspaper about Josh and his pregnant, underage girlfriend. Nobody even seemed to care that my baby's father was going to jail for making love to me. I was under the legal age of consent, so I was a nothing, a minor, a child.

But I didn't feel like a child anymore. Our fun days of hanging out in the shopping mall and being boisterous and rowdy were over. I looked back on those times and hated myself for being so stupid and foolish.

I cried over my lost innocence, thinking I could solve the problems of my life by getting married. How had I ever been so shortsighted?

I guess I should have realized I *was* a child if I thought getting married was a good idea at my age. But the worst part was that I had never known that having sex when you're below the legal age of consent is a legal offense.

I thought that law only applied to dirty old men. Sex offenders were sleazy old guys who molested innocent children, right? They weren't seventeen-year-old boys who got their fifteen-year-old girlfriends pregnant.

I felt so ashamed. I felt terrible that Josh was going through such a terrible ordeal on my account.

I have to give Mom a lot of credit. There she was, scarcely divorced herself, with her life in ashes, doing a crummy job that didn't pay well at all, but she tried hard that summer to cheer me up.

When she came home one day with a pretty little bassinet that she bought from someone at work, I began to realize there was another person involved in all this mess: my baby.

My heart about broke every time Mom would bring home something else she'd gotten from a coworker: baby clothes, toys, cloth diapers we'd have to wash, since there wouldn't be enough money for expensive disposable ones from the store.

It was nice the one time Josh's mom called to ask how I was coming along.

"Oh, she's outgrown all her regular clothes. The doctor even wondered for a while if she was having twins. She's due late July, he thinks now. Is Josh all right?"

I thought it was nice of Mom to ask Josh's mom about him. She listened and shook her head, and tears came to her eyes.

"Well, I'm so sorry, Janet," she said. "Tell him Lauren sends her love."

"What is it now?" I asked, wishing I could have talked to Josh myself.

"It doesn't look good," Mom said, wiping her eyes. "He's very depressed. It looks like it's going to be a real legal battle. There will probably be more publicity."

I didn't know what to say. It didn't matter what I said, anyway. When I was called into court the next time, it didn't matter that I said, "I *wanted* to make love with Josh. We were planning to get married. We love each other!"

The judge looked at me as if I'd said we were planning to go to the moon.

Had our ideas been that unrealistic? Well, maybe yes, considering the laws in our state. Maybe not, if we could've kept things within our families.

It didn't matter how unfair it all seemed to me. It didn't matter that I thought it was grossly wrong for Josh to be facing a jail sentence. The legal system was way bigger than me or my parents or Josh's lawyer.

Honestly, I had never thought what Josh and I were doing was illegal. I never could figure out if it would have made a difference. Maybe if we had known he might go to jail, we might have controlled ourselves. But we didn't know. I still find it hard to believe it all really happened.

By the Fourth of July, I was so big I was waddling like a duck. We had fixed up a corner of my room with the bassinet. I'd taken down most of my rock-star posters. I didn't feel like a teenager anymore.

With the help of a tutor from school, I completed my sophomore year and passed with good grades, but I didn't even feel happy about it. I still went to see the counselor once a week. We mostly talked about how I was going to cope with school in the fall while having a baby in day care.

I enrolled in some programs available in my town for teen mothers. There was a program at the time for financial assistance and food stamps. I was humiliated to use them, but it helped Mom a little.

My doctor bills were being paid for by my dad's health insurance, which helped Mom some also. We started going to church on Sundays. I had one talk with the pastor, but he seemed embarrassed by my condition. All he could suggest was adoption.

I thought about that one day and decided that so long as I couldn't talk to Josh, I wouldn't agree to anything. If I was too young to do what we'd done, I was too young to decide to give up our baby.

I still had a lot of anger inside about the whole mess. But mainly, I just had my mind made up that if Josh was going to be a registered sex offender for the rest of his life, I was going to be the mother of his child, no matter what I had to go through.

Mom warned me life would be hard.

"I know, Mom, but I want this baby. This is the baby Josh and I made out of our love. I can't give it up—not for anything."

One morning, I woke up feeling kind of crampy and uneasy. A few hours later, we were in the labor room, Mom and me, pushing and pushing and pushing. She was with me every minute. It was a hard labor, everybody said.

I kept begging Mom to call Josh so he could be there. I think she tried once, but Josh's mom still wouldn't let him come to the phone. I knew there was a terrible legal battle going on, but did she have to make it worse by keeping us apart? My baby needed a father.

So that's what I told the reporter—who came right into my hospital room—the next day when our baby, Shane Joshua, was a day old.

What I said made it to the newspaper, which made Josh's mom more furious than ever. But somehow or other, with the help of my mom's pastor and the counselor, I was allowed to call Josh to tell him our son had been born.

I will never forget how happy and sad I felt during that call. I felt like Josh was a million miles away from me, like he was already in prison.

"Maybe going to jail will be easier than living here at home," he said between sobs. "Mom's made my life a living hell. I wish I were dead. Don't forget me, Lauren. Tell little Shane about me, okay?"

"Josh, Josh!" I whispered urgently. "You've got to be strong for us. We're being strong for you. Maybe it'll be okay. But if it isn't, we'll be here waiting for you. We're going to get married, just like we planned—somehow, some way. I just know it."

I was telling the truth, mostly. I knew I'd always love Josh, and I'd be waiting for him. But I didn't know if we'd ever really get married.

I was afraid he would change. I didn't have much faith in anything anymore. If my parents and Josh's parents and his lawyers couldn't keep Josh out of jail, then I didn't know if anything would ever be all right again for us. All I knew was that I would keep my love for Josh alive any way I could.

There were reporters outside the hospital the day Mom and I took little Shane home. It was a hot, sunny day. Ordinarily, I love summer.

I was supposed to keep quiet, but I said to the reporters, "Please, somebody, help my baby's father stay out of jail!"

I figured they could keep us apart, but they couldn't shut off my love, and they couldn't silence me. I was trying to be an obedient person, but sometimes I think you have to speak up.

What I said made it into the newspapers again. At least if Josh was allowed to see that, he'd know how much I loved him.

Before I knew it, I had to go back to school. We found a woman Mom used to work with to look after little Shane. I didn't want to leave him to go to class. I cried an ocean of tears over that.

But finally, I just went to school. I'd sworn an oath to myself that no matter what happened, I was going to do everything I was supposed to do.

So I went to school and studied. Kids were nice to me at first and very sympathetic, but I was in such anguish about leaving little Shane all day that I could hardly be nice to anybody. Everybody seemed so shallow all of a sudden. They thought there was no tomorrow. I couldn't get anybody to listen to me.

I studied at night after Shane went to sleep. I got up with him in the night if he cried. I cooked supper. I helped Mom keep house. I got good grades. I just did it. Because by then, Josh was in jail. It was a special facility, a minimum-security type of place. But it was still jail.

Daddy made sure I was given information so I wouldn't go crazy worrying. But still I would think, *Josh can't go to the shopping mall. He can't leave his cell at night. Other prisoners might be tormenting him or abusing him.*

I went back to seeing the counselor twice a week for a while. We started having family therapy because we were all under such a terrific strain. Sometimes I'd just sit there while my mom and dad got into it together.

"We should've done this a couple of years ago," I muttered one time. Mom burst into tears, and Daddy had the decency to look sorry.

When my grades came back straight A's at midterm that year, I hardly smiled. All I wanted, all I thought about, was the day Josh would get to come home to me and our baby.

I wrote letters to Josh. I didn't know for a long time if he was getting them or not. It turned out that he was getting my letters, but Josh was so depressed in those days he didn't want to burden me with his dark thoughts. He was changing and didn't want me to see it. He was afraid

I'd stop loving him if I knew how angry he felt about everything.

At least he was able to finish his studies and get his high school diploma while he was in jail. His grades improved. He got some automotive training so that he'd have job skills when he got out.

It wasn't a happy time for me, but there were some happy moments—like when Shane smiled. He was so innocent. It made me really happy to look at his darling little face, but then I'd think about how he'd been born into such a mess. It wasn't fair.

But I was never sorry I had him—not once.

We'd be walking around the lake at the park, and I'd see Shane looking at the ducks or the colored leaves falling, and I'd imagine how fascinating the world must look through his innocent blue eyes. I'd start to think of ways to keep him happy and innocent for as long as possible.

Mom and I became very close. I began to understand her as a person. She wasn't my enemy anymore; we began to be more like friends.

I was asked to give a little speech in the health class one day at school about what it felt like to be an unwed teenage mother, and I told the truth: There were moments that were wonderful, but I was so very tired of crying. When I had my sixteenth birthday, I felt at least ten years older. There were times when I thought, *I wonder what my life would have been like if I'd never met Josh.*

I just couldn't figure out why Josh had to go to jail. I mean, I know it was the law in our state, but it seemed like somebody somewhere might have shown him some mercy. It was as though all the legal people wanted to make an example of us in order to keep other teenagers from doing what we did.

Well, maybe what we did was wrong and illegal and shortsighted, but I never saw any change in my classmates because of Josh going to jail or me spilling my guts in health class. The guys kept chasing the girls. The girls, some of them, got pregnant. There were five or six in school that year.

I kept on writing to Josh and sending him pictures of Shane. Shane was a good little baby who started babbling words and standing up before he was eleven months old. Mom and Daddy doted on him.

I even sent pictures to Josh's mom and Josh's dad. I never knew if they even looked at the pictures until one day, just before Shane's first birthday, when two big packages came. One had a rocking horse in it.

"Where will we put this?" Mom asked, laughing as she looked around our crowded living room with the swing and playpen and walker.

The other present was a snowsuit two sizes too big.

"This has to be from Josh's mom," I said, laughing.

It just seemed like the kind of practical thing she'd send. Of course, I'd be glad for it when Shane was two.

And then one day at school, the secretary came to get me out of class.

"There's someone here to see you," she said with a mysterious twinkle in her eyes.

When I walked into the school office and saw Josh sitting there, I felt like I did when I first met him. It was almost like he was back in school with me and just waiting to see the principal for some trouble he had gotten into.

As soon as Josh saw me, he stood up. He looked so different! Instead of a year and a half older, he looked five years older. His hair was real short and he was very thin. I could pretend he'd been in the Army or something, I remember thinking.

But it was his eyes that had changed the most. The wild, reckless boy I'd known was gone. He smiled and held out his arms to me, but the smile never reached his eyes. *They'd changed him,* I kept thinking. *They broke him.*

He was trembling as he held me. I didn't care if the whole school saw us like that. I didn't care if the principal came along and gave me a detention, I was going to hold Josh forever if I could.

But nobody came along to tell us to stop hugging. We were alone.

Finally, Josh pulled away. "I'm eighteen now, Lauren—almost nineteen. I'm going to try to get into the community college."

"Why did you come here?" I asked. "Won't your mother let you come over to my house? She hasn't even seen Shane. We invite her, but—"

He shook his head. "I still have a lot to work out with my folks. I came here because this is where *you* are. I'd like to get permission for us to go have an afternoon with Shane, if we can. I'll be looking for work tomorrow. I don't know how hard it's going to be to get a job, or to get into college."

He didn't cry, but I saw sadness in Josh's eyes that went so deep it scared me. He'd been ruined. He didn't have any hope left. I had thought I loved him before, back when we'd been making love. That was nothing compared to what I felt at that moment, looking at Josh's thin, sad face. I loved him so much, I felt like bursting.

We got permission to take the day off. I even made sure the school secretary called my mom so she wouldn't think I was getting into mischief again. Then we drove over to Mrs. Murray's house to get Shane.

Josh had only seen pictures of Shane, so our son wasn't *real* to him yet. We went down into the playroom in Mrs. Murray's basement. There were four other preschoolers there in the middle of a heap of toys.

Shane grinned when he saw me. He had two teeth coming in on the bottom and looked so cute. He crawled over to me and stood up against my leg.

"This is your daddy," I said to him. I started to choke up. "Walk to Daddy. Show Daddy what a big boy you are!"

As tears rolled down my cheeks, Shane took several steps all by himself into Josh's arms. Josh's face was a mixture of all he felt, his happiness at seeing Shane and the sorrow of all he had experienced since before Shane had been born.

We went for burgers and then spent a little while at the park, pushing Shane in the baby swing. Josh spent as much time watching Shane and me as he did looking around at the trees and sky.

We didn't do much talking at first. I couldn't, because the least little thing brought tears to my eyes. I was due to turn seventeen in a few weeks, but I felt like I had already lived a lifetime. I still had a whole year of high school to finish. We'd probably never even go to the prom—but, in a way, I wished we could.

We went home to my mom's place after that. Josh sat on the couch, playing with Shane, while I did chores and made supper. I pretended we were old married people, and it felt really nice. It seemed weird to think I'd have a test to make up the next day, and homework waiting—and another load of diapers to fold.

When Mom came home, she was really surprised to see Josh. She seemed awkward at first and hung back, but then after she got a look at Josh's ravaged face, she took him into her arms and held him for a very long time.

I saw Josh's shoulders shaking and knew he was crying. It meant the world to me that Mom could comfort him like that.

Later, I made sure Josh called his mom to let her know where he was. He didn't seem to want to go home, and I could hardly blame him. She wasn't all bad, but she was terribly difficult to deal with. I began to wonder if we faced a whole new set of problems now that Josh was out of jail.

He was able to get a job at an auto-body shop, where he did every menial job they could think up for him. He took a lot of ribbing about all that had happened to him. Didn't those guys understand what going to jail had done to Josh?

"Don't let it worry you," Josh told me one day. "Some of them have seen a lot worse. Believe me, I can take anything they dish out."

I began to see Josh in a new way that fall. He had changed, but he wasn't ruined. He was just a whole lot more mature. He worked very long hours and saved every penny. He registered for two evening classes at the community college, which meant when he wasn't in class or working, he was studying.

He never let up on his grueling schedule—and he never complained. If he couldn't hitch a ride to work or class, he'd walk all the way across town. He was patient and kind with his mom, even though she was still a pain. He spent every available moment with Shane and me. He even helped Mom hang wallpaper one weekend.

That Christmas was the first we'd ever really celebrated together. The Christmas before, Josh had been in jail.

Life kept rolling on. One day, I looked up and thought, *Things are better.* I hadn't cried in quite a while. I actually began to feel some hope.

But Josh and I didn't often spend time alone together. I wanted to do something special for New Year's Eve that year, but he didn't seem to want to do anything but watch television.

"I can't think of anything I want to do," he told me. "I'm not old enough to go to some bar or club to celebrate. That all-night party at the stadium for the high school kids doesn't appeal to me. I feel too old. Maybe we could see a movie, if you really want to. I even thought about driving out to the lake."

"And do what?" I whispered. "It's awfully cold."

Josh looked at me with a serious expression. "We've been to hell and back, Lauren. We're not the same as we were. If we go out to the lake, it's to build a fire maybe, not make love. I still love you with all my heart. If it hadn't been for you, I wouldn't have made it through the last year. But I'm done making mistakes.

"I know you're old enough now, but I've got legal red tape wrapped so tight around me, I'm not sure what I can and can't do. One thing I'm not going to do is get into any more trouble with the law. That means no sex for you and me until we're married."

I held my breath. We hadn't spoken of that since he got back. I didn't know if he still wanted to marry me.

Josh looked at me for a very long time. "That doesn't mean I don't want you, Lauren. I want you very much. But we're not going to get married until I have a job and can support us. If it takes one year or five, that's how long it's going to take to do it right. I had a lot of time to think this over. My mind's made up."

I felt a little disappointed, but I knew he was right. "Okay, Josh. I can wait as long as you can."

I realized in that moment that Josh had been just as worried about me standing by him as I had about him standing by me. When he took me into his arms, I knew we had survived.

That's what we did: we waited. Josh worked and I graduated high school. Shane was two and a half—and quite a handful during the graduation ceremony. I could hear him calling, "There's Mommy!" while I was on stage accepting my diploma.

Mom started dating a man from church that summer. It was really amazing to see the change in her. She looks years younger and a lot happier. Daddy got married to a woman he'd been dating from his office.

Josh's dad got divorced from his "bimbo." His mom was delighted. She never has been much easier to get along with, though. She never dates. She hates men, and I guess men don't like her much, either.

Josh lives with a couple of guys near his job. He's gotten raises and more responsibility there. But more and more, he's concentrating on his college classes. He gets good grades now, and that proves to me he is willing to take responsibility.

Since we're still not married yet, I've had to think about what I want for myself in life in addition to marriage. So I'm going to start college in the fall. Daddy said he would pay what he could. I'm trying for some student loans. Sometimes I wonder if I can do it all, four more years of college and day care. Shane will start kindergarten before long.

I look around and think, *My God, my life is so complicated!* But I'm handling it. I'm so busy, I can't think sometimes.

I learned I can do a lot more than I ever thought. And I do it all for love of Josh and my little boy. THE END

I'M STANDING BY MY RAPIST HUSBAND
Even his prison sentence
cannot dim the light of our love

I sat stiffly on a cold metal chair in a small room with walls painted a bleak shade of industrial gray. Although I was wearing wool slacks, a thick woolen sweater over a knit turtleneck, and beneath that, insulating thermal long johns, I was shivering uncontrollably.

And it wasn't simply because I was in Alaska in the middle of December.

Next to me, sitting on another metal chair, was my husband of thirteen years, Christian. He held my hand in his, trying to give me comfort that, under the circumstances, simply couldn't be given.

It hurt to look at him. And yet, I couldn't stop myself from giving him another swift glance to make sure that he wasn't about to fall apart. If that happened, God help me, I'd crumble like aged paper at the first touch of fresh air. Christian's strength, his steadfast belief that what he was doing was right, was the only thing keeping me from shattering.

His normally ruddy face was pale, his brown eyes somber as he stared into space. But he wasn't trembling like I was. His lips weren't bloodless with fear. Despite his pale color, and the haunted look in his eyes, he wore an expression of resignation, and . . . I couldn't deny it . . . peace.

And the truth hit me once again. Christian had made peace with himself, with his God. With whatever the future held for him.

Oh, how I wished it could be that easy for me.

Our time together was almost at an end. We'd said everything there was to say, cried all the tears there were to cry, and now, finally, had fallen silent. Now, we were just waiting for that last moment.

Waiting to say good-bye.

And once they took him away, I didn't know if I'd ever see him again without prison bars or a Plexiglas wall separating us.

It was amazing that four months ago—just four months—our lives had been so normal. So wonderfully normal. We'd lived in a little house just two blocks from the ocean in a small beach town in South Carolina—a town where everyone knew everyone, except in the summers, when the tourists came in droves. Although Christian and I were both transplanted westerners, he from Utah, me from Montana, we'd been accepted here as one of their own, mainly because of our work in the neighborhood parish.

We'd met in South Carolina, fallen in love, and were married in less than a year. By mutual agreement, we'd put off having children for six years, and then, when we were both ready to expand our family, Alexander was born. Three years later, Fiona came along.

In August, we'd been the perfect American family. Now, four months later, our lives were in shambles. Destroyed by something that had happened years before Christian and I had even met.

Really, I think I fell in love with him the first moment I saw him. It happened the summer after my first year of college. Growing up in the West, I'd always dreamed of the East Coast. I guess it's only natural to want to see what life is like someplace else. So, after graduation from high school, I did exactly that, having been accepted at a small private college in South Carolina. Instead of going home for the summer after my freshman year, I decided to take a job at a pizzeria on the boardwalk at Myrtle Beach. My college friend, Ashley, a Myrtle Beach native who'd worked at the pizzeria for years, got me the job.

I soon found out that the boardwalk was a great place to work, if you had to work. It was a twenty-four-hour party atmosphere, and there were lots of opportunities to meet good-looking guys. And I took advantage of it, dating one guy after another. Nothing serious, but I wasn't looking for anything serious. I was nineteen and I just wanted to have fun.

But fate had other plans for me. Ashley's older sister, Corinne, was getting married in June, and I was invited to the wedding. There I was, sitting in a pew at the Star of the Sea Catholic Church, waiting for Corinne to make her way down the aisle, when a young man wearing a tux stepped up to the dais, and in a pure tenor, began to sing "Ave Maria."

From the moment he opened his mouth and began to sing, I was lost, mesmerized. He was handsome—oh, so handsome, with his dark hair and beautiful brown eyes. But it was more than that. When he sang, he wore an expression on his face that I could only describe as rapturous. Everything about him, his voice, his expression, his very . . . essence . . . reached out and enveloped me, wrapping around me like a comforting cloak. I knew I had to meet him. I'd die if I couldn't talk to him, bask a moment in his presence.

That's all I wanted then. It wasn't even really a romantic thing. I just wanted to know him, to make some kind of connection. When we finally met at the reception, he was as warm and personable as I'd guessed he'd be. His name was Christian Bush and he was a construction worker for a local builder who specialized in beachfront homes. As for his singing, he did that only on weekends, performing at weddings and other functions for a small fee. He was a member of the Star of the Sea parish, and often sang during Mass.

We talked for hours that night, and were amazed at how many things we had in common. Both of us had come here from the West. Christian had grown up in a small town in southern Utah, and after graduation from high school, had drifted from place to place, living in places like Hawaii, Alaska, and New Mexico before finally coming east. He'd ended up here in South Carolina a couple of years before I did, and loved it enough to settle down.

But it wasn't just our western ties that we had in common. We both harbored a deep, earnest love affair with music. With Christian, it was his singing, of course. He told me he'd been singing in choirs since he was a young boy. During his years of aimless travel, he'd stopped singing, and it wasn't until he'd settled here that he rediscovered his love for it, and by doing so, his love for the Church.

"I guess you could say I had an epiphany," he told me that night, his face somber. "I found something I'd lost along the way, and now, I thank

God every day that He brought my voice back to me."

Ordinarily, I would've felt awkward around a near stranger's reference to his faith, but with Christian, I felt honored that he'd share something so personal with me. I hadn't been much of a churchgoer in years, even though I was raised by Roman Catholic parents. But, like Christian, I had a deep love of music, and a belief that the power of music was strong, that it could soothe troubled souls. From the age of eight, I'd taken violin lessons. By high school, I was playing in the school orchestra. And now, in college, I was a music major. I hoped to someday play in a city orchestra, even if it was a small one.

So, from the beginning, Christian and I had that musical bond between us. Maybe that's one reason why we fell in love so quickly. By the end of that summer, we were sleeping together, and Christian was talking marriage. I wanted that more than anything. I was so in love with Christian that I couldn't imagine going through life without him at my side. Back in Utah, my parents were adamantly against the marriage. Oh, not because they didn't like Christian. I took him home for Thanksgiving that year, and both my parents and my sister, Elspeth, adored him. But my parents wanted us to wait until I graduated from college.

Although I understood why they felt the way they did, I just couldn't bow to their wishes. Christian and I loved each other. We wanted to make a home together—a real home—and we didn't want to wait. We weren't satisfied with snatched moments together. I lived in the dorms, and Christian shared an apartment with one of the other construction workers at his job. Oh, I suppose we could've simply moved in together, but we just didn't want to do that. We knew . . . our deepest hearts knew . . . that we were soul mates. Marriage was the only option.

So, in May of the following year, less than a year after we'd first met, Christian and I became man and wife. We bought the small house just two blocks from the beach, and began our storybook marriage.

We were so happy, so incredibly happy, in those first years. During the day, I'd go to school, and Christian would go to work at whatever construction site he'd been assigned to. Nights, we spent on the living room sofa, snuggled together, watching TV, and later, making sweet love in our tiny master bedroom. On weekends, Christian was usually scheduled to sing at a wedding somewhere. As word of his beautiful voice spread, we traveled over the entire state so he could perform. And each time I watched him sing, tears would come to my eyes because I couldn't believe that he loved me. *Me.* On Sundays, we began going to Mass at Star of the Sea.

A little over two years later, I graduated from college, and just as I'd hoped, was taken on by a local orchestra as second violinist. Then one day, Christian asked me to accompany him on violin as he sang at a wedding for the daughter of a prominent mayor of a neighboring town. We were an overwhelming success, and from that time on, I began to accompany Christian on violin whenever he sang at weddings.

It was about that time that Christian was asked to sing a Christmas program at our church. The first time I heard him sing "O Holy Night," I was so overcome with emotion that I felt as if I could fall on my knees, literally. Christian's voice was that pure, that hauntingly beautiful. That first Christmas program began a new tradition, not only at our church, but also at others all over the state. Christian's mellow tenor, singing all the classic Christmas hymns, and the newer holiday songs, delighted listeners. The churches were filled to the rafters when he appeared.

After his third year of doing Christmas programs, I encouraged Christian to self-produce a CD of his favorite holiday music. Just two months before Christmas, my father had died after a long illness, and although he wasn't a wealthy man, he'd invested intelligently, and I'd inherited a generous sum of money. I wanted to use that money to produce Christian's CD.

Christian protested, insisting that we should put the money toward other, more practical, things. Perhaps we could put a down payment on a bigger house. But I was perfectly happy in our little home by the ocean. It was fine for the present, and it'd be fine for a while even after we had children. Anyway, I was convinced that Christian's CD would be a success, even if the only way we could market it was through a website on the Internet.

Christian finally agreed, and we began working on the CD. It took six months, but by the following Christmas, the website was up, and as word of mouth began to spread, the orders started coming in. Christian and I continued to do holiday concerts and weddings. Guests at these functions joined our mailing list, and the CD sales climbed. It took about eighteen months to break even, but finally, we began to show a profit.

In the summer of our thirteenth year of marriage, life was good. Our marriage was strong. Even with our children, Alexander, who turned four in August, and Fiona, who was thirteen months, we always found time for romance. I felt like the luckiest woman in the world.

Except for one thing.

In all the years I'd known him, Christian had had trouble sleeping. In fact, he barely slept at all. I couldn't understand how he could function with as little sleep as he got. Frequently, I awoke in the night to find his side of the bed empty. Investigating, I'd find him in his recliner in the living room, reading a book or listening to music through headphones. Even when he did manage to sleep, he'd often awaken with nightmares that he could never quite remember.

Strangely enough, his sleep disturbances grew even worse after the birth of Alexander, and then, came to a climax after Fiona was born. Christian's insomnia got so bad that he became a danger on construction jobs, not only to himself, but to others, as well.

We both knew it was time for him to seek professional help. So Christian began seeing a psychiatrist to try to work out the cause of his sleep disorder. The sessions continued over the winter without much result. The nightmares and insomnia continued. Finally, in the spring, Christian's psychiatrist decided to change tactics.

Dr. Greniere suggested that Christian begin a series of regressive hypnosis treatments to try and find the cause of the nightmares. So, once a week, my husband underwent hypnosis. I don't know what happened at that first session, but I saw the change in Christian as soon as he got home that evening. He was distracted and distant, and no matter how I tried to draw him out, he refused to talk about it. For the first time in our marriage, I felt shut out and rejected. It wasn't a good feeling, and I almost wished he hadn't started the regression therapy at all. But then, it *did* seem to be working. The nightmares had stopped, and Christian was actually sleeping better than ever.

But his personality was changing. Oh, he was still loving and kind, but only after I reminded him that we, his family, were around. Suddenly, he seemed to be going through life in a fog. His body was here, but his mind was elsewhere. And then, in September, he wasn't even around physically that much anymore. He took to spending long hours at the library after he got off from work, and even when he finally returned home late at night, he carried with him folders of papers which he'd shove into a drawer in the small spare bedroom we used as an office. After these mysterious trips to the library, he'd be more withdrawn than ever, his face haggard, eyes haunted. I begged him to tell me what was troubling him, but he simply wouldn't talk about it.

In desperation, I decided to do exactly what Dr. Greniere had warned me against—to confront the issue head-on. And to do this, I needed to know what was in those folders.

So, I waited until a sunny day in early December. While Christian was out working at a job site, I went into the office and began to look for the papers, feeling just the slightest twinge of guilt at invading his privacy. My husband was so trusting that he hadn't even thought about locking his desk.

Or maybe he *wanted* me to find them. Maybe it was Christian's way of getting it all out in the open.

The folder was right where I'd seen him put it, in the third drawer of his desk. It was full of photocopies of old newspaper clippings about a fifteen-year-old murder in Fairbanks. The victim was a twenty-year-old sorority girl at a local college.

I stared at the photo, my heart in my throat. Fallon Chase had been a beautiful girl with her long ringlets of blond hair and crystal blue eyes. Her body had been found in her dorm room by her roommate. She'd been strangled and raped. Although her college boyfriend had been investigated, no arrests were ever made, and her murder had never been solved.

So why was my husband so interested in this case?

It'd happened in the summer of 1984. Four years before Christian and I had met. Had he known Fallon Chase?

I tried to remember when Christian had lived in Alaska, but I wasn't sure of the exact dates. I knew he'd spent some time in Portland after Alaska. But where had he been when Fallon Chase was murdered?

I read the newspaper clippings a second time. The boyfriend wasn't named. Could that have been Christian? But he'd told me that he'd never gone to college. And the newspaper clippings said that Fallon's boyfriend had been a college quarterback.

So what was the connection between Fallon Chase and my husband?

That night after I put the kids to bed, I went into the office, grabbed the folder, and stepped into the living room, where Christian sat watching television—or, to be accurate—staring at the TV. I could tell his thoughts were far away. I stood in front of him and waited until he looked at me. Then I dropped the folder in his lap.

"You want to explain this to me?" I asked quietly.

The blood ebbed from his face. One hand covered the folder, but he didn't move to open it. He just looked at me, his eyes dark with pain. Moving slowly, he reached for the television remote and pressed the power button. The TV went black. Christian looked down at the folder in his lap.

"You'd better sit down, Eva," he said softly. "This isn't going to be easy. I've been trying to think of a way to tell you."

My whole body began to tremble. I sank down onto the sofa, my eyes on my husband. A new expression had settled on his handsome face—it looked almost like relief. For a moment, I wanted to go back in time. I wished I'd never pursued this. A premonition of disaster hovered over me, and it was already too late to turn back.

I licked my lips, my throat dry. "Who is Fallon Chase?" I asked when I finally managed to find my voice.

Christian's dark eyes met mine. "A girl I met in Alaska. But I have to start at the beginning. It's the only way to make you understand. I've only come to terms with it myself in the last few weeks."

"Okay. I'm listening."

But I didn't want to listen. I didn't want to hear what he had to say.

Because I knew in my gut that it would change my life forever.

"I was nineteen years old," Christian began. "I'd gone to Alaska to find work. It'd always been a dream of mine, to see Alaska. So I hitchhiked up there and got a job on a construction crew working on the roads.

"I'd been there about three months when it happened. It was an August night, and I'd gone to this bar with some of the other guys. It'd been a long week at work, and we were ready to party. The beer was flowing freely, and then one of the guys started passing out these pills. I'd tried my share of drugs before, but I wasn't heavily into anything. So, I thought, what the hell? And it gave me a good buzz.

"About ten o'clock, a bunch of sorority girls from the nearby campus came into the bar. They were all pretty drunk; I guess they'd just come from a party. I noticed Fallon right away . . . all that long blond hair. She was a showstopper."

I felt my heart spasm. It was stupid, I knew, but I was jealous of a dead girl.

"I edged my way over to her and asked her to dance. It was a slow song, and she slipped her arms around me as if . . . well, as if. . . ." Christian's face grew red. "It was like she knew me really well, you know? Oh, God, Eva—this is so hard to tell you—"

"Just tell me, Christian. She was coming on to you? She turned you on, right?"

He nodded. "I was only nineteen. I hadn't had too much experience with women before, and she was all over me. And the pills . . . they were doing all kinds of weird things to me. . . ." Christian paused and ran a trembling hand through his dark hair. The gold band of his wedding ring glinted in the lamplight. "She practically made love to me right there on the dance floor, Eva. She stuck her tongue in my ear and whispered all kinds of obscene things—things she wanted to do to me. Then she asked me to go back to her dorm room with her."

I felt an icy dread forming in the pit of my stomach, threatening to double me over. I wanted to scream out for him to stop talking—to quell this monstrous stream of words that was, I knew now, going to destroy everything that we had. But I just sat there, frozen solid, unable to speak, unable to swallow or force a sound of protest from between my teeth.

"I went with her, and as soon as we got to her room, she was all over me . . . doing things to me that I'd never dreamed could feel so good. I don't know if it was the drug, or if it was her . . . all I knew was that this animal instinct was taking over inside of me, pushing everything else aside. I had to have her. I thought I'd die if I couldn't have her.

"And she was wild, totally crazy for me . . . until . . . well . . . I don't know how to say this without sounding crude . . . until I . . . gave her what she wanted. And then, when it was my turn, she balked. It was like she suddenly realized where she was. She looked at me and saw a stranger leaning over her, and suddenly, she wanted nothing more to do with me.

"I . . . oh, God! I was mad with passion, with need. And when she said no . . . when she told me to get the hell out . . . I went crazy." Christian dropped his face into his trembling hands and began to sob. "Oh, God help me! It was so horrible—I completely blocked it out! But now I know—I know it's all true! God . . . oh, dear God . . . it's *true!*"

My paralysis ended, and somehow, I found myself on my knees in front of him, my arms around his shuddering shoulders, clutching him to me.

"It's okay, Christian. I'm here for you!"

Tears streaked down my face as my husband sank to the floor in front of me. We held each other, rocking back and forth as he sobbed out the torment in his soul. Finally, after a long, long time, he drew away and looked at me, his eyes wet and stricken.

"I raped her, Eva," he whispered. "And when she began to scream, I—I strangled her—with my bare hands." He shook his head as tears streamed down his bristled jaw. "I still—I can't believe that—that I was capable of such a monstrous act. But I must have done it. It all came back to me in hypnosis. I remembered it all. Oh, God, Eva, what am I going to do?"

My mind was racing as I held my broken husband in my arms. What were we going to do? I was still trying to absorb the shock of it all. Trying to make some kind of sense of it in my scrambled mind.

How could it be? This man . . . this gentle, loving soul with the voice of an angel . . . how could he be a cold-blooded killer?

How could I have lived with such a man for thirteen years, and never suspected a thing?

It just couldn't be true.

Could it?

"You can't know for sure that you did it, Christian. Can you?" I drew away from him to meet his eyes. "These memories . . . how do you know that's what they are? How do you know they're not just dreams that you've somehow absorbed from television or movies?"

He gazed at me sadly. "Because I started having the dreams years ago. Long before I knew the details of Fallon's murder. I completely blocked it all out. The whole evening with her. Then, when I went through the hypnosis, it all came back, and that's when I decided to do research through the Fairbanks newspapers, and I found these clippings. Don't you see, Eva? It all fits. Her photo looks exactly like the girl in my memories. I did it, Eva. I killed her. And it's a wonder I've gotten away with it for so long."

I bit my bottom lip. "It was a long time ago," I whispered, hardly able to believe I was saying it. "There's nothing you can do now but put it behind you. It was the drug that made you do it. And the girl—she shouldn't have led you on."

Christian was staring at me as if I'd lost my mind. "She shouldn't have died for it. There's no excuse for what I've done, Eva. And now—now, I'm going to have to pay for it."

My jaw dropped as I realized what he meant. "Christian, think about what you're saying. You'll be throwing away your life. *Our* life!"

He shook his head vehemently. "I've already talked to Father Nowicky. He agrees with me that the only way I'll ever be able to forgive myself is to give myself up."

"No!" I scrambled to my feet so quickly that dark spots danced in front of my eyes. "Christian, you can't do that! You just can't! They'll put you in prison! Our children will grow up without a father! I can't—I can't live without you!"

He stood, gazing at me with wounded eyes. "How can I be a good father to them when I'm living a lie? How can I teach them about the word of God, and recite the Ten Commandments when I've broken one of them, and never paid for it? How can I be a good husband to you when I murdered an innocent girl in a brutal, lustful fever for sexual satisfaction? How can I continue getting up in front of the congregation and singing about love and God and goodness when my soul is screaming out that I'm a hypocrite?

"Eva, I realize that what I have to do will change our lives forever. But I just can't live with myself any longer. Now that I know what I've done, I've got to face the consequences."

I stared at him, and I wanted to scream and shout at him, plead with him to reconsider, to not destroy our lives, our marriage—everything that we held dear. But I could see in his eyes that his soul was in torment. That if he didn't follow his conscience, his guilt would eat away at him until it killed him.

He gazed at me somberly and extended his hand. "Please, Eva. I need your support in this. Will you help me through this?"

I burst into fresh tears, and then I went to him. He enclosed me in his arms, nestling his chin against my cheek. I felt the warm wetness of his tears, felt the even thud of his heart under my palm, and breathed in his comforting scent.

I felt my heart breaking in two.

One phone call to a lawyer put everything in motion. Then everything happened quickly. Before I knew it, Christian was trying to explain to five-year-old Alexander why he was "going away."

He held our blond-haired little boy on his lap, stroking his rosy cheek and trying to find the right words to explain and make him understand. Alexander gazed up at his father, his brown eyes—eyes that were just like Christian's—huge and puzzled.

"But when are you coming back, Daddy?"

Christian shook his head, blinking back tears. "I don't know, buddy. Daddy did a bad thing a long time ago, and now . . . now I have to go to prison, and make up for that bad thing that I did."

"What did you do?" Alexander asked, his voice clear and pure. Like his father, he liked to sing hymns, and he already showed talent.

"I took somebody's life, Alexander. And I'm very, very sorry that I did it. But being sorry isn't enough. I have to show God that I'm sorry, and the only way I can do that is by confessing to the world about what I did."

Alexander's brown eyes filled with tears. "But I don't want you to go, Daddy!"

I swallowed hard, trying to hold back my own threatening tears. I could see Christian's throat working with emotion, and knew that he, too, was very close to breaking down.

"I know that, buddy," he said gruffly. "But you see, if I raise you by the word of God, and teach you the difference between right and wrong, and I don't follow those same rules myself, that makes me a hypocrite." He ran a trembling hand over Alexander's blond curls. "I have to go, buddy. God wants me to do this."

Alexander's bottom lip puffed out. Tears began to stream down his round, red cheeks. "Will you be gone a long, long time, Daddy?"

That was Christian's undoing. He folded his arms around our son, snuggling the boy to him, and wept into his blond hair. My heart aching, I turned away and hurried from the room, leaving them to share their last moments alone.

The next day, we took the kids to the sitter's, where they'd stay until I got back to South Carolina, probably within a week or two. Christian took Fiona from my arms, and held our wriggling two-year-old, his lips skimming her pale blond head, breathing in her baby-powder scent. He closed his eyes for a long moment as if he were memorizing the feel of her in his arms. Then finally, he handed her to the sitter, and then knelt on the floor in front of Alexander.

"You're going to be a strong little man for me, right, buddy?" he asked quietly, gazing into our son's eyes. "Take good care of your mommy and your little sister for me, okay, Al?"

Alexander nodded, his chin quivering. It wrenched my heart, seeing our little boy striving to make his father proud and not give into tears.

"Okay, buddy." Cupping his small, heart-shaped face, Christian kissed him, then hugged him close. The boy clung to his father as if he were a piece of driftwood in the ocean, the only oasis of safety within grasp. Christian practically had to peel himself away. Then, with a final ruffle of his blond curls, he stood and turned to me. "We'd better get going," he said.

I kissed the kids and followed Christian out the door, forcing myself not to look back to see the grief on our little boy's face. I wondered if he really understood it all. Or did he just understand that his father was going away and might never return?

The flight to Fairbanks was long and tiring. We didn't talk much, for what was there left to say? It was agonizing, being so close to my husband, and knowing that the time was ticking away—that soon, very soon, I would be alone. It was unbearable to think about, so I pushed it from my mind, telling myself to take things moment by agonizing moment.

Christian held my hand through much of the flight, almost as if he needed the connection of touch. As did I. Everything about these last moments with him was magnified. All my emotions, my needs, and fears had crystallized into this one sensation—the touch of his skin against mine.

I knew he was a murderer. I knew that he'd killed that sorority girl in cold blood. And yet, I couldn't stop loving him. Because I knew with every fiber of my being that he was a different man from the one who'd committed that awful crime. I knew it as well as I knew my own name. And knowing that he was turning himself in, despite the pain it was causing our family, only made me love him more.

Yes, the flight was long, and I was glad of it. We flew to Atlanta and caught a connecting flight to Seattle. From there, we'd fly to Fairbanks. All the important discussions had taken place. Before leaving South Carolina, Christian had gone over everything with me—the insurance policies, the investments we'd made, pertinent information about his CDs, which were still selling briskly. I'd always paid the household bills, so that was nothing new to me. But other things, like household repairs, taxes . . . things like that, Christian had always taken care of. He wanted to make sure that he explained everything to me so I could take it over, or, in the case of our taxes, be able to find someone to do it for me.

Now, there was just silence between us. Silence, and the connection of touch.

When we reached Fairbanks, reporters were waiting for us in the airport. Word had leaked out that there'd been a confession in the

Chase murder case. Still, they didn't know who we were until a man in a dark suit approached us at the gate.

"Mr. Bush? I'm Graham Hennessey." He extended his hand.

We'd hired an attorney on the recommendation of a Fairbanks builder for whom Christian had worked years ago. He and Christian had already spoken on the phone several times. As soon as the throng of reporters heard the attorney speak Christian's name, they swarmed all over us, shouting out questions.

"Don't say a thing," Graham Hennessey advised, elbowing his way through the reporters, clearing a path for us.

Suddenly, a short, pudgy man with thinning white hair stepped in front of Christian. Through wire-rimmed glasses, his dark eyes glimmered with emotion. He was a good four inches shorter than Christian, and he was forced to look up to meet his eyes.

"I'm Morris Chase," he said, his voice trembling with rage. "I'm Fallon's father. You took my little girl away from me, you bastard. And my wife died of a broken heart because of it. You've taken everything away from me!" His hands clenched into fists and he began to pummel my husband.

I screamed and tried to wrench the man away from him, but he was too strong for me. Christian didn't even try to defend himself. He just stood there and took it, until finally, three bystanders managed to pull the enraged father away from him.

"Bastard!" the man screamed. "You filthy monster! I'll see you in hell! I hope to God you rot in prison for the rest of your miserable life!" As the men dragged him away, the man's face crumpled and he began to sob uncontrollably.

The blood had drained from Christian's face as he stared after the weeping man. "I'm sorry," he said softly—way too softly for the man to have heard.

They took us directly to the police station, where Christian and Mr. Hennessey disappeared into the interrogation room. They wouldn't let me sit in on the deposition, and I didn't know whether to be glad or not. On the one hand, I didn't really want to hear the horrible details. But every minute I spent with my husband was now precious, even if it was time spent in the company of others. So, I resented that time when he was in the other room, away from me.

It took about ninety minutes to complete the deposition. Afterward, Christian was arraigned, and incredibly, released on bond until the sentencing. That was something that neither of us had expected, or even planned to ask for. But Mr. Hennessey was a good lawyer, and he bought us some time. The sentencing was scheduled for a week later—one whole week that we'd have together. It was a gift, pure and simple.

Time flew like I'd never seen it fly before. December in Fairbanks was not a time to be outdoors, so we spent that precious, bittersweet time in our hotel room, just the two of us, and it was as if we were on our honeymoon, really. We ordered room service for most meals, and spent our time just holding each other, savoring every moment together, making slow, sweet love, memorizing each other's bodies as if it was the first time we'd ever been intimate with each other. We held each other, comforted each other, and very often, wept together. And the days passed.

Our last night together was the most painful. We stayed awake all night, making love, each time knowing that it might be the last time. Finally, toward morning, we lay entwined, exhausted and sad beyond reason. I'd vowed to be brave, as brave as Christian was; I knew that if I fell apart, he would lose it, too, and that I couldn't bear.

So, I was really trying to put on a brave face for him. But as the hours slipped by, and the hands of the clock crept closer to six, I felt desperation well inside of me. I'm ashamed to write of what happened next.

I began to cry, and, clinging to Christian, I pleaded with him to run away with me. We'd go across the border into Canada—somewhere far away where no one knew us. Somehow, we'd find a way to send for our children, and bring them up to join us. We'd live out the rest of our lives in a foreign country, in absolute hiding, but even that would be better than living without each other.

Christian didn't answer me. He just gazed at me with wounded eyes, and finally, my pleas faded away as I realized how impossible it all was. I collapsed against him then, as slow, silent tears traced down my face. For the first time in my life, I really understood what it feels like to have a broken heart.

A few hours later, Christian was sentenced to life imprisonment. At the very least, he wouldn't go up for parole for thirty years. He'd be sixty-five when, or if, that happened.

So, now, we waited in the small room with the industrial gray walls, the anteroom of the penitentiary. They'd be coming to take Christian away soon. His hand enclosed mine, warm and reassuring. We were silent. There was nothing left to say.

The door opened, and my heart plunged. A uniformed guard stepped into the room, his face expressionless.

"It's time to go."

To me, his voice sounded like a death knell.

Christian's hand tightened on mine, and we stood. He turned to me, his eyes sweeping over my face, as if trying to memorize it. My heart was pounding like a kettledrum. I still couldn't quite believe that this was really happening. Biting my bottom lip to control its trembling, I gazed up at my husband.

He leaned toward me then, and, cupping my face in his trembling hands, he kissed me. Softly, sweetly. Then he drew away and gazed at me again for another agonizing moment. A tear slipped down my face and he brushed it gently away with his thumb.

"I love you," he whispered. "Take care of our kids. And take care of yourself."

I nodded, biting down harder on my bottom lip. "You, too. I'll write you every day."

Weeks ago, knowing that he'd probably receive a life sentence, Christian had offered to divorce me. I'd gazed down at my wedding ring, and then looked at him.

"When I married you, I married for better or for worse. I plan to keep that promise, Christian."

Divorce was never mentioned again.

The guard cleared his throat. "Time to go, Mr. Bush."

My hands tightened on Christian's arms. A wave of indescribable anguish washed over his face.

"Oh, Eva!" He wrenched me to him and kissed me again—this time, hungrily, desperately—like a man drowning. Then he tore himself away and strode over to the guard without looking back.

Seconds later, the door closed behind the guard and my husband.

I was alone.

Only a year has passed since that horrible day when I left my husband in an Alaskan prison. One year down, twenty-nine to go until the possibility of parole.

It might as well be an eternity.

I've been to visit Christian once this past summer. He hadn't changed much—just grown a bit thinner, with a touch of gray glimmering at his hairline. The guards allowed us to spend an afternoon together, but although we were allowed to touch, a conjugal visit was forbidden. Christian told me that he was attending church services in prison, and that he'd started singing in the choir. He's also writing a book—not about the murder, but about how God has changed his life.

He never talks about the ugly side of prison, about the violence and rape that take place inside those walls. I can only hope that he hasn't been the victim of any of that, but I don't dare ask, because I honestly don't know if I can handle the truth.

The kids are doing fine, even though they naturally miss their father. I encourage them to draw pictures for him that I send along in my daily letters. At Christmastime this year, we baked cookies and sent them to him. Christian is allowed to call home once a month, and those few moments on the phone are very precious to us. Alexander and Fiona so look forward to hearing his voice. I'm torn as to whether or not to take them with me to visit him next summer when I go. On the one hand, I think it would be good for them to see their father, and I know that it would mean everything to Christian. But on the other hand, I wonder if visiting their father in a prison would negatively impact the kids. I just don't know. But I've got a few months to think about it before I make a decision.

The one thing I know for certain is that I still love my husband. Yes, he did a monstrous thing. But he is not a monster. In fact, in my eyes, he's a hero. Because he could've chosen to stay with his family and live out his life, fighting his demons and struggling with his conscience. So many years had passed that, undoubtedly, he could've lived the rest of his life without being charged with Fallon Chase's murder. But instead, he chose to give up everything he held dear to atone for his crime.

And no matter what happens—whether or not he ever walks the streets as a free man again, I will always love him. And no one can ever take that away from us. THE END

I'M A GOOD GIRL GONE BAD
I couldn't keep my panties on, and now I pay the price every single day

If someone had asked me, even a week before, if I'd ever contemplate being unfaithful to my husband, I would've gasped a horrified no!

But that was before I accepted a temp job at Zip Comm, Inc. and met Ilya Gordiyeva, a twenty-eight-year-old Russian with jet-black hair and ice-blue eyes.

From the minute our eyes met, I was lost.

Let me tell you how a happily married woman—a good woman—can cross over to the dark side with almost the same ease as which she'd go into a Baskin Robbins and order a triple-scoop sundae, knowing it would add all those extra pounds. It happened to me, and I believe that under the right circumstances, it could happen to any woman.

Up until I met Ilya, my life was pretty ordinary. I grew up in a small town in Kansas, the eldest daughter of three. Our family was a traditional one—an old-fashioned one, some would say. Daddy was a minister in the Methodist Church, and Mom was a homemaker. I'm the first to admit that I had a blessed childhood. My sisters, Sandi and Caroline, each of us two years apart in age, adored each other, and we never had the power struggles or sibling rivalry that a lot of sisters do. Our parents were wonderful, too, always willing to lend an ear when something was troubling us, and offering love throughout the years. In addition to the strong support we had at home, we also had both sets of grandparents still living, and numerous aunts, uncles, and cousins living in our small town, and they were always available to us. So if anyone said I had an idyllic childhood, I'd have to agree.

That good life continued on through high school. At Westmont High, I was a varsity cheerleader for four years, and reigned as homecoming and prom queen for two years in a row. But I never allowed my popularity to go to my head. I made it a point to be nice to everyone, whether they hung out with me or not. In fact, I had friends in all the different cliques at school. That's how I met Trent, and that's how we fell in love.

Trent wasn't the good-looking quarterback of the football team or the star basketball player. In fact, he wasn't a jock at all. He was the good-looking nerd in my biology class. Of course, none of the other girls were smart enough to see that Trent Thatcher was good looking behind those thick glasses and quiet demeanor. I didn't, either, at first—not until we became lab partners for the semester. Only then, after we'd gotten to know each other, did I notice that besides his dry sense of humor, he had the sweetest smile and the warmest brown eyes I'd ever seen. We were sophomores when we began dating, and from that time on, I never looked at another guy.

We were very much in love, so much so that we got married right after graduation, and in the fall, we left for college, where Trent would be starting his freshman year. Even though I'd done well in high school, graduating with a three-point-eight average, I really had no desire to go to college. My plan was to get a part-time job to help Trent out, and when the time was right, have his children. Then, maybe once the kids were older, I'd take a few courses at the community college. I know it sounds old-fashioned, but all I really ever wanted out of life in those days was to be a wife and mother.

And that's exactly what happened. I found a part-time job as a receptionist at a small office in the town while Trent went to school. We lived in a tiny, one-bedroom apartment off campus until he graduated. A few weeks later, he got a job at a research lab in Mount Pleasant, a town about thirty-five miles away. We moved into a small, but charming, two-bedroom house in town, and within a year, I was pregnant with our first daughter, Lindsay.

The following six months were some of the happiest times of my life. I felt healthy and beautiful—like I was the most special woman in the world to be blessed with such a loving husband and the imminent arrival of our first child.

Because Trent coddled me so much during my pregnancy, I had plenty of time on my hands, and I spent much of it reading romance novels. I'd joined one of those mail-order book clubs, and every three weeks, a half-dozen romances arrived in my mailbox. I devoured them, living vicariously through the spunky heroines, falling in love with the tall, dark, and handsome—and rich!—heroes. Of course, I had my own hero, but Trent and I had been together since I was sixteen. Could I help it if I wanted to "fall in love" all over again?

Then, in my seventh month of pregnancy, the 1980 Winter Olympics were broadcast from Lake Placid, and I was *hooked*. I especially liked watching the figure skating competition. One Russian ice-dancing couple intrigued me the most—especially the male partner. Something about him—his long, flowing dark hair and crystal blue eyes, his lean, hard thigh muscles straining as he moved across the ice—held me absolutely enthralled.

That's when I got the idea to write my own romance novel. Of course, the Russian ice dancer would be the hero. I wrote feverishly on *Ice Palaces* for the next two months, and by the time I started having labor pains, I'd written four chapters of my first novel.

Of course, after I came home from the hospital with Lindsay, my novel was dropped into a desk drawer and forgotten. Not only did I not have time to write anymore, but I was too wrapped up in being a new mom to really care.

Still, as Lindsay grew older, and I finally began to get a full night's sleep again, I started working on my novel again during her afternoon naps. Every day, I found myself increasingly excited about getting back to my writing. It was almost as if my characters were real people. Especially Vassily, my Russian hero. It took me almost a year to write that first novel, but I did it, and I was proud of my efforts. And encouraged enough that I immediately started a second book!

By the time Lindsay started kindergarten, I'd written five novels, but it never occurred to me to submit them to publishers. Writing was fun, a hobby. Besides, I still thought of myself as more of a reader than a writer. How could my work possibly compete with those wonderful books already on the shelves? But Trent thought that I should take my writing more seriously. He suggested that I hone my skills with a creative writing course at the community college. I had to admit that I found the idea intriguing.

But it wasn't to be. Just around the time of registration for the fall semester, I found out that I was pregnant again, and unlike the easy pregnancy I'd had with Lindsay, this baby was a completely different experience. Morning sickness hit me hard and didn't let up until my fifth month. I guess it was a sign of things to come.

From the very beginning, Laurel was a daddy's girl. The difficult pregnancy should've been a warning to me, because unlike her older sister, Laurel was a cranky little thing from the moment we brought her home from the hospital. No matter what I tried to do to soothe her, nothing worked. She fussed constantly, and barely slept more than three or four hours a night. In fact, she only seemed to be happy when she was in her daddy's arms.

Maybe that was part of the reason why my life didn't seem so fulfilling after Laurel was born. Suddenly, there seemed to be a real void in the middle of everything that I did. Something essential was missing, but I didn't know what it was. I had a wonderful husband who provided well for our family. Yes, he worked long hours, but when he was home, he was attentive and good to me. I had two beautiful daughters whom I adored. In the little spare time that I managed to eke out from my busy schedule, I tried to start a new novel, but it just wasn't happening.

And that wasn't the only thing not happening. After the births of our daughters, the romance had somehow gone out of our marriage. I still loved Trent dearly, and there was no question about his love for me, but the spark just wasn't there anymore. Kids, dirty laundry, and carpools had combined to leach every bit of romance out of our lives. And if I had no romance left in my life, how on earth could I possibly write about it?

Not that my imagination was lacking. At night, lying in bed beside my snoring husband, I'd fantasize about being in love again, and my hero was always the same man—Vassily, from my first novel, *Ice Palaces*. I'd created other handsome heroes in other novels, but none seemed quite so vivid—or as sexy—as the big, dark Russian did.

When Laurel finally started kindergarten, I had more time on my hands, and one day, as I was cleaning out my desk, I came across the manuscript of *Ice Palaces*. I hadn't read it in years, so I skimmed through the first pages and was surprised that it was better than I'd remembered. For the rest of that afternoon, I reread the novel, and by the end, I was excited about writing again.

From that day on, I wrote while the girls were in school. Glancing through the newspaper one day, I saw an ad for a romance writers' group that met twice a month. Summoning my nerve, I went to the next meeting, and immediately felt at home with my fellow romance writers. I started attending the meetings on a regular basis, and once I got over the initial stage fright of reading my novel aloud before a group, I enjoyed sharing my work with the other women. They were encouraging, yet, gently critical when they felt I could improve upon something. It was with their encouragement that I finally got up the nerve to send my polished manuscript to a publisher.

It was around this same time that I started doing temp work to make extra money. I was beginning to discover that writing to sell can get costly. What with sending out three-hundred-page manuscripts on a regular basis, postage costs were adding up. So, I started working occasional temp jobs—usually receptionist positions—to pay for my writing habit.

Unfortunately, I wasn't having much success at selling my novel. One publisher after another rejected it, but sometimes they sent very nice letters saying how the writing showed "great promise." So, I just kept plugging away.

The following autumn, with both girls in school—Laurel, a first-grader, and Lindsay, a tall, gazelle-like sixth-grader, I accepted a month-long position at a company called Zip Comm. On my first day there, I met Ilya, and my heart jolted to life.

Ilya was my Vassily come to life! He was tall and dark and

gorgeous—and best of all, he was Russian. But he spoke perfect English—delightfully accented, of course! Not that I heard it that much—he barely spoke to me that first day. I thought it was because he was shy. But every time I passed by his open office door, he glanced up at me and gave me a soft smile. I was working the receptionist's position, but there were always reasons to run an errand to his office or past it. I had no idea what kind of company Zip Comm was, or what they did. I just knew it had something to do with the Internet. It was a small company; there were only about ten employees, and the phones weren't terribly busy.

On the first Friday I worked there, only a few employees were in the office, and all of them, except Ilya, went out to lunch together. I was nervous and jittery, knowing that Ilya and I were the only ones in the building. My imagination started running wild as I fantasized about going into his office and coaxing him into making love to me right there on his desk.

The phones were quiet, even more so than usual, and I'd finished all my routine duties, so I sat at my desk and wrote a love scene for the new novel I was working on, all the time imagining Ilya as my hero.

Suddenly, I heard footsteps coming down the hall. I stiffened, my heart suddenly pounding. Ilya walked into the reception area. His usual shy smile was nowhere to be seen. In fact, he looked rather pale.

"Adrienne, where is Shaun?" he asked, referring to the president of the small company.

"He went to lunch," I said. "All of them went to lunch, as a matter of fact. Are you okay?"

He shrugged and summoned a half-smile. "Not really. I have a bad sinus headache, and I am going home. Will you tell Shaun, please?"

"Sure."

He gave me another wan smile and left the building. I watched him through the glass doors until he was out of sight.

Oh, Ilya! Let me take care of you! I've always read that a good roll in the hay takes the edge off a headache!

Immediately, I was ashamed of myself for having such lascivious thoughts. But I couldn't seem to stop myself from fantasizing about the sexy Russian.

And what harm did it do as long as that was all I did?

Still, once Ilya left the office that day, five o'clock couldn't come fast enough for me. But after I got home, the weekend dragged by, and I found myself actually *anxious* for Monday morning. I just hoped that Ilya was over his sinus headache.

Monday, the first chance I got, I went down to his office on some pretense, and breathed a sigh of relief when I saw that his light was on. He looked up when he noticed me standing in the doorway, and I paused, smiling.

"Hi." My voice sounded breathless, even to my own ears. I felt the blood rush to my face. I sounded like a lovesick teenager! "How's your head?"

"Good, thank God. It was a horrid one. Did you have a nice weekend?"

"Oh, it was okay. My husband worked, of course, so it was just the girls and myself. Anyway, they kept me busy driving them all over the place. You know what that's like, I'm sure. You have kids?"

He stared at me, a blank look on his face. I felt my color deepen.

"I'm not married," he said finally, and that's when I noticed the glimmer of amusement in his eyes.

Oh, God! I wanted to fall through the floor! He'd seen right through my clumsy attempt at discovering his marital status! And I was *sure* he knew I was flirting with him—and he thought it was *funny*! How mortifying!

"I think the phones are ringing," I said hurriedly, and rushed off down the hall.

What was I doing, anyway? I was a married woman. I didn't even *know* this man. Just because he looked and acted *exactly* like my imagined character, right down to his sexy accent, didn't mean that I *knew* him.

Still, I couldn't stop thinking about him during that second week at Zip Comm. At night, lying in bed next to my unsuspecting husband, I fantasized about Ilya, playing out sexy scenarios of him making mad, passionate love to me. Just like the other day, everyone except Ilya would leave the building. I'd go back to his office, maybe take him a package that UPS had delivered for him. And then our eyes would meet—his, smoldering—mine, naked with longing. He'd cross the room and take me into his arms at once. His mouth would cover mine, and I'd melt against his lean, hard body.

"Adrienne?"

Startled, I looked up. Shaun, the bearded young CEO of the company, stood at my desk, a wry smile on his face. "You looked really far away just now."

"Oh, I'm sorry," I said quickly, feeling my face flame. "Can I help you with something?"

"I just wanted to tell you that I'm leaving for a meeting in Nashville, and I'll probably be gone all afternoon. Do you know where Kristen is?"

I checked the "In/Out" board for the whereabouts of his secretary. "She just left for lunch, and I think she said something about having a doctor's appointment this afternoon."

Just as I spoke, three other employees stepped into the reception area.

"Hey, we're going to lunch," said Keith, the carrot-haired accountant.

Shaun cocked a black eyebrow at me. "Well, looks like you're in charge of the company this afternoon, Adrienne."

"Ilya's here," Keith said.

Shaun laughed. "Like I said, Adrienne's in charge of the company. And if Ilya gives you any trouble, you just tell him I said so."

Laughing and chatting, the four of them left the building together. I scanned the "In/Out" board, and my pulse jumped when I saw that, indeed, Ilya and I were the only ones left in the office.

I don't know what I thought I was doing, or if I was thinking consciously at all. Maybe I was just allowing my id full rein, and it was acting on impulse. Whatever—I left the reception area and walked down the hallway toward Ilya's office. As I got closer, I smoothed my hands down the front of the snug black dress I was wearing. I'd bought it the weekend before at the mall. It was a sexy dress, even though it was long-sleeved and square-necked, and perfectly appropriate for office wear. Maybe it was the four-inch side slit that revealed an enticing glimpse of my black-stockinged leg that made it seem so seductive. On some level, I know I'd had Ilya in mind when I'd bought it. I looked great in it, especially with the strappy black heels I'd bought later that same day.

Ilya looked up as I appeared in the doorway of his office. His blue eyes appraised me, and a shiver of excitement snaked down my back as I recognized the appreciation in them. He looked incredibly handsome in a chili-red turtleneck and jeans.

"Hi," I said, standing on the threshold. "I was just wondering if there was anything I could do for you."

He gave me a slow smile. One dark eyebrow lifted. "What do you have in mind?"

I felt hot color flood my face. "I—I'm kind of bored, you see," I stammered. "I'm all caught up on my work, and the phones are quiet. I just wondered—I was wondering if you have any busy work you'd like me to do."

He leaned back in his chair and studied me. My body temperature rose a notch, and I wondered if this was what it felt like to have a hot flash. Finally, he spoke.

"Yes, I believe I can find something for you to do."

I held my breath, waiting. He stood up and pushed his chair back.

"Would you mind taking a letter for me? I speak English fairly well, but writing it is still difficult for me."

"Sure."

"Please. Take a seat, and I will get my thoughts in order."

I sat down, opened my steno pad, and poised my pen over it. Ilya began to pace his small office, tunneling his hands through his thick black hair. Finally, he began to dictate a long, boring letter about stock options and financial matters. It didn't matter to me what the content was, though; I was simply mesmerized by his voice. I'd just finished a full page when he walked over behind me, placed his hands on the back of my chair, and leaned over my shoulder to peer at what I'd written.

"Let me see what I've got so far," he said.

I sat motionless, my heart thundering as his intoxicating scent washed over me. Sandalwood aftershave and Irish Spring soap. He was so close, I could hear his breathing, could feel his warm breath on my cheek. If I turned my head, my lips would be just inches from his sexy, Russian jaw. My fingers loosened around the pen, and it dropped to the floor, rolling under the desk.

"Oh, sorry!"

I scooted the chair back, and sank to my knees to go for it. But Ilya was already on his hands and knees, reaching for it, too. I grabbed it first, and just a second later, Ilya's hand covered mine.

Electricity arced between us. Our eyes met and held; both of us grew still. For a long moment, we just stared at each other, his hand covering mine as I clenched the pen. Breathless, I heard blood rushing through my brain, drowning out all other sound. Time seemed to stand still.

Then Ilya leaned toward me, and I felt myself swaying to him as if he were a magnet and there was no possible way I could resist his pull. The next thing I knew, his lips were locked on mine, his tongue gently seeking. It was a sweet invasion that demanded total surrender. And I was lost. Totally, and irrevocably, under his spell.

Slowly, we stood, facing each other. He reached out and brushed a stray tendril of hair away from my face. I stared up at him, barely breathing.

What, now?

He stepped away from me and went to his door. For a moment, I felt a sense of relief, mingled with sharp disappointment. He was putting an end to this madness right now, and rightfully so.

But then, I saw him shut—and lock—the door, and my heart began to pound even harder. He strode back to me, his blue eyes simmering. I caught my breath as his hand entwined itself in my hair, tugging gently to expose my bare neck to his gaze. He lowered his head, and his lips skimmed my throat in leisurely, blood-churning kisses. I moaned softly as he took me into his arms, and finally, his mouth returned to mine with renewed fervor.

Oh, Vassily! You have come to life for me! This was meant to be.

Still kissing me, he eased me back, down onto his desk, his warm hands sliding up my thighs under my dress. I was mindless with passion, even when I knew he was tugging down my panty hose and unzipping his jeans.

He never spoke a word, and neither did I. We were like two animals in heat. Nothing in the world meant anything; nothing else existed but this sheer, animal urgency to mate.

And so, there, in that office, just like in my fantasies, Ilya made love to me right on his desk. It was quick, urgent, and very, *very* good. I'd never been with any other man but my husband before, and I'd always thought we had a good sex life. But our sex had never been like this. I never knew it could be like this.

That was the beginning. As Ilya left the office that afternoon, he dropped a note on my desk:

I want you again. Here's my address. Please say you'll meet me there after you get off work.

After making love, I'd adjusted my rumpled dress and returned to my desk, torn with guilt, thinking of Trent and the girls.

How could I have done such a thing?

It wasn't like me at all. I'd never, ever been ruled by my passions before. But for whatever reason, with Ilya, I'd been ruled by nothing *but* passion—and need and desire. It was insane—and depraved. And it could never, ever happen again.

But as soon as I read Ilya's note, my whole body began to tremble, and I felt a slow heat rise inside of me as I remembered how good—how incredibly *fantastic*—the sex had been with him. I knew then that once wasn't enough.

I had to have more.

My stomach churned as I dialed my home number. Trent picked up the phone on the second ring.

"Hi," I said. Guilt ate at me, but it didn't stop me from lying. "I didn't think you'd be home so soon. Hey, I'm going to the mall after work. I'll probably be there for a couple of hours. Why don't you and the girls order pizza for dinner, and I'll heat it up when I get home?"

"Sure, babe. See you when you get home."

Just as I'd expected, Trent was his usual, easygoing self. He didn't have a suspicious bone in his body. And that made me feel even guiltier.

But not guilty enough.

Fifteen minutes after I left the office, Ilya met me at the door of his apartment, looking devastating in sweatpants and a Tennessee Titans T-shirt. His hair was damp from the shower, and the scent of Irish Spring encompassed him.

He invited me in and closed the door behind me. "Can I get you a drink?" he asked. His eyes swept over me, warming my blood to a fever pitch.

I felt like a character in one of my books. A beautiful, sexy heroine—a single woman who was *very* much attracted to the male hero. And this new woman that I was becoming would do things that Adrienne Thatcher would never even *dream* of doing.

I shook my head and stepped closer to him, trailing a finger down his firm, hard bicep. "No drink," I murmured, holding his eyes with mine, pursing my lips in a small, cat-like smile. My hand skipped over to his chest, flattening against his heart so I could feel the rapid thud of it against my palm. "Just you. That's all I want—just you, Ilya."

He smiled. His reached around to cup my bottom in his hands, wrenching me to him so I could feel his heat and arousal. Then his mouth took mine in a savage kiss, and once again, I was lost in him.

Our affair continued through the rest of the month. And, yes, I suffered guilt. Horrible guilt. Especially when I was lying in bed next to my husband at night. Or when I helped the girls with their homework, or made their lunches for school the next day. In fact, when I was at home with my family, guilt was my constant companion. But as soon as I went to the office, the moment I saw Ilya, it went right out the window, and all I could do was think about when we'd get our next stolen moment together.

We made love in his office when everyone else was gone, which, incredibly, happened once or twice a week. When we couldn't wait for those times, we'd take our lunch breaks together and head for his apartment, which was close by. Sometimes, we'd meet after work . . . after I'd left a carefully rehearsed message on the answering machine at home: "I have to work late tonight," or, "I've got some errands to run after I get off. There's a casserole in the fridge, but don't wait for me."

In anticipation, I'd made a few meals ahead on the weekends. Of course, at the time, I'd told myself I was doing it just to make my life a little easier after getting home from work at night, but the real reason was so I could go to Ilya without worrying about what my family would eat that night. Generous of me, huh? Oh, I was so totally bewitched by Ilya by that time.

I'd even started thinking about staying on at Zip Comm permanently. After all, I knew Shaun was looking for a permanent receptionist. In fact, I was surprised they hadn't found one yet. But then, maybe he was hoping I'd agree to stay on. Even though my conscience told me that would be the worst thing in the world for me to do, I knew deep down that if he asked me, I'd readily agree.

That's why I was so shocked on that Monday morning—the last week of the month—when Kristen, Shaun's secretary, led a pale blonde into the reception area and introduced her to me as the new receptionist.

"We're going to have you train her this week, Adrienne," Kristen explained, smiling. "You've done such a good job this month. I'm sure you'll have Caitlin ready to be on her own by next Monday."

For a moment, I could only stare in astonishment. I'd been so sure that they were going to ask me to stay. Finally, though, I remembered my manners and forced a smile.

"No problem," I said. "Caitlin, have a seat, and we'll get started right away."

I realized quickly enough that no one was going to be making "dumb blonde" jokes about the new receptionist. Not only was she trim and pretty, but Caitlin was also intelligent and polished. In an hour, she was answering the phones as if she'd been doing it for years. By Wednesday morning, she was pretty much handling the reception area completely on her own, only occasionally asking me questions as certain circumstances came up. I wanted to hate her, but I couldn't. She had a vivacious, bubbly personality that was impossible to resist, and I knew that everyone at Zip Comm would love her.

At that thought, my stomach plunged.

After Friday, what would happen with Ilya and me? Would we be able to continue our affair? Really—was that all it was to him—just an affair? After three weeks of sex with Ilya, I'd convinced myself that what I felt for him was much more than lust. He was the hero of my romance novel. If I'd thrown caution to the winds and betrayed my husband and family, then, surely, I must be in love.

Only love could make someone act so abominably.

It was almost three o'clock on Wednesday afternoon. Caitlin was handling everything at the reception desk, and I hadn't been with Ilya since the previous Friday night. I'd hoped that morning we'd arrange a "lunch date," but he'd gone out alone at twelve-thirty, barely speaking to me as he'd passed the reception area.

"I'll be back in a few minutes," I said to Caitlin, and headed down the hallway to Ilya's office.

But he wasn't there. His computer was on, though, so he hadn't left the building. I did a U-turn and headed to the break room. As I approached, I heard male voices inside, raised in laughter.

"I'll bet a hundred bucks, Ilya, that you can't get into the new blonde's panties within two weeks!"

That was Keith's voice—the red-haired accountant. My steps slowed as I eavesdropped. Even my heartbeat seemed to slow in anticipation of Ilya's response.

"Ah, Keithie . . . you make it so *easy* to take your money. Did you not learn your lesson with Adrienne?"

At Ilya's mention of my name, my heart practically stopped. I leaned against the wall, trying to choke back the nausea suddenly churning in my gut.

Keith laughed. "Hey, how was I to know she'd turn out to be such a slut? Did you see what she looked like the first day she worked here? Hair all pulled back like a librarian's. High collar. Long skirt and low heels. It wasn't until she laid eyes on you that she started wearing those tight, short skirts and clingy tops. How was I to know the schoolmarm would turn into a man-hungry ho?"

"I guess that's why they call me a babe magnet," Ilya said in a smug voice.

They both laughed. Then Keith's voice lowered. "So, how was she, Ilya?"

Although I couldn't see his face, I heard the smile in Ilya's voice when he answered Keith's question. "Oh, she was a hot little minx. She couldn't get enough."

My face flamed with humiliation. Blindly, I turned and stumbled back down the hallway toward the reception area. Caitlin looked up and her china-blue eyes widened.

"Adrienne, what's wrong?"

"I feel sick," I mumbled. "I'm going home. Tell Shaun and Kristen, okay?"

"Well—sure." She looked concerned. "Gee, I hope you feel better."

Somehow, I got home, but I don't remember the drive. It was only three-thirty, and the girls were still at the sitter's. Trent would pick them up on his way home from work.

I was glad the house was empty. All I wanted to do was bury myself under the covers and sob out my pain and humiliation.

And my guilt.

I'd almost thrown away my marriage and family for a sexy Russian playboy. And I probably would have done it if I hadn't overheard that awful conversation in the break room—if Ilya had given me any kind of indication that he wanted our affair to continue.

Oh, God! What kind of a horrible woman was I? To give up a man who loved me? To risk losing my daughters?

All because of lust?

And now, what? It was over with Ilya. Not because I'd come to my senses, but because I'd realized that he wasn't whom I'd imagined him to be. That didn't make me an honorable person. No, it just made me an idiot—an idiot with bad judgment and an overworked sex drive.

I tossed and turned in my bed once my tears were spent. Should I do the right thing and confess all to Trent—give him the choice to throw me out or to forgive me for my infidelity? Yes, if I was going to be brave and honorable, that's exactly what I should do.

Unfortunately, not only am I an idiot, but I'm a coward, too.

By the time Trent brought the girls home that night, I was in the kitchen preparing dinner. I greeted my husband with a big smile and told him that I'd left the Zip Comm job early because the new receptionist was doing so well on her own.

And that was the truth, wasn't it?

Part of it, anyway.

I've never confessed my affair to Trent, and every day, I pay for it. I don't sleep well at night, and even though I hide it well, my stress level is high whenever I'm with my family. It seems like I'm always on my guard with Trent these days, trying too hard not to say the wrong thing—anything that might lead to suspicion.

And here's the most ironic thing: I can't write anymore. Since Ilya, my characters always seem cardboard thin.

And love scenes?

Forget it. I can't write them. Maybe because I've become so cynical. How can I write about love and romance when I feel like such a hypocrite?

And, to make matters worse, just the other day, I got a letter in the mail from one of the publishers I'd sent a partial to. They want to see the complete manuscript, but I don't know how I can possibly finish the book. Not with this cloud of guilt hanging over me.

So, readers, I ask you, what should I do?

Should I cleanse my soul and confess everything to Trent?

I know that the knowledge of my infidelity will devastate him. And even if he can somehow find it in his heart to forgive me, how can he ever trust me again?

As it is, I don't even know if I can trust myself. I don't think I would ever again do anything as crazy and wrong as what I did with Ilya, but who knows? Before I met him, I never dreamed it would be possible for me to sleep with any man other than Trent. I've always

been a good girl, always prided myself on doing the right thing.
  So how could I have gone so terribly wrong?
  I leave it up to you, dear readers. Tell me what I should do.
  Live with the guilt, or confess all to my husband?
  You decide. THE END

THE TRUTH HURTS!
Why do I destroy the people I love most?

It was a party from hell. On the drive home, I sighed with relief and turned to look at my husband, Grant.

"Whew! I am glad this night is over."

"You were right in there with the best of them," he said in an even tone. "You were lying through your teeth by pretending everything was just fine."

"What were we supposed to do?" I asked defensively, sitting up straight and uncrossing my legs. He studied the steering wheel, and I noticed how tight his grip on it was.

"You could have told the truth," he said simply.

I snorted and laughed unpleasantly. "Oh, sure. I should have told Simone that we all know her husband is making it with Michelle, while Michelle sits there looking like Alice in Wonderland, so pure, so blonde. That would really be cool, Grant. It would even be more awful than sitting there pretending everything is just fine!"

"This whole evening just gave me the creeps," he said as he parked the car in the driveway. "I wonder when it was that honesty became something to avoid at all costs."

I shrugged and followed him inside. In bed later, I tried to joke with Grant about his remark. "You can't handle the truth," I said lamely, trying to imitate Jack Nicholson in a movie Grant loved.

"Maybe *you* can't," he said, ignoring my attempts to make him laugh. He obviously was not in the mood for jokes.

I reached over and pressed my body close to his. "Can you handle *this*?" I asked softly.

"I'm not in the mood, Wendy."

Being turned down hurt my feelings, but I was tired so I didn't mind all that much. I figured after a good night's sleep, Grant would be fine.

Before I fell asleep, I thought about Simone and her wandering husband, Nate. I did feel bad about the secret because Simone was my best friend, but there was no way I was going to hurt her by telling her the truth. I didn't much like Nate, anyway. I always had the feeling he was laughing at me.

Simone and I are opposites. She is short and dark, and I am tall and fair-skinned. She loves sports, and I love to be at home. Our friendship started because we have kids the same age. My daughter, Lucy, and her daughter, Krista, are both five.

We took our kids to the park together for them to play and discovered over time that we were friends, too. Her attempts to get me to exercise and run with her were useless, however. My idea of exercise is to walk from the car to the mall or the grocery store or the house.

When the news got out that Nate and Michelle were seeing each other, I didn't want to believe it. I never mentioned any of the gossip to Simone, and she never said anything to me about trouble at home. Then one day, Grant came home and told me that Nate admitted to the affair at a golf game the guys all went to.

"He was actually laughing about it," he said. "He was comparing Michelle's lovemaking skills to Simone's. It made me sick. I had to leave."

I was proud of my husband for doing that, but I still could not bring myself to tell Simone what everyone was saying.

"I just can't tell Simone," I told Grant.

"She probably already knows," he answered quietly.

I looked at him, surprised by his words. "What makes you say that?"

Grant's face turned red, as if he were embarrassed. Sometimes Grant blushes if someone catches him being "sensitive."

"I don't know." He shrugged. "Just a guess."

"I don't think she does. Simone would confide in me if she knew or even suspected. I know her too well. She can't keep a secret."

"Forget it," Grant said. "It doesn't really matter."

I didn't forget about it, though, and a couple of days later, I asked Grant again why he thought Simone already knew about the affair.

Grant looked strangely tense. "Could we change the subject please? I hate talking about all this crap."

I started to say more, but I could tell by Grant's face that he was through with the subject, so I didn't press on.

The next morning was frosty, a sure sign that winter was coming. Lucy chattered and sang over her breakfast, and Grant buried his head in the paper and drank his coffee. Lucy had been invited to a birthday party that afternoon, so she was very excited. She hurried away from the table finally, wanting to get ready for the big event.

When she was gone, I sat down next to Grant with a cup of coffee. "If I were being totally honest, I would tell you that I wish you would put down that paper and talk to me."

Grant lowered the paper and looked at me. "You couldn't be totally honest if you tried." He wasn't smiling.

"I beg your pardon?" His words made me suddenly very angry and defensive. "Are you calling me a liar?"

His jaw tensed in an all-too-familiar way. "I'm not saying that," he snarled at me, "but you and I play the same game as everyone else. We lie automatically. Hell, our lives are all lies, if you really want to be honest about it."

"Where did all this come from?" I was astonished by his words. He was usually so nonjudgmental.

He sighed. "Let's just drop it, Wendy. I really don't want to talk about this anymore."

"No, no," I continued. "You can't tell me I'm dishonest and then tell me to forget it."

So we continued on, back and forth like this, for about fifteen minutes. What I intended to be a discussion had developed into an argument. By that time, we were both angry and we were saying things we really didn't mean.

About that time, Lucy came running into the kitchen clutching her favorite pink dress. "I want to wear this to the party," she announced, waving the dress in the air.

She stopped and looked at us. "Are you having a fight?" Only a five-year-old would be so blunt, and my immediate reaction was to deny it.

"No, we're not fighting." I gave her a hug. "Yes, you may wear the dress."

She smiled and looked at her dad. "Are you fighting with Mommy?" she persisted.

"Yes, I am," he answered simply. He gave me a defiant look.

"Well, stop it," Lucy said, wrinkling her face into a frown. "I don't like it when your voices get red."

Grant and I both smiled. "Getting red" to Lucy meant anything disagreeable. When she left the room, though, the tension between Grant and me deepened.

After about five minutes of arguing back and forth in whispers so Lucy couldn't hear, Grant stood up.

"I don't want to fight with you, Wendy." He threw his arms up in the air as if he were surrendering. "But we are what we are, and none of us is very honest, including you."

"I don't know about you, Grant," I said in a prissy voice that I hated the sound of, "but I consider myself to be a very honest person."

Grant sighed. "Even that's a lie."

"How is that a lie?" I asked, almost shouting again.

"You don't really believe you tell the truth all the time. I know I don't."

"I *am* honest," I said proudly. "I would like to know what you are dishonest about, since you seem so ready to admit it."

"No." He had a sad look that frightened me. "You don't want to know, Wendy."

Maybe it was because he scared me with that look and those words or maybe I was just reveling in a good argument, but I kept pressing him.

"Come on, Mr. *Honesty*," I prodded sarcastically. "Give me the benefit of your total candor. Tell me your pathetic little secrets."

Grant's face was as rigid as a board. His eyes were dark with fury.

"All right," he finally said. "You want me to tell you the truth about our lives, about me? I will. I have been sleeping with your best friend, Simone, for about six months now."

He may as well have slapped me. The effect was exactly the same. My first reaction was to gasp, then for some reason, I laughed.

"That is a terrible thing to say," I sputtered, unable to believe at that moment that Grant might be telling the truth. I thought he was just trying to shock me in order to stop the argument.

"But it's the truth, Wendy. If you want more of the same truth, I am in love with her and I want to be with her." With those words, he bowed his head, but I could see that his face was gray and sad.

I sat down on the chair, since my legs no longer could support me. I looked at Grant, and I knew that what he had just told me was the truth and that the truth was more awful than anything I'd ever imagined.

Lucy came running into the kitchen with another dress to show us. She stopped suddenly and looked at us.

"Uh-oh," she said. "Red again."

Grant walked out of the room, and I guess my automatic mother pilot clicked on, because I dealt with Lucy in a calm way. I reassured her that Mommy and Daddy weren't fighting, and then I left the house. I had no idea where to go. When I was upset, my first inclination had always been to seek out my friend Simone, but how could I do that now?

I drove around for a while in aimless shock, but then I did turn to Simone. I drove down her familiar street, not knowing what I would say when I saw her, but knowing I did have to see her and hear the words from her.

Nate answered the door. "Saturday morning and it's Wendy," he said in his glib, mocking, slightly insulting way. I looked at him with disgust, not only for what I believed was going on behind Simone's back with him and Michelle, but for what was going on behind his back with his wife and my husband. So I glared at him and asked to see Simone.

"Won't I do?" he asked with a grin and a wink.

My increasing glare stymied him apparently, and he turned to shout for Simone.

Simone came out of the kitchen looking comfortable and familiar. "Ah, Wendy," she said, reaching her arms out to me. "You came to help in the post-party cleanup. Bless you."

I looked at my friend and fought back the tears. Even in her sweatpants and tee shirt, she was adorable. Her dark curls fell across her face like ribbons. Her cheeks were rosy, even though her eyes looked tired.

"Can I talk to you in private?" I asked in a shaky voice.

Simone's face immediately changed to one of concern. "What's wrong?" she asked. I saw fear in her face now, maybe even guilt.

"Could you just come outside and sit in the car with me, Simone?" I asked.

Nate was watching from a distance. "Go ahead, honey. I'll take over in the kitchen."

Simone followed me out to the car silently. When we got inside, I turned to face her.

"You know," she said softly, turning her head away from me.

I clenched the steering wheel in front of me, watching the icy rain streak down the windshield. I died inside.

"Is it true?" I managed to ask.

Simone put her head into her hands and started to sob. "It's true. Oh, Wendy, I am so sorry."

"Get out."

"Wendy, please," Simone pleaded, reaching over to touch my arm. "It just happened. I was so miserable about Nate and Michelle, and I couldn't talk to you—I just couldn't. Then one day I ran into Grant and he listened and he seemed to care, and it just happened, Wendy."

I kept staring out the window. "You knew about Nate and Michelle?" For some reason, that piece of information enveloped my brain at the moment. "Why didn't you tell me you knew?"

Looking back, I realize how ridiculous it was for me to ask Simone about that when my world was turning to ashes.

"I had this other thing on my mind, Wendy," Simone said in dry, choking words.

I turned to look at her. "This other thing being my husband," I said sarcastically.

"We never meant for it to go on, Wendy," Simone nearly moaned. "We just couldn't stop. I love Grant, Wendy, and that's the awful truth of it. God help me, but I do."

"Well, I love you both," I said, still staring out the window. "Or at least I *did*. So, like the song says, what has love got to do with it? Now get out of my car."

Simone got out, but she leaned in the window. "Are you going to tell Nate?" she practically whined.

I sped out of the driveway without answering her. Experts say in times of great stress or tragedy, the body locks down to protect itself, and that is what happened to me. I drove home and went into the house. I had to get my daughter ready for the party, and that is all I could deal with at the moment.

I said only two words to Grant during the hubbub of getting Lucy ready: "Start packing."

As she was leaving for the party, Lucy turned to me. "When I get back home, no red, okay?"

I smiled and hugged her, fighting back my tears.

Grant came out of the bedroom with a suitcase in his hand. "I'm going over to stay at Mom's house for a while. If you need me, that's where I'll be. Are you sure this is what you want to do, Wendy?"

"No, Grant," I practically spat out. "I don't have any choice, though."

He turned to leave.

"One more thing before you go," I added.

He stopped, with his back to me, and waited.

"Is Simone the only one you've been with since we were married?"

Grant turned to look at me, and I almost laughed for one insane moment at the shocked and offended look on his face.

"There could have been others," he said in a stiff, self-righteous tone. "I held out until Simone and I found each other. God knows I had reason to look around. You made it clear to me once Lucy was born that I was unimportant to you."

"So much for honesty," I managed to say between my sobs. "I'm sorry I asked."

Then Grant left our home. The next two weeks are a blur in my mind. My mom came to my rescue, bless her heart. Once she found out what was going on, she came to the house and stayed.

"Dad will be all right on his own for a while," she insisted. "It will do him good."

"That isn't true, Mom," I protested weakly. "I know how much he depends on you."

"He told me to come, Wendy." She took my face in her hands. "You need to grieve a while."

It was amazing how my friends stayed away. There were a couple of calls at first, curiosity calls mainly, and then the phone was silent. I did hear through the grapevine that Nate had moved out and that Simone and Grant were living together in her house.

Then the inevitable happened: Grant called to see Lucy. I knew I couldn't deny him that. Lucy was very confused and missed her daddy. I tried to explain to her in simple terms why her daddy was living in Krista's house with Krista's mommy, but I could tell by the blank, hurt look in her eyes that she couldn't make sense of it. Neither could I, as a matter of fact.

"Everything's red in this house," Lucy muttered one day.

When Lucy came back from her weekend with her dad, she seemed happier and calmer.

"We had a lot of fun," she told me. "I like being Krista's sister."

Her innocent words stung my heart. I knew enough about kids, though, to know that now was not the time to give into petty jealousy and make some caustic remark about Grant and Simone that would only confuse Lucy again.

"That's good, honey," I finally said.

Grant filed for divorce, and I accepted the fact that my life as I knew it was over. Along with that acceptance came a new resolve that I would always tell the truth and be honest in the future. Lying, or ducking the truth, never gets anyone anywhere, I said over and over to anyone who would listen.

I avoided telling Lucy about the divorce, though, as long as I could—but I knew I had to do it. Without a doubt, it was the hardest thing I ever did in my life.

"I don't know what that means—divorce," said Lucy. "But I know it's red."

"It just means that Mommy and Daddy will live in different houses, but we will both always love you," I explained.

"Did daddy divorce *me?*" Her blue eyes were so sad, so scared, all I could say was a simple no.

"Just make the red stop, Mommy." Her eyes begged me to make everything all right again, and I knew I couldn't do it. It was hard knowing how much truth could hurt Lucy, so sometimes I made an exception in her case and gave up my determination to be totally honest.

"I will try," I promised, knowing only time would make things better.

After about a month of "grieving" and self-pity, I sent Mom home and started looking for a job. I landed a good job pretty quickly. I have a degree in public relations and a good resume. Felton International hired me on their publication team, and a retired neighbor lady agreed to come and take care of Lucy after kindergarten each afternoon.

Those were days of barely making it. I went through what I had to to survive.

When Grant came to pick up Lucy, we were polite but cool to one another for Lucy's sake. I gave him plenty of looks, though, and he had the grace to blush and look away. Mercifully, he never came with Simone. I had not spoken to her since that winter morning months ago.

Then one day, Grant came with Simone. She waited in the car, but I saw her. He told me they were married. I sat home that day and did nothing but think and examine my life.

I decided I had to live in this world, but I didn't have to trust anyone ever again. Again, I made an exception for Lucy and possibly my folks. A new hardness set into my heart, like cement, and I felt safe knowing I would tell the truth, even if everyone else did not. It was something to hang on to.

I went to work every day with that steeliness in my heart. I rarely smiled, and I developed a cynical attitude toward everything. My coworkers avoided me at breaks or lunchtime, since I was apt to tell them the truth, such as the fact that their new haircut was awful—or if they asked, that, yes, they did look like they were gaining weight.

One night, Lucy and I were watching a Disney video together, and Lucy sighed with happiness when it ended.

"Now everyone is happy," she said. "No more red."

"No one is ever happy for long." I turned to see the startled, frightened look in her eyes and was immediately ashamed of myself. She was so young; she had a right to believe in happy endings. Then I reminded myself of how cruel the world could be, reminded myself of the truth about people, and I refused to retract my statement.

"Happiness is just pretend," I explained, pulling my child to me. "It lasts a little while, but it never stays."

Lucy pushed me away and ran from the room crying and holding her ears. "Red, red, red!" she screamed.

I started to go after her but stopped myself. I knew I couldn't lie to my child about what life was really like, so I let her sob herself to sleep. The truth really hurts, I decided, but not as much as the lies.

At work, I noticed that my habit of telling everyone exactly the truth as I saw it was starting to come back to me. Instead of compliments, I started getting critiques about my own appearance, and I didn't like it very much.

"Your hair could use some styling," my assistant told me one day.

I just stared at her, surprised and speechless.

"Well, you know, you told me how bad my haircut was last week, so I thought I would return the favor. I know how much you value honesty." Then she gave me a sweet smile and walked away with a toss of her hair.

"Thank you for your honesty," I called after her, but I didn't mean it. Her remarks had hurt my feelings. I went to the mirror and realized she was right. "She told the truth," I whispered to my reflection.

Fair enough, I told myself. *I give the truth and I get it.* Somehow, though, I found those words less than consoling. I made an appointment to get my hair styled later that day.

My mother called a few days after that incident and asked how I was. "I feel unhappy and miserable most of the time, Mom, so don't ask me those questions if you expect me to lie and say everything is fine."

"Oh, Wendy," she sighed. "I am so sorry this has happened to you."

"I believe you are, Mom. But there's nothing anyone can do about it now."

The odd thing about the whole situation was that I actually missed Simone more than I missed Grant at times. I was so angry and hurt about what she did to me, but I still missed the fun we'd had together when I thought she was my friend.

Then one day at work, someone with an old, familiar face walked into my office. It was Nate Hunter, Simone's unfaithful ex-husband.

"Hi, Wendy," he said, holding his hand out to me.

I shook his hand and asked what he was doing there, and he told me he was going to be working for the company as a temporary consultant.

I stared at him, thinking he was even more handsome than I remembered. His dark hair and good body brought back memories of the old days. My dislike for him at that time ruled out acknowledging his good looks. Now, numb and wounded as I was, I saw him in a more objective way.

I invited him to come into my office and have a cup of coffee with me to catch up on old times.

"You look good, Nate," I said, looking into his eyes. "Divorce must agree with you."

"So do you, Wendy." He smiled. "You've lost weight, haven't you?" He was so charming and personable, but his eyes were taunting me, just the way they always had.

I shrugged. "I guess so, about twenty pounds."

"Well, it suits you. How are you? How is Lucy?"

"We're getting by a day at a time, Nate. It isn't easy."

"Tell me about it," Nate agreed. "I go to pick up Krista, and there is Grant, mowing my lawn."

I raised my eyebrows. "I had no idea your yard meant so much to you," I said sarcastically.

"Come on, Wendy." Nate leaned back in his chair and studied me. "I am not a bad person. I don't know what you think you know about me, but I was totally shocked about Simone and Grant. I thought our marriage was going all right."

I snorted, spitting some of my coffee on my desk, which I quickly mopped up with a tissue.

"How could it be going all right if you were having an affair with Michelle right under everyone's nose?"

"That meant nothing." He blushed and lowered his eyes.

I stared at him. "I value honesty a lot these days, Nate. Please don't tell me your adultery meant nothing, but Simone's did."

"Well, believe what you want, Wendy. You never really liked me, anyway."

I couldn't deny that. "Simone was my friend. I thought you were treating her horribly," I said.

"She never told you she was having an affair with your husband, did she?" Nate asked, his eyes taunting me again.

"*Touché*," I barely whispered.

Nate stood up. I felt his presence in the office. He was so masculine, so good-looking. I automatically sucked my stomach in as I got up to walk him to the door.

"Let's go to dinner," he said suddenly. He stopped to look at me. "We ought to be friends. Who knows better than you and I what we have gone through?" He smiled a crooked smile, and I liked the way he looked that moment.

"I guess I could have dinner with someone I never really liked," I said with a smile.

"That's right," he agreed. "We'll make a good pair. I don't like myself much, either, so we have something in common."

I raised my eyebrows. "All right. Let's go to dinner. Why not? Maybe we can be friends," I added.

"Or we can pretend to be." Nate pursed his lips and nodded his head, then winked at me and told me to be ready Friday at seven o'clock.

Mom came to stay that weekend and to sit with Lucy. She was very excited to hear that I was going out, but when she heard it was with Simone's ex-husband, she hesitated a little.

"Are you sure it's a good idea, dear?" she asked. "I think it's time to move on with your life in a whole new direction. Won't this just bring back memories?"

"It doesn't matter, Mom," I reassured her. "Nothing is going to come of it, anyway. I just hope Grant and Simone find out we're out together."

"Oh, Wendy," my mother sighed.

Nate took me to a lovely restaurant, and sure enough, some people we knew from the old days saw us out together. We clinked our glasses in a toast as we chuckled with glee, thinking the news was sure to get back to our mutual ex-spouses.

Actually, despite myself and my newfound cynicism, I had a very good time. Nate wined and dined me and whirled me around the dance floor. I felt good in his arms, and I closed my eyes as he held me close and we swayed to a love song I knew and loved.

On the way home, he asked if he could see me again.

"I don't really see the point, Nate. I will never trust you or believe anything you say."

Nate looked at me. "You never really knew me, Wendy. Hey, you're into honesty. Why don't you give me a chance?"

"Look, Nate, I'm tired of people and their promises and lies. I don't trust or believe anyone anymore. The truth is something most people want to avoid. I happen to think it's the only way to survive. I made up my mind when Grant left that I was going to tell the truth and face it for the rest of my life."

Nate was silent for a moment. "Well, that's commendable, but why can't I be part of it?"

"No offense, but I don't think the truth is very high up on your priority list."

"Not always . . . but sometimes. I can put it up there for you."

"I don't think you understand the concept, Nate," I said in a sarcastic tone.

Nate just laughed. When he walked me to the door, I took his hand and shook it.

"Maybe I'll see you around work," I said.

Nate took my hand and pulled me to him. He wrapped his arms around me and pressed me close. I could feel his warm breath on my neck, and I went limp in his arms. It felt so good to be held, and he was so attractive.

He touched my lips gently at first. Then he pressed his mouth down on mine, and I was lost in a delicious ecstasy. The kiss was long and wonderful, and when it was over, Nate looked at me.

"Can I see you tomorrow night, Wendy? Will you go out with me again?"

"Yes," I answered simply. "I think I want to."

"Good," he replied. "I'll see you tomorrow night."

Mom was still awake watching television when I came in.

She smiled when she saw me. "You look happy."

I sat down beside her and sighed. "It's probably just the wine."

Mom stayed with Lucy again on Saturday night while Nate and I went out to a play. It was a comedy and it was funny, and I felt lighthearted and younger than I had for a long time.

Nate kept touching me in little ways—a brush on the hand, an arm around my shoulder. I felt my defenses melting away when I was with him, but I would remind myself that nothing was as it seemed and that I certainly could not trust Nate.

We sat in the car in front of my house and necked like two teenagers when we got home. The windows of the cars were steamed up, and we were both breathing hard.

"Whoa," I finally said, pushing Nate away. "This is getting out of hand."

"Shall we go back to my place?" he asked.

"No, no, no." I felt horrified at the thought. "This can't go on. I don't trust you."

"What don't you trust?" He let me pull away from him. "You are a woman, I'm a man, we're attracted to each other, and both of us are free. What are you afraid of?"

"Do you want me to be honest?" I asked with a sly smile.

Nate shrugged. "I guess so."

"I think you could really mean something to me. I don't want to get hurt again."

Nate sighed and started tracing my eyebrows with his finger. "Wendy, I can't promise you that you won't get hurt if you see me. I can't promise you everything will be wonderful. I can't promise you that I will be totally truthful with you. I *can* promise you that I won't hurt you deliberately, and I *can* promise you that I will always try to tell the truth. Isn't that enough?"

"I don't believe you."

Nate was silent, and then he said softly, "Okay, I give up, you win." With a sigh, he got out of the car and came around to open the door on my side.

I got out and stood by him, and I felt a magnetic sexual pull. I wanted to wrap myself around him, pull his body into mine. I was filled with such a strong sexual urge that embarrassed me. I turned away from him and walked a little ahead of him to the door.

"You think about things and call me if you change your mind," he said as I put the key in the lock. He pulled the collar of my shirt up around my chin and smiled down at me. "You're too nice to hurt, and too pretty."

I watched him walk back to the car, turn, and wave goodbye to me. I wanted to run back to the car and climb inside, to go home with him, but I didn't.

I went into the quiet house and stood in the hallway, motionless, staring into the blackness. At that moment, honesty was not nearly so much on my mind as making love, and making love with Nate was what I wanted to do. I was embarrassed by the truth of what I felt.

I spent the next few days thinking. I went to work and went through my duties like a robot. I thought about Nate every moment. I knew I wanted him physically, but I had to admit it was probably a situation that would start, remain, and end on a physical note.

I didn't trust him at all. In fact, I still felt he was taunting me at times, and I was uncomfortable around him because I never knew what he was really thinking or feeling about me.

About three days later, I had just gotten Lucy settled down and asleep when my doorbell rang. I put down the newspaper I was reading and went to the door. I gasped to see Simone standing there. She looked the same, except that her hair was longer. She smiled that old familiar smile at me.

"What do you want?" I gasped.

"I came to talk to you as your friend, Wendy."

I let out a snort of disbelief. "Oh, please. Give me a break."

"Will you let me in and just listen to me?"

My curiosity overcame my anger, and I motioned her inside. We sat down on opposite sides of the couch.

"Well?" I prompted.

"How are you?" she asked.

"How do you think?" I replied in an acidic tone. "How do you imagine I am?"

"Please, Wendy," she said in a soft whine, "try not to be so bitter."

"No, Simone. I won't try. I have a right to be bitter."

She stood up and walked over to the mantle. Her back was turned to me. "I hear you have been seeing Nate."

Her words surprised me. I was expecting her to talk about Grant, not Nate. "Yes, yes, I have. Do you have a problem with that?"

She turned around and gave me a big smile again. "Of course not," she cooed.

"Baloney," I replied.

Simone's smile vanished. "Look, Wendy." She walked over to sit on a chair by the window. She looked very pretty with her dark curls shining in the lamplight.

"Nate is no good for you," she continued. "He will hurt you. He simply has no character. Grant and I are very worried about you. We do care what happens to you."

"Pardon me for laughing at your being an arbiter," I said in an ugly, snarling voice. I was furious. I walked over to the front door and opened it. Simone stared at me like a little girl.

I motioned for her to leave by sweeping my arm toward the porch. "Please go."

Simone stood up and came to the door. She started to go outside, then turned to me.

"You think you want honesty, but you don't, Wendy. You are so busy being the victim and holding your head up high for all to see how noble you are, but you are to blame for some of this, too. I was as good a friend to you as you were to me. I think you liked knowing my husband was unfaithful and not telling me. I think it made you feel superior."

"At least *I* wasn't having an affair with your husband!" I cried, breathless with rage. "I was a better friend than to do that to *you*."

Simone's chin went up as if I had hit her. "You were to blame for that happening, at least partly." Her voice was quivering. "You just won't admit it."

I reached over and shoved her out the door. "I was not to blame, and I didn't deserve it." I slammed the door shut.

I heard Simone shout from outside, "Well, you're with my husband now, aren't you? I guess we're even."

I laughed without humor at her pathetic remark. Obviously, being seen around town with Nate had gotten back to Simone and Grant, and they didn't like it. That was all I needed to make me go to the phone.

"Hello, Nate? I made up my mind. I do want to see you. Let's just see what happens, okay?"

Nate was very cheerful and arranged to meet me for a drink the next night. I dressed carefully, wanting to be sexy and classy at the same time. My message to Nate was just that: sex with class. I wore a white pants outfit with a low-cut neckline. I pulled my hair over to one side and let it fall to my shoulder.

A neighbor girl came to baby-sit Lucy and she commented, "Wow, Mrs. Osborne. You look beautiful."

The nice thing was, I felt beautiful, too.

"Yes, yes. Mommy is gorgeous!" Lucy squealed.

When Nate came to pick me up, he gave a low whistle and rolled his eyes. "Do I have your permission to leer a little?" he asked with a sexy laugh.

"Yes," I replied, looking into his wonderful blue-green eyes. "You may leer."

At dinner, I flirted with Nate and finally, as we drank our coffee, he leaned back and asked, "Okay, Truth Girl, what's going on?"

I blushed. "I guess I'm trying to tell you that I want to have a relationship. That is the honest truth."

"Ah, yes, the truth," he said with an exaggerated sigh.

"I want the truth from you, too, Nate. How do you feel?"

He looked a little uncomfortable, but then after a moment's silence, he said, "I want you. I don't know what lies ahead, Wendy. Let's both be the best people we can be to each other. That's a good way to start."

I knew he was ducking my question, but I let it go. I couldn't wait to be alone with him.

We went back to his condo and made love. It was wonderful. As his hands caressed my body, I realized how much I missed the passion and gratification of being physically intimate with a man. Despite the passion, though, I couldn't quite connect with Nate on a personal level the way I had always done with Grant.

When our lovemaking was over, I sighed with pleasure as I laid back on the pillow, turning my head to look at Nate. He was so handsome. His eyes were closed, and he had a smile on his full mouth.

I leaned over and kissed his forehead. "That was marvelous."

Nate groaned in response.

"Was it great for you, too?" I asked in a teasing voice, but I wanted the answer.

Nate opened one eye and looked at me. "The truth?"

I was startled by his words, and I felt immediately on the defensive. "Of course." I tried to sound more sure of myself than I was.

"Well . . ." He sat up and looked down at me. "I don't like so many directions."

I was humiliated. I had encouraged him during our intimacy to do things I particularly enjoyed. I had always done that with Grant. It worked so well with us, I thought it was the best way to make love.

"I'm sorry," I mumbled. "I won't do it again."

Nate laughed and pulled me into his arms as he slid down beside me. "It's no big deal. But next time, not so much talk and more action, please. Now, how about you? Was I okay?"

"You were perfect." It was a lie. Nate had actually disappointed me in a few little ways, but I could not bring myself to say so. It was our first time together, and I suspected he would improve. I didn't dare tell him otherwise, especially after his comments about me.

Our relationship never really got off the ground. The next time we were together, I kept my promise and only moaned or sighed, and Nate was even less perfect than he had been the first time. He was sulky and subdued that second time, and I was miserable not knowing what was wrong.

"Maybe I just need some time alone, Wendy."

I was humiliated and got up to dress. "Let's go." Nate was staring at the television. "Will you drive me home?"

"Oh, sure." He stood up and grabbed a shirt off the back of the couch. "Next time, why don't you bring your own car?"

I will never understand why I didn't just tell Nate to take a hike. I went from being overboard on honesty to the depths of kidding and lying to myself. It was as if I was desperate to make Nate be something he wasn't, to make him feel something for me he never could.

So we kept seeing each other for about two months. I was even more of a wreck than I had been before he came into my life. I had no appetite, and I was shaking all the time from nerves. I was short-tempered at the office, and my work was shoddy, too.

Then Nate just stopped calling. Lucy was away with her father and Simone on a trip, so I was really alone. I called his place and got nothing but the answering machine over and over. I drove by his house, I am embarrassed to say, but I could never see any lights on in his place and his car was nowhere in sight.

I was filled with panic, and I didn't know why. I was at least honest enough to know that Nate no longer stirred feelings of admiration or even much lust in me. But my relationship with him had become something of a battle, and I wanted to win. I did not want to be dumped so suddenly and unceremoniously.

I was sitting at my desk when the phone rang. "Hi," Nate said casually. "Can I meet you for coffee?"

"Where have you been?" I demanded.

"Meet me for coffee in an hour, Wendy. I'll explain everything."

I left work and headed for the coffee shop. I was shaking all over. I did not know what to expect, but I was so happy to hear from Nate, I didn't really care.

He was waiting for me when I got there, grinning like a kid, as if nothing in the world were wrong. I sat down and waited. He ordered our coffee, then turned to me and took my hands in his.

"I need a favor, baby."

"I want to know where you have been." I tried to make my voice sound cold. Actually, I was so happy to see him, it was difficult to be angry with him.

"I took a trip." He shrugged.

"And you didn't bother to tell me you were going?" I asked.

When the coffee came, we stopped talking for a moment.

Then Nate said, "Look, I took a trip I'd planned a long time ago with a lady friend. I didn't want to hurt you by telling you the truth, so I just didn't say anything."

Out of the corner of my eye, I saw people moving around the coffee shop. I heard the clatter of dishes and the murmur of voices, but it was as if I was not really there. I couldn't focus, and it felt as if I had no breath left. My face must have shown my distress, because Nate leaned across the booth and grasped my hands.

"Are you all right?" he asked.

I stared at him. I couldn't speak.

"Do you need to go home, Wendy?"

Finally I got my voice back. "You went away with someone else when we were so involved? I can't believe you would do this to me."

Nate looked amazed. "But I spared you the truth," he stammered. "I thought that's what you wanted."

I laughed wryly. "No, that isn't quite what I meant. The truth doesn't give you a license to be cruel. You just don't get it, do you?"

Nate leaned back in the booth and watched me. "I guess I don't." I could tell by his body language that he was bored with the whole subject.

"What's the favor?" I was trying hard to follow the conversation and to stay calm, but I wanted to scream and hit him. I was beyond hurt and mortified. I could not comprehend someone as insensitive as Nate was, but I still didn't get up and leave. I couldn't, because I was afraid of being alone again.

"I want you to marry me," he said with a smug smile.

I sat back in the booth, my heart pounding. "You want me to *marry* you?" I repeated, unable to believe his words.

"Yes, yes, I do." He leaned even further across the table. "Listen, this woman I went away with is convinced she should leave her husband so she and I can get married. I don't want to marry her. I'd rather marry you. If you and I could get married, the problem would be solved and she would leave me alone."

"Do you love me?" I was clutching the handle of my coffee cup so hard, I thought it might break off in my hand.

Nate laughed. "Sure, I guess I love you in a way. But you and I both know—we've talked about it—love comes and goes. We wouldn't have to stay married," he added, as if this might be the final inducement I would need.

"Is this what you call being honest?"

"Sure," he replied. "You and I aren't kidding ourselves the way the rest of the world is."

He smiled at me. I looked at him and smiled back. Then I lifted up my cup and threw my coffee right into his beautiful, smiling face.

"You want honesty?" I asked, standing up as he gasped and wiped his face with a napkin. "Here's honesty. Love *does* matter, and so does respect—and you have none in either category!"

Then I walked out of the coffee shop as people sat there and stared. I felt good and free, like a heroine in a movie. I was proud of myself at last.

I actually laughed all the way home. It was so obvious that I picked Nate for reasons other than I would admit. I wanted to get back at Simone and Grant. If Simone had not come over that night, I probably would not have decided to get involved with Nate, despite the physical attraction.

Now, with the passing of time, I am not sure I will ever totally forgive Grant and Simone and Nate for what they did to me.

The good news is that I am past all that. Each of them took my love and made a mockery of it, but I wasn't perfect, either. I have faced some truths about myself and my own life. It is and always has been much easier for me to tell the truth than to hear it or face it.

Honesty is still a big part of my life, but it is only part of the package. Honesty shouldn't be a weapon to use against others to hurt them or to be cruel.

I am dating an impassioned attorney right now. He and I have long debates about truth and justice, and we go round and round. We don't agree on everything, but I trust him and I like his fire. He doesn't mock people the way Nate always did. He tries to make the world a little bit better in any way he can.

We have a lot of fun, but we are careful with one another, too. When I don't look my best, he fibs and tells me I look wonderful. When he loses a case, I fib and tell him it wasn't his fault. We both know we are lying, but to tell the truth, those lies are sometimes necessary, just for the sake of kindness.

When he takes me in his arms and his breath is warm on my lips, when he whispers that he loves me and that he needs me, I know he is telling me the truth and that I really do matter to him. I tell him I love him right back, and there is no doubt in my mind when I say those words. We are getting married in the spring.

I knew I was really back on the road to my own happiness the other day when Lucy smiled at me. "Want me to tell you something that is really true, Mommy?"

"Sure, honey."

"There's hardly ever any red times in this house anymore."

I realized how true those words were and how free they made me feel. THE END

WE SAW A MURDER AND DID NOTHING
It changed our affair forever

"You lousy bastard!" The deep voice came from the woods.

"You don't understand! It meant nothing." This was a different voice, softer than the first, with a pleading tone.

"It won't mean anything when I'm done with you!" the deep voice answered.

"And what are you going to do?"

The two figures emerged from the woods in front of us. The darkness of the old country road hid us from them. The moon was full, though, and we saw their silhouettes before us.

The first one, the one with the soft, pleading voice, was tall and thin. Glasses were falling down the long bridge of his nose. The second one, the one with the deep voice, was older, shorter, with a stocky, powerful build, shadows playing on his grizzled face. His stomach flopped out of his shirt in a lazy manner.

"You'll pay for it!" the short man yelled. He raised a baseball bat into the air.

The thin man raised a hand up to ward off the bat. The short man, though, brought it down hard. A thud cracked through the night, and the thin man fell to the ground. He crawled, his hands reaching out to the dirt around him, trying to pull himself out of harm's way.

I grabbed hold of Mitch's arm. "Are we just going to sit here?"

He did not answer me.

The thin man was half crawling, half flopping now as the short one raised the baseball bat up in the air again. He brought it down with all the force his thick body could muster. Another curdling thud sounded.

"Aren't we going to do something?" I whispered.

Mitch said nothing. He was focused on the scene outside as if he were watching a pulse-stopping horror movie.

Once again, the bat was raised and it came down, crashing hard against the struggling man's head. This time it was a crack, not the dull thud of before. The man on the ground stopped crawling. He stopped flopping. He lay in the spot, silent as the night that surrounded us.

The short man raised the bat again, a number of times, bringing it down with less force each time until he stopped. He kicked at the thin man once.

"That'll teach you to mess around with my wife," the short man said, spitting on the ground. He turned and walked back into the woods, taking the baseball bat with him.

I shivered but it was not because of the chilly fall breeze coming through the cracked windows of the car. I knew we had done something wrong. It was not as simple as stealing a piece of pie before dinner or sliding another piece of paper into the bulging trash can. We had watched. We had sat and watched.

The slumped man did not move, not even in the small way that breathing moves a body. We had watched someone being murdered.

"That was something," Mitch said.

The silence had stayed with us long after the man had disappeared back into the darkness of the woods. I stared at the man in the road, hoping to see some signal that he was still alive. But there was no movement at all.

"Shouldn't we go out there?" I asked.

"No, Laura. We can't go out there. Soon enough, someone's going to find him. How's it going to look if we said we'd seen the whole thing?"

"What if he's still alive?"

Mitch shrugged his shoulders. "He's alive then. We can't do anything to help. This has to be between us. This is one of those things I would never be able to explain to Nina."

"We can't just leave him."

Mitch reached an arm out to me. I inched farther away from him in the seat, pressing myself against the metal door.

"We have to leave him." Mitch took his outstretched hand away and started the car. He pulled away from the woods and eased around the man's body.

The headlights picked up an image of the man, and I knew then it was something that would stay with me for the rest of my life. The thin man would be embedded in my mind forever. I would see him when my dreams turned into nightmares, and in the daytime I'd see him whether my eyes were open or closed.

The man's glasses lay beside him, one lens shattered, the other intact. The glasses, though, were nothing compared to the man's face. His eyes were open in terror. A small line of blood trickled from his nose and his mouth and even out of his ears.

It was through the man's unseeing eyes that I knew there was nothing we could do for him. He was dead. Nothing we did now would bring him back. Had we simply flipped on the headlights at the height of the battle, simply yelled something out at them, we may not have been driving past a dead man. We could have driven down the same dark and deserted road we had come down.

Mitch turned on the blinker once we emerged from the small back road, heading towards the bank. There, he would slide in his car, and I would drive back home alone.

If Mitch would have said something at that point, he would have made the small remark, "Like nothing ever happened." It was something I was unable to pretend, though, because the image had embedded itself into my mind like a fossil's imprint in stone.

He said nothing to me, though, and I said nothing in return. I think at that point there was nothing we could say to make it better for each other. We had sneaked off to be alone as we had done a dozen times before. This time, though, everything had changed for us. We were coming back different people than when we had left.

In my mind, if I replayed the whole thing over again, I did not see it happening in the same way. I did not believe Mitch would sit idly by and watch a man as he was being murdered. I did not think I would, either. I thought we were better people.

We pulled up to the bank, and Mitch got out of my car. He shut the door and then opened it again, leaning his head inside.

"We can't talk about this, Laura. You know that, right? It would ruin both of us."

I nodded my head. I left, glancing in the rearview mirror at Mitch. I watched his car door slam and then the headlights flick on. It was as I was watching it all that I realized he was not the man I wanted to believe he was.

Everything had begun so simply between us. We had not been planning anything, but things do not need to be planned in order to happen.

He was working late at the bank one night, preparing some loan papers for some new clients, and I was working late typing some papers for the president of the bank, something I had volunteered to do. I needed the extra money, since I had recently separated from my husband and was trying to make it on my own.

I was at the Xerox machine, copying the letter, when he came out of his office. In the whole time I had been there, the door had remained closed and I often glanced over at it, knowing there was another person working late, but not seeing him.

"Oh, you're using it," he said, sticking his head out.

I had seen Mitch at the bank before, ushering multitudes of people in and out of his office. I had come to the point where I could tell whether the loan was approved or denied by the look on the customers' faces. I had not talked to Mitch much, though. Every once in a while, we gave each other a short hello as we passed by, but I knew nothing of him and he knew nothing of me.

"It'll only be a minute," I answered, shuffling some papers around in my hands.

"I didn't know there was someone else working late tonight," he told me. "Otherwise I would've been a little friendlier. I'm just used to having the place to myself at these hours."

"I hope I'm not invading," I said.

"Oh, no. It does me good from time to time to have someone else around. I say we blast the music, I'll tear my tie off, and we'll have some fun as we finish up."

"I'll change the radio station," I offered, heading off to where the radio controls were located. Sometimes there was no music playing overhead and other times it was on the classical station, so I switched it to the station I listened to most of the time, hoping it was something Mitch wouldn't mind. I envisioned him to be an old rock-and-roller, but country was my taste.

Much to my surprise, Mitch was nodding his head to the upbeat song playing across the speakers. I stood there in the doorway, where he did not quite see me, and watched him, not wanting to invade on the moment, knowing this was a side of Mitchell A. Lawson that not too many saw.

He was a handsome man, with dark hair and equally dark eyes. It was as if someone had matched him up in the way people match their socks and shirt. He was tall and a little on the stocky side, but he was borderline fit.

"You still have your tie on," I said.

He slid two of his fingers underneath it and tore it off in the manner he had spoken of earlier, throwing it across the room onto a chair.

"I think you're done," he told me.

"What?"

He smiled and won me over in the same second. "The paper—it's done copying."

"Oh." I walked across the room as gracefully as I could with him staring at me. I thought it would be the perfect time for me to stumble or fall on my face as I so often did when there were eyes focused on me, especially the eyes of someone like Mitch.

I managed to make it across, scooped the papers out of the tray, and did not fumble with anything until I tossed the lid of the copier up to retrieve the paper I was copying. Somehow my hand missed the edge of the lid, and I fell towards the copier. I stood up and slowly grabbed the lid, tossing it up, reaching in for my paper.

I did not look up at Mitch, afraid that he would be laughing at me—or trying hard not to. I shuffled the papers into a straight pile and stood away, letting him use the machine. I was getting ready to walk back into the office where I had been working, when he called out to me.

"What does your husband think of you working late?" he asked.

I wandered back over to him, the stack of papers still in my hands. I had yet to sort them and stuff them into all the envelopes sitting on my desk. I shrugged my shoulders, opened my mouth to talk, and then closed it. The music blared overhead, a slow song about leaving and heartache. I did not answer.

"If I were him, I wouldn't like it, not one bit."

"We're separated," I finally said. "He doesn't know what I do—or doesn't care."

"That's a shame. Any kids?"

"None." I sank down in a chair behind him.

He worked over the Xerox machine, making copies of stacks of documents.

"It's only been a few weeks. He walked out on me, said something about needing his space and his freedom. I think he was just sort of pissed that I didn't want him going to the bars anymore, or out with his friends every night, or whatever it is that he's been spending all of his time doing."

"Do you think he was having an affair?" he asked.

That was where he got me. Paul and I had been married for three years, and during that time, Paul had never been able to completely settle into the marriage. I had loved him, still loved him at that moment, and missed the feel of his body laying in the bed next to me every night.

"I don't want to believe that he was." Tears came to my eyes in a flood. "Gosh, I don't want to believe that. I want to believe that while we were together, everything was right, you know?"

"I know." He was no longer standing over the copier machine. He was standing right in front of me, his hands stretched out to me in a comforting manner. He took my hands in his and squeezed them softly, pulling me up to him.

He held me tight. He let me cry and I realized, as I was wrapped up in his arms, that it was the first time I had cried since Paul had left me, the first time I had spoken the truth to someone who seemed to understand the words I was saying.

"It's all right," he whispered in my hair as he rocked softly back and forth to the sound of the music. "Let it all out. This has been so hard on you. It's been so tough. You have a right to cry."

I do not know how long I cried. I do not know how long it was that he held me tightly in his strong arms, but when at last my tears stopped and I backed away from him, I stared into his dark eyes. He stared back.

"I'm sorry you ever had to go through something like that," he told me. "I'm so sorry. I know what it's like to love and lose. It's not like the person just went away; it's as if they died, isn't it? Things will just never be the same. That time in your life is over, and it's hard to start a new life, a different life, but that's just exactly what we have to do: start a new life, without that person who has played such a big part for so long."

"That's exactly it," I agreed. "But no one understands me. No one understands what it is that I'm going through. They all think that I should just be able to do things as I always did, except without Paul."

"I understand."

While we were talking, while I was feeling more comfortable in his presence than I had ever felt around another person, I could not help but glance down at the small wedding band on his own hand. We had talked about love and loss, but we had not talked of his wife. I took his left hand in my own and let my hand circle around the band.

"You haven't lost your wife, though," I said.

"I have—in a lot of ways. We still live in the same house, still sleep in the same bed, still share our meals at the same table, but I don't know when the last time was that we talked. We talk about the weather, about the scandals at the White House. We talk about things that don't hurt us one way or another, you know."

"That's how it was with me and Paul the last few months. Our conversations were basic, just to fill up the quiet that always lingered between us. They never had a thing to do with either of us, but it was safe talk. Neither one of us would get hurt as long as we kept it within the boundaries."

"She cringes away from my touch," he said suddenly. "At night, I turn to her, just wanting to hold her, be with her the way we once were, but she moves away."

"Paul and I never even reached out to each other. It's awful, isn't it? You're with someone for so long, and it all just ends. He didn't say anything to me, just packed his things up one day while I was here at work and left. I came home, and there was a message on the answering machine explaining it all to me."

"At least he could've talked to you. It might not have been so hard if he'd talked to you instead of ignoring you that way."

"It would've hurt just the same." I shrugged and took my papers into the office to start sorting through them, getting them ready to mail, but I could not stop thinking about Mitch.

It was weird that someone I did not know yesterday, someone who had only been an acquaintance the day before, was now someone I had opened up to not just a little, but in the way the wind smacks a door open in a storm. I had even cried, feeling the comfort of his arms tight around me.

I was halfway through stuffing the envelopes when he stuck his head in my door. "How's it going?"

"Fine," I replied. "I just wonder why I ever let myself volunteer for this stuff. I could be home, kicking back, watching some Monday night football, burping up some beer."

"You do that?"

"No," I laughed. "But it sounds like a heck of a lot more fun then sitting here stuffing these envelopes."

"Want to go for a ride after you're done? I just stuck my head out a second ago and there's a north wind blowing in, giving the air just the right chill to make it seem like fall."

"It *is* fall," I told him.

"Yeah, but it hasn't seemed like it, has it? It's been much too warm."

"Guess you're right."

"So what about it?"

"Okay, Mitchell." I smiled. "Maybe a nice little ride isn't a bad idea."

"It's Mitch," he corrected me. "Most everyone calls me Mitchell, but a few select people, well, I let them call me Mitch."

We rode out into the country after I finished getting the envelopes stuffed. We rode out to where the darkness filled the land around us, only opening up from time to time to the light of a house that we passed. I was not sure exactly where we were. I had let Mitch drive my car. The car windows were open and the breeze blew in around us, washing us with the coolness that had pervaded the night.

He turned on a small gravel road after some time, and slowly we crept down it.

"Where are we going?" I asked.

"We'll see where this road goes," he replied.

We drove for some time, and then he pulled over to the edge of the road, towards the trees whose leaves were falling down in the October breeze. He switched the headlights off.

"What are we doing here?" I asked.

"Enjoying the night."

I did not resist when he reached over and kissed me. His lips found mine and we locked together, both of us needing the other in a way that I did not understand—and yet I did. Maybe it was the loneliness that had become a part of my life since Paul had left. Maybe it was the coldness that came from Mitch's wife when he needed a warm touch. Maybe it was nothing more than a need beckoning from the deepest parts of ourselves.

The spot we stopped that night became our spot. We found ourselves there a number of other times. The trees let go of their leaves, and in time, winter came. Sometimes the whiteness of the land washed over us as we parked in our little quiet spot.

It was those times in his arms that I felt my safest, as if no harm could ever come to me. We no longer talked of his wife, but I knew in the way that he touched me, hungered for me, that things had not changed at all at home. Paul called me from time to time, but at that point, I was so busy giving myself to Mitch that I did not wish to talk to him anymore. After some time, he stopped calling.

Of course, we could have made our excursions to my house, where it was warmer, where there was more room to wander over one another's bodies, but neither of us were ready to give up our spot for anything else. We never even suggested going somewhere else.

He talked of leaving his wife. I thought of a life shared with him and everything seemed perfect . . . until the night of the murder.

That night was horrifying enough as I watched a man being murdered. I had seen a special on television about dog fighting, and I had watched as two pit bulls, with their trained instincts, fought to death. I had watched as one dog lay on the ground, the light leaving his eyes and saw the other, his jaws clamped on the other's neck, his eyes huge as animal instinct washed through him.

I had wondered why not one person moved to save the dying dog, especially when it was a show trying to make a statement on the cruelty of it. I had sat there, wanting to take my eyes away from it all, to walk away from it and think of something else entirely, something as simple as watching the flowers come up from the ground outside.

I had not moved but had watched down to the dog's last breath, watched as the other dog was at last pried away from the dead dog. I watched it all. It was one of those images that sticks with you forever, but no matter how awful it had been, how terrifying to watch, that night with Mitch was even worse.

I had watched a man kill another, watched as all rationalization left him, as everything human about him disappeared, and instead he became an animal, protecting his mate from another.

And there was more to that night than the murder. At that point in my relationship, something was going to happen. We were either going to become closer or be pushed apart. I did not believe we would ever be pushed apart.

As the two men emerged from the woods, I thought Mitch would get out of the car and defend the downed man. I had thought something would be done, in the same way I had thought something would be done that day I'd watched the two dogs fight to death.

On television, there had been something to prove. They had wanted to show the gruesome details of a cruel sport taking place in closed-off places in the country. That night, though, there was nothing to prove, nothing to gain, except maybe the realization of the lie I had lived with Mitch.

He said it all when he said he could not explain it to his wife, Nina.

Sometime in between witnessing the scene and driving back to the bank, I asked him something and I will never forget how he answered, because it was the final words of the night that at last made me cry.

"Was there ever anything between us, anything real?" I asked.

"It was good, Laura—wasn't it? We had some good times, but it's time for us to admit it's over. We can't go back there, not after that, and there's nowhere else for us to go. We played a good game right up to the end."

A good game. So that's all it had been to him, a game, and I no longer knew whether or not to believe the tales he had told of his wife, or if his stories, too, had been part of the game. I realized then that he had never once planned to leave his wife for me. That, too, had only been part of the game.

The next day, there was a story in the newspaper about the murder. The details of it all were there, letting me fill in the empty spaces of the night. The man murdered was named Anthony. The murderer was a man by the name of Marty. The two had been neighbors for some time, had even been friends. Marty began to suspect Anthony of having an affair with his wife.

It was the wife who had relayed the events leading up to the murder, and even she had been somewhat vague with the details. She did not say in the countless interviews I watched, or on the talk shows she appeared in, if the affair was something that had really happened. I wanted to know whether the man had been killed for something he really did, or senselessly blamed for something he didn't do.

Whatever the case, though, those lives were ruined. There was a man who had died as the pit bull had on television. There was another man who would be serving time behind bars and would never be able to wash his hands of the murder. And there was a wife who had a husband behind bars, and maybe a lover, too, who was now buried at the local cemetery.

It was my life, too. I came to accept things the way they were without questioning them. The night had brought the relationship Mitch and I had to an end, but had it not been then, I knew it would have been another night, with or without some tragedy.

Losing Mitch was only part of it. I also had to deal with the guilt on a daily basis and had to wonder if I had done something, whether things would have been different. There was a teacher I had some time ago in school, and from time to time, I still think of the words she once told me when I was scared to climb a rope.

"There are doers and there are watchers. You'll never regret *doing*, even if you don't climb the whole way up the rope. At least you did your best."

That night, I was only a watcher, and every day I will live with the regret.

Sometime after we had left, another car, of a person who lived farther down the road, had seen the body strewn across the gravel and had stopped. He had walked to the nearest house, which happened to be the one where Marty and his wife lived, to call someone. The police showed up, and after the neighbor relayed the events of finding the body, Marty confessed to doing the job.

It was open and closed. It was simple, or appeared to be simple, when they relayed the news in the paper or on television.

That morning, the morning after, I walked into Mitch's office and laid the newspaper on his desk. He nodded at it but said nothing.

"Look at it," I told him.

"Why? It has nothing to do with me."

"It has everything to do with you," I insisted, my voice growing louder with every word I spoke.

He looked behind me at the rest of the employees of the bank, the ones visible through the door. They were busy, acting as if they were doing something, but more anxious to hear what was being said. Everyone had seen me as I rushed into work, and instead of hanging my coat in the employee room, I had lunged towards his office, the paper clutched in my hand.

I stepped back and slammed the door shut with the heel of my foot.

"Now doesn't *that* look good to everyone," he said sarcastically.

"What does it matter? What would everyone think of you if they knew you had watched this poor man murdered? What would—"

He stood up from his desk. "This has *nothing* to do with us. There never was an *us*. I'll ruin you if you ever spill a word of this to anyone. You won't have a job, you won't have a house. I can make your life hell."

I did not care to publicize it myself. I did not want anyone to know of the affair I had had with Mitch, did not want one person to know of my own stupidity. I did not want anyone to cast sympathetic glances at my own foolishness. He said he was going to leave his wife for me, and in lust, I believed him.

We had witnessed something together. We had both sat and watched, and Mitch was the one person who would understand the feelings that were raging through me: the guilt, the sleepless nights I was sure were to come, the nightmares even when sleep did find me. I wanted him to understand in the same way he had understood when I had told him of Paul's leaving.

He stood at the door of his office, his hand resting on the knob. "It's over between us, Laura. You have to realize that."

"But—"

"What we had was a lie, anyway. I lied to you. I lied over and over about my wife, about everything."

He flung the door open, and I left. I did my job, waiting on the customers as they came along to make deposits or withdrawals. From time to time, I would catch someone looking over at me, and I knew they were wondering what exactly was going on. I had no close friends at work, and even if I had, they would not have known. It was something I would have to keep inside me forever.

I stayed at the bank another few years, but in that time, Mitch asked to be transferred. He left to work at a branch on the other side of town. He used his moving as an excuse, said the other bank was a better commute for him, but I knew the real reason. Each time he saw me, just as each time I saw him, it was an awful reminder of that terrible night we had witnessed.

Paul started to call me again, and we even started to go out. We took it slow. We talked for countless hours on the phone or over the kitchen table. We talked about what we needed to do to bring us back together and keep us together, and months later, he moved back into the house.

Although we drew closer and our bond became stronger than it had ever been, there was one thing I was not able to tell him— about the night I watched a man murdered in cold blood.

It is something that has become a part of me that no one else can know about. Part of it is the shame that comes with being involved with a married man, and part of it is the guilt. I see it, though. I see it when I am drifting off to sleep, and I see it when I am deep in sleep and sometimes when I am awake. I see their faces and I see Mitch. I see myself, too, watching, always watching—just watching. THE END

NAUGHTY ORGASMS WITH MY EX
They're getting me in hot water!

"Please tell me you're joking," my friend, Janine, pleaded. But though she acted appropriately shocked and mortified by my confession, I knew she was very curious and wanted *all* the juicy details.

"Since when do I joke about something as serious as sex?" I gave her a naughty grin and winked.

"But technically, it wasn't sex, was it?"

I thought for a moment before I answered. "Well, we were a hundred miles apart, and I don't have to be concerned about getting pregnant or catching a nasty venereal disease, so what do you think it was?"

Janine folded her arms across her ample bosom and replied, "I think it's dangerous. Very, very dangerous, and I would be careful if I were you."

Her words had an ominous sound to them, but I didn't take her warning seriously. After all, whom did it hurt? I hadn't *intentionally* set out to have phone sex with my ex-husband. And it wasn't like he was physically present or anything like that. We were just having a normal conversation and it just sort of . . . happened.

"So did you have . . . you know!" Janine asked, her eyes wide. We'd been best friends since junior high school and we shared most every detail of our typically boring lives with each other. Since Janine was single and hadn't had a date in three months, lately, it was usually my life that was fodder for our discussions.

"Did I have what?" I plopped down on the floor and began painting my toenails a bright shade known as Passion's Red. A very appropriate color for the way I was feeling.

Janine looked at me as though I knew perfectly well what she was talking about. "You *know*," she prompted. "*The Big O.*" She sat down beside me and craned her head at an odd angle to force me to look into her eyes.

"So what if I did?" I cleaned a spot of polish that had dripped onto my skin and acted nonchalant about the whole matter.

"Oh, my God! You're going to have to go to confession on Sunday for sure!" She paused and looked thoughtful. "How many Hail Mary's do you think Father McCullough will give you for this?"

I rolled my eyes and continued painting my nails. Janine and I both came from very religious backgrounds, and sometimes, she fell back into the old guilt mode. She couldn't help it; it was just something she did on occasion—kind of like a bad habit she couldn't quite shake. Sometimes I followed her down the familiar road, but usually, I let her make the pilgrimage alone.

"Seriously, Shannon, do you realize you committed two sins at the same time?" She had two fingers extended out in front of her for emphasis. I guess she thought I needed the visualization to understand the extent of my transgression. Well, she was right on that count, but I held my hand up to halt her explanation.

"Well, even if you *are* in denial about the seriousness of this, Father McCullough won't be. He's going to have a heart attack for sure!" She clutched her hand to her chest in mock agony.

"Cut it out, will you? There's no *way* I'm gonna share this with anyone but you. And don't you *dare* take this outside of this room!"

"Don't worry. Your tawdry little secret's safe with me." She wrapped her arms around her bent legs and rested her chin on her knees. "But, I *still* think you should consider doing some penance."

Though I didn't totally agree with her, Janine's words did start me thinking about things. What I'd done wasn't exactly adultery. Or was it? Didn't two people have to physically be in the same location for that to happen?

I chided myself on my lack of remembrance concerning my religious training. My parents had made sure that I attended church regularly as a child, and here I'd gone and rewarded them by forgetting something as elemental as one of the Ten Commandments! At least, I *thought* adultery was one of the Ten Commandments.

Unwittingly my mind drifted back to the events of the morning that it all started. . . .

That day had begun like any other typical Friday. I woke up early and got my daughter, Tara, ready for school. It was her final day of kindergarten, and she was so excited about the little graduation party her class had planned. Like usual, we chatted and laughed as I got her dressed. Both of us really enjoyed our mornings together, and sometimes we had our best discussions while I combed and styled her long, dark hair.

Finally satisfied when her braids looked presentable, I sent her to look for her backpack while I made waffles and bacon for my husband, Jimmy. It was his favorite breakfast, and since we'd argued the night before, I wanted to do something special to show him how much I cared. Though we'd made up quickly after the fight, I still felt a lingering sense of guilt.

Usually, when I wanted to make someone feel better, or in this case, make up to them, I offered food. That morning was no exception. It was an old habit I'm sure I picked up from my mother. Mom was a large, friendly woman who spent a lot of time cooking and baking, whipping up many tasty delights. Of course, that meant that there were always loads of cookies and candies that had to be sampled and eaten. Thank goodness I inherited my father's slender build and his lack of a sweet tooth!

With pleasant memories of Mom in my head, I put an extra waffle on Jimmy's plate.

"Wow, honey! This looks great!" he said when he saw the spread I'd laid out in front of him. "You shouldn't have gone to so much trouble."

In spite of his words, I knew he appreciated a good meal and would enjoy every bite of it. He gave me a quick peck on the cheek and dug into his food with relish.

Later, when Jimmy had left for work, I dropped Tara off at school and ran to do a few last-minute errands. I usually wasn't very organized, so to make sure I didn't forget something important, I'd made myself a list before I'd even left the house. Dutifully, I crossed off each errand as I completed it. I sighed with relief when I got home and looked at the small sheet of paper riddled with black lines running through the words. A phone call to Tara's dad, and my chores for the day would be complete.

Donny and I had been divorced for three years. Though we didn't always agree, we kept things pretty amicable for our daughter's sake. Tara absolutely adored her father, and I didn't want her to feel torn between us. And since both Donny and I'd come from broken homes, we'd vowed to make things as easy as possible for Tara. After all, she was the one thing in our lives that we could agree on. And so far, things had been working out fairly well. So, I had no reason to suspect that they wouldn't continue on in the same manner when I made the phone call that day.

Though I had custody of Tara, I was pretty flexible when it came to letting Donny see her. Unfortunately, this wasn't always easy, since he lived two hours away from us, and Tara was in school full time.

That's why, since summer vacation was starting, I'd relented when Donny asked if he could take Tara down to Florida to visit his parents. They hadn't seen her since the divorce, and they were quite anxious to be reunited with their only granddaughter.

Because Donny had a small car and I knew they'd be gone for over a week, I called him that morning to find out how many and what kinds of clothes to pack for Tara. The conversation started out innocently enough, even if Donny was being his usual, annoying self. As it was, he had the ability to get under my skin and make me angry about the smallest thing. And that morning was no different, as I found myself getting irritated with him right off the bat.

"I *know* it's hot in Florida, Donny. That's not what I'm asking." I was busy folding a load of laundry and was holding the phone precariously between my chin and shoulder. Finally, tiring of the balancing act, I picked up the basket, walked into my bedroom, and put him on speakerphone. Then I turned my attention back to our conversation. "I just wanted to find out if you have enough room for her heavier clothes and her skates. Also, maybe a few toys and books would make the trip a little easier on her."

"Use your own judgment, Shannon. How hard can it be to pack for one small child?" Donny's husky voice exited the tinny speaker and filled the room.

"Oh, Donny—you can be so annoying!" I folded a few undershirts and put them in the appropriate pile. Then I started balling up socks.

"Actually, Shannon, it's your blasted speakerphone that's annoying. I can hear my voice echoing. Why are you using that thing, anyway?"

When I explained that I was trying to talk to him and fold clothes at the same time, he chuckled.

"What's so funny?"

"I was just remembering those white cotton panties that you used to *insist* on wearing. Do you remember them? Man, how I used to beg you to wear thongs!" He chuckled again. "Old habits die hard, I guess."

His teasing brought up an emotion in me that I couldn't easily identify. I was offended, for sure, but I was also surprised that he remembered a tiny detail like the type of underwear I'd preferred when we were married.

"Well, I'll have you know that I threw out my old, white undies a long time ago—right along with my cheating ex-husband," I answered with a bite.

"Ouch!" He was quiet for several seconds, and then he said, "You know, I never cheated on you, Shannon."

"You mean, I never *caught* you cheating on me. There's a big difference, Donny, even if you don't want to admit it."

I was quickly tiring of this conversation. Whether or not he'd cheated during the course of our marriage was a moot point at this juncture. After all, Donny was in my past, and I knew I wouldn't go back to my old life for anything. I was married to an *honest* man now, and I was so thankful that I could trust Jimmy implicitly.

I finished the laundry and started packing Tara's clothes inside a small, slightly tattered suitcase. I was about to bring our conversation to a close when Donny asked me something that stopped me cold. I put the stack of clothes down and eased myself down onto the bed.

"What did you say?" I asked incredulously. I couldn't have heard him correctly.

"I *said*, if you don't have those little white panties anymore, what do you wear now?"

I don't know what ever possessed me to play along with his silly game. It seemed innocent enough, but for some inexplicable reason, I also wanted to get back at him. Maybe it was simply because he'd teased me about my taste in underwear. Then again, it could've been because he was right, and I resented him for it. Even then, I knew that underneath my loose, navy blue running shorts, I had on a pair of plain, white cotton briefs. Donny knew me all too well, and that made me uneasy.

"Well, aren't you gonna tell me what you have on?"

Before I could even stop my mouth from speaking, I told him that I had on a tiny, lavender thong.

"You're kidding, right?"

"No, that's what I'm wearing."

"Tell me more," he encouraged, his already deep voice lowering even further.

"Well, they're kind of soft. They're made out of that silky material that you used to like."

He groaned. "Can you slip them off for me?"

I just about choked on my tongue. My mouth suddenly turned dry, and I didn't know what to say. What had started as a joke was quickly getting out of hand.

"You're so quiet, Shannon. Does that mean you're out of them?"

"Uh . . . yeah . . . yes, I am," I stammered and stuttered, still not believing what we were talking about.

"Good, now tell me: Do you still have that cute little mole on your inner thigh?"

We continued on like this for several minutes. Before I knew it, I'd been drawn into his game and we were both nude, throwing sexual suggestions back and forth over the phone!

"*Wow*," Donny sighed heavily when it was over. "That was almost as good as the real thing was when we were married!"

Reluctantly, I had to agree. Sex had always been *fantastic* with Donny. And though what we'd just done was altogether very different, I had to admit that it'd been *very* enjoyable, too.

Leave it to Donny to lead me down an unfamiliar path yet again.

"Shannon, are you listening to me?" Janine tapped me on the arm and brought me out of my reverie. "What were you thinking about? Whatever it was, it must've been heavy. Your upper lip's breaking out in a sweat!"

I swatted her hand away and pretended to be irritated. "I was thinking about how crazy you are if you think I'm going to go to confession and tell Father McCullough about this! You're the only person who will *ever* know, Janine." I paused and contemplated my words. "Besides, I wasn't *really* being unfaithful."

Janine rubbed her two index fingers together in a "shame on you" gesture while she admonished me with a tsking sound. "I'm not so sure Jimmy would feel quite the same way about it if he ever found out about your long-distance rendezvous."

I bopped her on the arm. "That's exactly why he *won't* find out!"

I knew she was absolutely right about the situation . . . at least— part of it. Jimmy would *definitely* have a hard time with this. Even after a year and a half of marriage, he still had an occasional pang of jealousy concerning Donny. I didn't really blame him for it, either. Since we all knew each other from our years at Trafalgar High School, I knew it was hard for Jimmy, knowing that I had a past with Donny. As a matter of fact, the two men had been friends at one time. But that was before I'd come into their lives. Nowadays, they simply tolerated one another.

No, Jimmy *definitely* wouldn't appreciate the intimate "exchange" that Donny and I had shared on the telephone.

The next day when Donny came to pick up Tara, he acted fairly normal. Besides a sly grin and a wink, he didn't let on that we'd done anything out of the ordinary. I was very relieved that he obviously hadn't taken it seriously and had put the experience behind him. After all, that was where it belonged.

He and Jimmy talked for several minutes about Donny's new job managing a nightclub, while I said my teary good-byes to my little girl. The truth is, I was slightly apprehensive about letting her go. We'd never been apart for longer than a weekend, and I was feeling a tad overprotective. Oh, I knew she'd be in good hands with Donny and his parents, but it was still hard to say good-bye, even if it was only for a little while. Still, in spite of his shortcomings as a husband, Donny was a terrific father, and he really doted on Tara. I knew I needed to get a grip and relax or I'd go crazy during her absence.

Honestly, the only two things that my marriage to Donny had produced were a wonderful child and incredible sex. I thought I'd forgotten about most of the latter years ago, but our naughty phone call reminded me suddenly of just how *good* sex with Donny had really been.

"Honey, you can call me anytime if you need anything," I told Tara as she tried prying my fingers loose from her arms. "Any time of the day or night, I'll always be here for you. If you're lonesome or scared—"

"I'll be okay, Mom," she groaned, cutting me off. "Daddy will take good care of me. And I'll get to see Grandma and Grandpa, too."

I knew then that I needed to lighten up and let her go. My worries were misplaced; Tara would be absolutely fine. I gave her one last kiss and watched as she walked out the door, hand in hand with her father. The two of them shared so many traits that it never ceased to amaze me. They had the same stance, the same walk, and the same, strange habit of arching a single eyebrow when confused. With a slight pang of sadness, I realized that my daughter carried very few of my own traits; honestly, Tara was almost a miniature version of her father.

"Well, here it's barely lunchtime, and we're all alone." Jimmy came up to me as Donny's car pulled out of our driveway and wrapped his arms around my waist.

I was still standing at the door, watching the car disappear from sight. I was trying not to regret my decision of allowing Donny to take my baby so far away from me.

"Hmm?"

"I was saying that it's just the two of us now. How often does that happen?" He dipped his head down to trail a few hot, moist kisses down my neck. I closed my eyes and felt him put his hands under my T-shirt, touching me through my bra. "So, why don't we take advantage of this time? What do you say we go upstairs?"

Even though I wasn't especially in the mood, I relented and joined him in our bedroom. It was so much easier to just go along with him rather than explain why I wasn't very interested in making love right then. Truthfully, though, I hadn't been interested in *weeks*, and it was troubling me.

However, this time, it was different. As Jimmy touched me in the same old, familiar way, something strange happened. My mind shut everything out, and I remembered and focused in on all of the sexy words that Donny had whispered to me on the telephone. Suddenly, I found myself incredibly aroused—and very, *very* willing.

"Wow! What got into you?" Jimmy asked me afterward. "That was fantastic!" We were lying in bed, still holding and touching each other. "You were so wild, Shannon—so kinky!"

I shrugged and gave him some excuse about it being so long since we'd last made love that I was just crazy hungry for him. Jimmy believed me. I knew that he would. He didn't have any reason not to.

The truth was, sex had never been very exciting between Jimmy and me. It was the same old routine, time and time again. And I probably wouldn't even have ever known the difference if it weren't for Donny and the past we shared.

Sex with Donny had been anything *but* boring and routine. I don't think those two words were even in his vocabulary. Donny knew more variables than our old math teacher did, and he was more than eager to try them out anywhere and anytime. Too bad our marriage outside of the bedroom had been so lousy. We'd argued from the time we got up in the morning until late in the evening. Usually, though, we worked out our differences before bedtime, just so we could fall into bed and have hot, lusty sex again. Of course, sometimes, we had great sex even before we'd made up.

Then the inevitable happened, and our marriage went south. Part of it had to do with rumors circulating of Donny's supposed infidelities, but most of it I blamed on Donny's lack of ambition. While I worked two jobs to make ends meet, he partied and ran around with his buddies. I finally tired of it and filed for divorce. By that point, I'd been more than ready to move on with my life—a life that now included Jimmy, as well as Tara. The three of us were very happy together.

Jimmy and I'd had a good marriage right from the start. We got along extremely well, and it didn't hurt that we both liked doing a lot of the same things. Also, Jimmy was a wonderful stepfather to Tara, and really, that was what mattered to me the most. Jimmy loved children and was truly looking forward to the time when we would have a baby of our own to share. For now, though, we were content to be a family of three.

Whereas my marriage to Donny had been constantly filled with loud fights and endless shouting matches, Jimmy and I hardly ever argued. Of course, we had very little passion, either. Honestly, I often wondered if there was a connection between the two. Don't get me wrong—I loved my husband with all of my heart and I really wanted my marriage to last a lifetime. It's just that sometimes, I wondered how much longer I could tolerate the lack of excitement in my life.

My agitation concerning Tara vacationing with her father was groundless. Every time she called, she was happy and sounded like she was having the time of her life. Her grandparents were thrilled to have her with them again, and the four of them were even planning a repeat visit for the following year.

Thankfully, the days without her went by quickly enough. My job as a receptionist at an insurance agency helped pass the time. And when I wasn't working, I spent a lot of time outside, either gardening or sunbathing.

"Wow! You have a better tan than we do," Donny commented when he brought Tara home ten days later, "and we spent most of our time at the beach!"

I could feel his eyes watching me as I picked Tara up to give her a huge bear hug and a kiss. Finally satisfied now that I had her home again, I put her down and told her to go unpack.

"Would you quit staring at me?" I hissed at Donny when Tara was out of earshot. The way his eyes kept sweeping over my body was making me very uncomfortable. "I don't like it."

"There was a time when you loved my eyes on you . . . on *all* of you," he said suggestively. His eyes narrowed and he moistened his lips with the tip of his tongue.

"You're doing it again," I complained.

He held both of his hands palm side out up in front of himself. "Hey, don't take it so personally. You just look really nice today." He paused, and then added, "I'm just trying to figure out if you have any tan lines underneath that pretty sundress."

I looked down at the flowered, sleeveless shift that I was wearing. I knew it looked good on me; its form-fitting design hugged my slender curves and fell to just above my knees.

Donny's gaze followed mine. "Or maybe a teeny, tiny, lavender thong?" he asked seductively.

"Cut it out," I snapped. "Tara might hear you." I glanced around the corner and saw my daughter cheerfully putting her clothes away while singing a Christina Aguilera song in tune to her CD player.

"Relax, Shannon—I'm leaving. But I need you to call me later."

"About what? Can't we just talk about it now?"

"No, I still have two more hours of driving ahead of me, and I'm tired. I need to get going. Just call me tonight." He combed his fingers through his dark hair and glanced at the door.

He did look tired, and I really didn't want to talk to him right then, anyway, so I agreed.

I tried not to stare as he made his way down the sidewalk and eased his muscular frame into his car. Donny had always taken excellent care of himself; his fit body attested to the many hours he spent in the gym. When we were married, I'd always thought he was overly conceited and way too concerned with his looks. Now, however, I found myself appreciating the way his tight jeans rode low on his narrow hips.

I shook my head to clear the unwanted image from my mind. I hated that I found myself thinking about my ex-husband in such a way. After all, I was happily married to Jimmy now; I didn't need distant memories of wild times to drive a wedge between us.

Later, I made Tara's favorite dinner to celebrate her return home—macaroni and cheese with extra cheddar, hot dogs, and strawberry ice cream for dessert. Not a particularly favorite meal for Jimmy or me, but it was Tara's night. I wanted her to know how much we'd missed her.

After dinner, I loaded the dishwasher, dressed Tara in a pair of brand-new pajamas, and read her a couple of stories before tucking her in for the night. When I came back downstairs, I found Jimmy reading the sports section of the newspaper and halfway engrossed in an old movie on cable.

"What do you say we go upstairs and take a bubble bath?" I walked up behind him and massaged his neck, hoping I could entice him to put down his paper and join me. I didn't want to admit it to myself, but I was still preoccupied with Donny. I figured a little TLC from my husband might help to get my mind back on track.

"Oh, honey, I'm really beat. I'd just like to sit here and drink a beer and watch a little TV. Do you mind?" Not bothering to wait for my answer, he grabbed the remote and turned the volume up a notch.

I dropped my hands from his shoulders, feeling disappointed, but understanding. Jimmy worked long, hard hours as a construction worker. Some nights, he was too tired for much of anything.

"No, it's okay." I gave him a small, forced smile.

Well, since I was going to have to bathe alone, I decided to take the cordless phone upstairs with me and kill two birds with one stone. I would soak in a scented tub while getting my phone call to Donny out of the way.

I sighed as I lowered my weary body into the warm, blue water. Then I dialed the phone number I knew by heart. I closed my eyes and sighed with contentment as I waited for him to answer. I was about to give up and put the phone down after the tenth ring, but then I heard his voice come on the line.

"Hello?"

"Hi, Donny—it's me." I sank down deeper into the water and massaged my sore calf muscles with my free hand. A bike ride with Janine that afternoon had given my legs a real workout, and I knew I was going to pay for it in the morning.

"Well, well, well—this is a surprise! I didn't think you were gonna call."

"Of course I was going to call," I retorted, feeling a little testy for some reason I couldn't quite put my finger on. "After all, you made it sound so important! Does it have something to do with Tara?" My voice rose and I started talking fast. It was a nervous habit I'd never been able to shake.

"Relax, will you? You're running at the mouth again. I remember when—"

"Donny, let's just cut the chitchat. Tell me why you needed me to call you."

"I just wanted to see if you wanted to go dancing with me." He chuckled in the way that I'd once found endearing. That night, though, it set me on edge.

"Will you get real, Donny? I wouldn't go dancing with you even if Jimmy and I divorced and you were the only remaining upright man on earth!"

He chuckled again. "Okay, okay—I get the idea. I was only joking. Hey, what's that splashing sound in the background? Are you washing dishes?"

I went on to explain that I was taking a bath. Of course, that was a big mistake on my part; I instantly regretted saying it. I knew right away that Donny would take the opportunity to jump on my words, which is exactly what he did.

"So, you're talking to me while you're naked in the tub? I suppose you're surrounded by bubbles, too, right? You know, that kind of turns me on. . . ."

I sucked in my breath and considered hanging up on him, but then I stopped myself. Because I couldn't kid myself—I'd chosen to call him at this particular time. The question was: Why did I do it—and what did I want?

Maybe I was a little angry with Jimmy for not joining me in the tub and I just didn't want to admit it. But before I had a chance to examine my motives, Donny started talking again.

"You know what *really* turns me on, though?" He didn't wait for a response from me before he continued in a low, seductive voice. "It's the way you make that soft, sighing sound—"

"Stop it!" I ordered. "I didn't call you for this."

There was silence on the line for what seemed like several minutes. In reality, it was only a few seconds. When Donny spoke, his voice was steady and well controlled.

"Listen, Shannon—I don't want to force you to do anything you don't want to do. So I'll stop if you want me to . . . but that's not what you want, is it?"

I thought about what he was asking me for all of three seconds before my lips answered without consulting my brain.

"No, Donny—that's not what I want."

I'm not proud of what I did that night, but I did go to bed feeling more satisfied and satiated than I had in *months*.

"How could you have done it *again?*" Janine asked incredulously when I told her of my bathtub exploits of the previous evening. "And you *initiated* it?"

"I didn't *mean* for it to happen." I was lying through my teeth and we both knew it. "Donny said he had something important he wanted to talk to me about."

"Yeah, I'll just bet he did! He probably wanted to talk about his big, hard—"

"Janine!"

I watched a scowl descend over my friend's face.

"Well, Shannon, how can you be so naïve? Why is it you could see right through him in the past, and now, it seems like you're blinded by lust and can't see his real motives? Donny's a *player*, Shannon. He always was, and he always will be."

"I thought you *liked* Donny!"

"I did. But that was before he hurt my best friend. And if you're not careful, he'll only hurt you again." Janine twirled a piece of her long, curly hair between her fingers. I could tell she had more to say.

"Okay, out with it," I ordered. "Speak now or don't ever bring it up again."

"I was just thinking—maybe you and Jimmy just need to have a little more . . . you know."

My eyebrows shot up even as my mouth flew open. "We have *plenty* of . . . *you know*, thank you very much! It's just that when we *do* have . . . *you know*, it's rather—well . . . *dull*."

We talked a little while longer about the expectations I had about marriage. Maybe I was expecting too much from Jimmy. From what I heard, a lot of married couples had lukewarm sex lives. My problem was, once you've experienced the peaks of pleasure, it's hard to trudge back down the mountain and live in the valley.

Nevertheless, the next few weeks were happy ones. Jimmy, Tara, and I spent a lot of time together. We swam, played softball, and went on picnics in the country. Though summer was usually a very busy season for him, Jimmy still made sure that he took a lot of time off for leisure activities that we could enjoy as a family.

We even discussed having a baby.

I still wasn't quite certain that we were really ready; however, Jimmy brought up some very good points to support his position. Tara was getting older, and he felt it would be harder for her to adjust to having a new sibling if we waited too long. We were also experiencing a renewed sense of freedom since she'd started school. If we didn't have a baby soon, it might be difficult to give up that freedom. What Jimmy said made sense; however, what won me over to his side was his excitement and enthusiasm. His eyes sparkled when he talked about me getting pregnant and both of us experiencing parenthood together. I really wanted to make Jimmy happy, and if that meant having a baby, I was willing to do it.

I guess I also had some lingering guilt over what had happened with Donny, though a part of me justified what I'd done. Maybe I was just getting rid of some leftover lust that I'd been carrying around since the divorce. So maybe, getting it out of my system wasn't such a bad thing, after all. Still, the other side of me said that I'd deceived my husband, and that he'd be very hurt if he ever learned what had transpired between Donny and me.

Yet, as the days and weeks passed, I got over my fear of Jimmy finding out. After all, I hadn't seen Donny since he'd returned from Florida, and when he called, I quickly passed the phone to Tara. I decided it was just too risky to fool around with him anymore, even if it *had* only been through words, and not actions. Then something happened that had the power to rock my world to its core.

Donny called out of the blue and suggested that instead of him driving out to pick up Tara, that I make the drive and drop her off at his place on Friday.

"Come on, Donny. I can't take time off work to do that. Why don't you just wait until Saturday and pick her up then?"

"Because I got to thinking. If you told Jimmy you had to drop Tara off at my apartment as a favor to me, it'd give you an excuse to get away."

I fidgeted in my seat, suddenly feeling very uncomfortable with the direction our conversation was taking. "And just why would I need—or want—an excuse to get away from my husband?"

"So we can be together," he answered simply. "I've been thinking a lot about us lately, you know. What we did on the phone was nice, but it's made me realize just how much I miss being with you. I'm tired of just talking dirty, baby. I want the real thing."

"Are you *insane?*" I practically yelled into the phone. I jumped up from my chair and began anxiously pacing around the living room. "I'm not going to jeopardize my marriage just to have a cheap little fling with you, Donny, so you can forget it!"

I heard him exhale harshly. I knew he was mad, but I didn't know the extent of his anger until he dropped his next bombshell.

"And what if I go to Jimmy and tell him all about our little sex chats? I bet he'd love to hear about the things we discuss." He paused to let his words sink in. "You don't want me to do that, do you?"

"Jimmy would never believe you," I shot back. Suddenly, all the thoughts and fantasies I'd had about Donny in the past few weeks disgusted me. I was thoroughly disappointed in myself. I didn't know what I'd ever even seen in him in the first place.

"Oh, he doesn't have to believe me, baby," he drawled, with a touch of humor in his voice. "But I'm sure I can plant a nasty little seed of doubt in his mind. Jimmy might just find out that you're not as sweet and innocent as you pretend to be."

Donny's words were bitter and ugly. I lost all respect for him, right then and there.

"You wouldn't dare do that, Donny." Though I kept my voice steady, cold fear descended over me. I felt myself tremble.

"Go ahead and try me, Shannon."

Suddenly, any desire I'd ever felt for Donny flew right out the window. I saw him for what he was—a player—just like Janine had said. Only this time, I'd played right along with him. Now, though, I wanted out of the game.

It took me about a nanosecond to figure out what I wanted to do about Donny's cheap attempt at blackmail. I would never consider doing what he'd proposed. I knew now that I'd made a mistake in renewing an intimacy that should've remained in the past; I wouldn't compound it by having sex with him just to cover it up. I'd call his bluff and live with the consequences, whatever they turned out to be. Even if it meant that Jimmy would find out, then I'd deal with that, too.

With a renewed sense of courage, I gripped the phone tightly, and when I spoke, my voice was calm. "Listen to me, Donny. If you go ahead with your little plan, several things are going to happen. First of all, you're right about Jimmy. He's going to be suspicious. Who knows? He might even believe you." I went on to explain to him that Jimmy would probably take it out on him, rather than me . . . maybe even do something really stupid. Next, I told him that I'd quit being so accommodating where Tara was concerned. As it was, I had full custody, and I'd see to it that he didn't get to see her again.

"Yeah, well—I could always take you to court and get our custody agreement revised," Donny interjected.

I felt myself tense, and then I shrugged it off. I'd come this far; I wouldn't back down now. "You could try. But it does cost a lot of money to do that, and up until now, you've never had to worry about it. We both know I've been more than generous where Tara's concerned. But even if you did succeed, you'd eventually lose her."

"What are you talking about?" He nearly spat the words out at me.

"When she finds out that her own father was responsible for the breakup of her very happy home, she'll never forgive you, Donny. Especially now that she's going to have a brother or a sister."

"Are you telling me you're pregnant?"

"I just found out this morning. I won't hold my breath waiting for your congratulations." I could tell I'd gained the upper hand; our conversation was finished.

Donny uttered a soft curse and hung up fast. I wasn't quite sure what he'd do, and for several minutes, I gave in to my feelings of anxiety. Then I brushed them aside. If Donny acted according to character, he'd move right on and find another woman for his amusement, though I pitied anyone who'd be stupid enough to get involved with him.

Jimmy and Tara were thrilled when I told them that we were going to have a baby. Personally, I struggled with feelings of ambivalence—not about whether I wanted the child or would love it, but whether or not I was ready to have a baby so soon after deceiving Jimmy.

Jimmy chalked up my sadness and depression to being pregnant. However, when I told him that I felt I needed to see a therapist to work out a few issues before the baby was born, he gave me the go-ahead. He'd never been anything less than supportive of me, and this also added to my shame.

The therapist I chose was a middle-aged woman who had a good reputation as a marriage counselor. Her name was Sandra, and I liked her from the start. True, I didn't feel very comfortable about going to a stranger with my problems, but I knew I needed to talk to someone. I couldn't continue to carry the guilty burden I was shouldering without sharing it with someone else.

During our very first session, I told her everything—all of my doubts and fears—and, more importantly, I told her about the mistakes I'd made with Donny. Sandra listened without comment or judgment, and I felt so relieved that she didn't seem at all shocked by what I'd shared.

"I can tell you're confused and that you're carrying around a lot of guilt, Shannon," she said when I'd finished. "But I wouldn't recommend telling your husband."

I was shocked by her words, and my face must've reflected it.

Sandra smiled. "I never advocate lying to a spouse, and in the end, it'll be your decision. But when infidelity's involved, and it's in the past, it's usually best not to unload on an unsuspecting partner."

I blanched at what she said. It wasn't like I'd had an *affair* with Donny; it'd only been a couple of phone calls! And hadn't I cut it off immediately when he'd demanded more? Sandra noticed my reaction and commented on it.

"Shannon, you may not have been *physically* unfaithful to your husband, but in your heart, you suspect you've been untrue to your marriage. If not, you wouldn't be here. Am I right?"

I nodded. I was tired of lying to myself. I wanted to feel secure in my marriage again, like I used to. I only hoped it wasn't too late to get the old feelings back.

"Telling Jimmy might make *you* feel better, Shannon, but only because you'd be transferring part of the burden to him." She sat back in her chair and looked thoughtfully at me.

"Then what can I do?" I asked hopelessly.

"You and I need to work on finding out *why* you did what you did, and to help you not be vulnerable to this sort of thing in the future."

Oh, I knew I'd never repeat that mistake again. I knew that for sure. I also knew why I'd succumbed to temptation in the first place. So did Sandra, once I told her about my sex life with Jimmy. With openness I hadn't even known I possessed, I explained to her how it'd been in the past with Donny, and how it currently was with Jimmy.

"You're a follower, Shannon," Sandra commented when I was through.

"What?" I asked, feeling confused by the way she perceived me.

She smiled and looked at me intently. "Donny was wild, adventurous—maybe even a little dangerous."

Boy, she had *him* pegged correctly. I nodded in agreement.

"Donny was the leader, and you didn't have to take any chances emotionally. You simply followed him down the path, whichever one he chose."

I bristled at her description. "And is there something wrong with that?"

Sandra shook her head. "Of course not. But Jimmy is different. He's strong, dependable, and laid-back by nature. Once again, you're following someone else's lead in the bedroom, but now, you're resenting him for it."

I sat up straight in my chair and stared at her.

"If you want something different, Shannon, why don't *you* initiate? Why don't *you* try to be the leader for a change? You never know—it could really turn things around for you and your husband."

Sandra went on to explain how most men were very receptive to their wives taking the upper hand and being more aggressive in the bedroom. When I complained that I didn't know if I could do that, she had a hard pill for me to swallow.

"Then you don't have any right to judge Jimmy, do you?" She paused and pushed a strand of her black hair from her forehead. "Shannon, both you and Jimmy are responsible for the state of your sex life. Why is it that you could be brazen and free with Donny?"

"Because he did it first," I reluctantly admitted.

"My point exactly. The leader takes all the chances. The person who makes the first move is the one who risks rejection. No one wants to be rejected by the one they love most, Shannon. You know, maybe Jimmy even *shares* some of your fears."

In my heart, I knew she spoke the truth. Sandra and I went on to talk about other things. She made me see that my problems hadn't originated because of a dull sex life. They went much deeper than that, and had to do with my self-esteem and how I viewed myself as a person. At some point in my life, I'd begun to judge my value as a human being by what others thought of me, not by what I thought of myself.

I really got my money's worth out of that therapy session that day. I drove away from Sandra's office feeling like a salve had been applied to some of the wounds I'd been carrying around for far too long. I knew it would take several more visits before I could totally deal with the issues that were haunting my mind and attempting to destroy my happiness and my future. But at least I was headed in the right direction.

Today, I'm five months pregnant, and we just found out that we're having a little boy. Jimmy's ecstatic about having a son, though Tara had her heart set on a little sister. Personally, like most mothers, I just want a happy, healthy child, regardless of its sex.

Donny still sees Tara, though we've never again talked about what happened between us. We're polite to each other, yet distant, and that's the way it needs to be. Our relationship has forever changed since we crossed that line, and I never want to make myself vulnerable to that kind of temptation again.

I did take Sandra's advice to heart and took on a more active role as "the aggressor." I'm happy to say that it's working. Jimmy was pleasantly surprised, and lately, he's been following my lead! After the baby's born, I suspect that things will get even better between us.

THE END

HIS MISTRESS IS BI— AND SO AM I!

I wasn't exactly surprised to find out that my husband, Bill, was having an affair. I guess it took away some of the tension and guilt I had been feeling, since I was also having one . . . in a manner of speaking.

Bill and I both worked and we had no children. We still had our romantic moments, but for the most part, our marriage had become one of convenience. We'd basically settled in and become comfortable and complacent with each other. Neither of us was working at keeping our marriage alive. We took it and each other for granted. Suffice it to say, we were bored.

I'm convinced that both of us would've worked harder on our relationship if we'd never gotten married. I'm sure neither of us would admit this to anyone, probably not even to ourselves. But how else, and why do things like this get started . . . affairs?

Maybe my own reaction at finding out surprised me a little. I wasn't angry with Bill—or her, whomever she was; I was disappointed in both of us. Ours was a good and loving relationship.

We'd both had past experiences, enough to be well informed before deciding to take each other down the aisle. We loved each other and wanted to be married, to forsake all others, to cling only to each other. What had happened to us?

I hadn't been honest with Bill—or myself. I wasn't spending long afternoons in hotel rooms with out-of-town salesmen. I was repeatedly committing an indiscretion with one other person, and that meant I was cheating on Bill. I had been from the very beginning.

It's the kind of thing you always want to explain, but the time was never right, or I was afraid he wouldn't understand. If I was feeling bored, or that something was missing and needed to change, why hadn't I told him?

We used to talk. We still talked, but we weren't really communicating. I often wondered, *What does Bill need that I'm not aware of, that I can't—or don't—provide for him?*

Our tastes were similar in many things. Our sex life was more than adequate, as far as I was concerned, and had been from the start. We were considerate, well-matched partners, and we knew it. Maybe we knew each other too well. How do some marriages go on and last for decades if ours was stale after only four years?

I was curious, of course, but I didn't really care who the other woman was. I just wanted to know how I could save our marriage.

My stomach was full of butterflies and knots when I arrived at Caroline's. She and I had been great friends since college. Our on-again, off-again relationship had been going on since before I had met Bill, and Caroline was the only person I'd ever cheated with.

I had been cheating on him all the time we were dating and living together, but it didn't affect our relationship. It was an outlet, an alternative that I needed. I didn't see how it could be a problem for Bill and me. I was always there for him, and Caroline was always there for me.

I still needed her in my life. I convinced myself I had given Bill everything, withholding nothing from him, and had provided a good home. What else did he need?

Tears glistened in my eyes when Caroline answered the door. Once I was inside, the floodgates opened. There was no stopping my crying. She guided me to her bed, where I proceeded to collapse and sob uncontrollably.

"Feel better now?" She asked about an hour later, when I came out of the bedroom, all red-eyed and puffy.

"Want to tell me about it?" Caroline knew me and had prepared the herbal tea I always wanted whenever I was upset. She poured a cup as I settled on the sofa in the living room.

I dabbed at my eyes while I waited for the tea to steep. Somewhere, halfway through the tea, I managed to smile weakly at Caroline.

"Thanks for being so patient with me. I must've come in here raving like a crazy woman." Actually, I hadn't talked at all. I hadn't been able to. She still hadn't a clue what had upset me.

I put the cup down and surrendered to her open arms, accepting the comfort I had come for in the first place. I found myself clinging to her desperately. I hadn't said a word to her yet and already she knew.

"You're welcome to stay here as long as you need to, Emily. You know that, don't you? Whatever it is, I'm on your side, and together we'll get through this."

Caroline's soft voice whispering in my ear had a wonderfully calming effect. That and the tea unraveled the knots in my stomach. Having her arms around me and feeling the heat of her breath on my neck was definitely turning me on. I took several deep breaths before starting to tell her what had happened.

"Emily, you don't have to tell me anything if you don't want to. I'm still on your side."

"Bill's having an affair! I don't know with who, but—"

"With *whom*," she corrected.

"I don't know," I insisted.

"Forget it! Tell me what you do know." Caroline kissed me gently on the forehead, like a loving parent.

"Well," I began, "I've been getting a lot of hang-up calls. You know, when somebody's there and won't say anything, and then they hang up."

"That's it? No telltale lipstick smudges on his collars? No late nights out? He's not telling you he's working overtime, and then you call and find out he left at five?"

"No . . . nothing like that. Do you suppose I'm wrong? Am I just acting like a jealous wife or feeling guilty because of what you and I have?" I snuggled closer to Caroline. My entire body was shaking. I needed reassurance, and I usually got it from Caroline, not Bill.

Without saying a word, she got up, encouraging me to rise with her, and we went into the bedroom. I felt safe in her arms—maybe safer than in Bill's, at that moment. The emotional roller-coaster ride had left me drained.

Now I wasn't sure, though. Was Bill having an affair, or had he gotten into something else—something over his head? Was I overreacting, without getting the facts first? Should I have come right out and asked him?

I was tired and almost asleep in Caroline's arms when her soft voice, close to my ear, whispered to me.

"I do love you, Emily, and I never meant to do anything that would hurt you."

I awoke fully in an instant. "What? What are you saying? Do you know something about this? Do you know who Bill's seeing? He *is* seeing someone, isn't he?"

"There's no easy way to tell you this, Emily. *I've* been seeing Bill. We're having an affair. Believe me, I was hoping you would never find out, but since you suspect, I'll be honest with you."

I was dumbfounded. I sat up and stared at Caroline. Without a thought crossing my mind, I slapped her across the face.

"Bitch!" I screamed at her. "I thought we had something. I thought you were mine! I thought you were . . . "

"I'm bisexual, Emmie, just like you."

"With any other man in the world, I wouldn't care, but Bill? My husband? We met him at the same time, on the same night. Why did you wait until now? Or maybe I should be asking how long this has been going on!"

Caroline sat up next to me on the bed, the left side of her face swelling and turning red where I'd hit her. She didn't seem to notice it, though it must have hurt. While my tears over Bill and his affair had dried up and I was now furious, hers were shining in her eyes.

"I'm sorry, Emily. I can't tell you how sorry I am."

"Try," I said coldly. "When did you two hook up, anyway? I'm curious."

"It was on a Saturday morning, last winter. I dropped in to see if you wanted to go shopping, but you had gone to your sister's that weekend. You left Friday night. I woke Bill up, and he answered the door half asleep, in his boxers. I guess he hadn't been to the bathroom yet, either. It was kind of obvious. He invited me to come in. I mean, there was no way he could hide it."

"So you came right on in!"

"I've known Bill as long as you have. Why shouldn't I have come in? I didn't know that you were out of town."

"Did he tell you?"

"Yes—almost immediately. He went and put a pair of pants on first."

"I kidded him that he was a party pooper, so he called my bluff by dropping his pants and hanging them over the kitchen chair.

"So you decided to make yourself at home?"

"I've been in your home a thousand times, before and after you two were married," she went on. "Why shouldn't I be? Neither of us planned for anything to happen, you know."

"It just did, and both of you were too weak to stop it?"

"Something like that." Fresh tears welled in Caroline's eyes. "He is a handsome man, Emily, you know that."

"I do. And I know that he's married, too—to me!"

Caroline pulled back at my raised voice, afraid that I was going to hit her again. But I wasn't. Hitting her the first time had been impulsive and had drained all the anger and rage out of me.

I loved Bill *and* Caroline, and I didn't want to lose either of them. But what was I supposed to do? How was I supposed to react to the news that my best friend—my lover—was sleeping with my husband? I was angry with both of them and myself and the whole situation, but hitting her certainly wasn't the answer.

I hated that they had gone behind my back, but these were the two people in the world I loved the most, and Caroline had been right earlier when she said that somehow we were going to get through this. I wasn't ready to accept it yet emotionally, but intellectually I knew that we could remain together, except that now there would be three of us.

I got up and went to the bathroom to get a cold washcloth to put on Caroline's face. She accepted the gesture of good will and held it to her cheek.

"Am I forgiven?" she asked.

"Not so fast. I want to know what you do for him that I don't. I want to know how this all happened in the first place. Wasn't he happy with me? Have there been others besides you?"

"I doubt that, Emmie. Bill loves you very much. He also enjoys making love to you—and me."

"He told you that?"

"Not in so many words, no."

"Talk to me, you bitch! What happened while I was away all that weekend? And how many times after that?"

"Do you want some more tea? I could use a cup now myself."

We both needed a break in the action, a chance to step back and reassess our situation. We got up and went to the kitchen to make a fresh pot.

The water boiled and we took the tray back to the bedroom to wait for the tea to steep. I touched Caroline's cheek lightly with my hand. It was still red.

"Will you hold me, Emily?" she asked tentatively.

We cuddled and let the tea take its time brewing. We both fell asleep for a while and awoke together. Caroline and I were going to make it. We would be all right.

The next question was Bill. What was I going to do? I wasn't crazy about the idea of knowing I was sharing him with anyone, not even my best friend. I couldn't really get angry with him for falling for her, though. Still, didn't I have the right to go on enjoying the relationship I was having with Caroline?

I drove home without making any decision. I would simply maintain the status quo for the time being, until I had the chance to sort this out and make up my mind.

"Hi! I'm home. Sorry, I've just been running around like crazy. I should've called. Have you eaten? Want something?" I tend to rattle when I'm nervous, and I was rattling.

"I called Caroline," Bill answered when I stopped long enough to let him get a word in. "She said you two had been together all afternoon, and that you were on your way home. I waited to see what you wanted for dinner. Any suggestions? Something you want me to make?"

"Reservations!" I called back from the bedroom.

He laughed.

I changed into a T-shirt and a pair of khakis and took a couple of deep breaths to keep from rattling on. Bill knew me well enough to pick up on that behavior. I wasn't ready to get into this issue with him, not until I was sure of myself and what direction I expected the situation to take.

He took one look at the way I was dressed and asked, "Table for two in the Boom-Boom Room here at home?"

"You got it."

Bill and I had a warm and loving marriage. He hadn't a clue that anything had changed that afternoon. We always were able to entertain ourselves when we were home together, borrowing lines from television comedians and old movies, improvising our own.

We'd been together for two years and married for four, and we had done a lot of laughing in those six years. No, I couldn't give this up.

Bill had the freezer door open and was surveying the contents. "How about fried clams and French fries? We can start with an order of clams oregano. That only takes a few minutes to zap."

"Sounds good," I answered. "I could go for some of those. Say, when did the Boom-Boom Room add clams oregano to the menu?"

"The last time I did the shopping. These have been in there for two administrations," he teased.

There was a wonderful, warm feeling spreading over and up from within me. I loved Bill and he loved me. This was what our marriage was supposed to be like—always! I made some garlic bread and slid it into the oven beside the browning clams and fries.

"What are you drinking?" he asked.

"Iced tea for me," I answered.

Bill poured me a glass and took a bottle of water out of the refrigerator for himself.

"Bill," I murmured after dinner, when we were in bed and both nearly asleep, "can I take the car this weekend?"

"Sure, why not? Where are you going?"

"I'm going to take the camera and drive upstate to see the fall colors. I'll probably stay in a motel and be back Sunday."

I didn't want to run aimlessly. I wanted to take a retreat to regroup before deciding what to do next.

"We could go together, make a little holiday of it . . . "

"The only fall colors you appreciate are on football jerseys on television. I'll be fine." This was one of the few areas where our tastes differed widely. I'd do anything to get out of watching another weekend of football.

"Okay." There was no protest coming from Bill. He wouldn't want to miss all the action to go tramping through the woods. "Is Caroline going with you?"

It should have been an innocent enough comment—Caroline and I spent a great deal of time together—but Bill was checking to see if Caroline would be available while I was away.

A chill went through me. All the loving warmth of a moment ago drained out of me as if someone had pricked a balloon. I'd be damned if I was going to be a pawn in his game.

"I'm not sure. I'll have to ask her." *There, you son of a bitch! That'll keep you off balance, until I come up with something to keep her out of your reach.*

I wanted to be alone that weekend; that was the whole purpose of going. I didn't want either of them with me, but I didn't want them to be together, either. Bill began snoring softly, but I lay there for hours, wide awake, thinking.

"Hey!" Bill shouted to me a few days later as he came in from work. "I've been thinking. Why don't the three of us—you, me, and Caroline—plan a getaway next month? We'll go up to the ski lodge where we all met the first time. There'll be some snow by then, and we can all find out how rusty we are. How about it?"

I was taken aback by that announcement. "I don't know, let me think about it. I'll have to ask Caroline, too." I was desperately stalling for time.

I hadn't seen Caroline since the day I found out about them, and the thought of us all spending a weekend together wasn't too appealing. We left the subject at that and didn't get back to it for days.

One night when Bill and I were in bed, I brought up the trip. "I spoke to Caroline today. She said she can't go skiing with us next month. She didn't say why." I figured that would break up his little game plan. I could have cared less why she said she wouldn't be able to go. Maybe she was feeling guilty and wanted out. *Good!*

"I know." Bill's voice dropped to an ominous tone. "She can't go skiing, but she could still come with us if she wanted to. She's pregnant."

"Pregnant! I just spoke to her today. She didn't say a word about it. Why would she tell you first?" The shock had catapulted me into full babble mode.

"She wanted me to know . . . because I'm the father. I'm sorry, Emily. I should've told you sooner."

As I looked at him, the color drained out of Bill's face and out of the room around him. I became briefly aware of having tunnel vision, then wave after wave of blackness washed over me, each darker than the last, as I slowly sank into unconsciousness.

I was swimming up out of the blackness, back toward reality, even though I didn't want to. My wonderful world had crashed and burned. I didn't think about dying or causing anyone the inconvenience of having to arrange my funeral. I just wanted to sink back into the blackness, to pull it in after me. Caroline was going to give Bill a baby.

All this time, I had been stubbornly putting myself and my career in retail ahead of family. I'd never even asked Bill if he wanted children. I wasn't able to have a child for medical reasons, but I'd never actually considered asking Bill about his feelings on the matter.

The next thing I felt was a cold compress being laid across my forehead. I opened my eyes, though I really didn't want to. Caroline was sitting on the side of the bed. Evidently, she was the one who had gotten me the compress. Bill was standing right behind her, looking down at me.

"You scared the hell out of me. I didn't know what to do," he said.

"*I* scared *you?*" I was barely conscious and yet full of anger. "What do you think you did to *me?*" There was venom in my every word. Here were two caring, soon-to-be parents—where was I supposed to fit into this?

Disappearing seemed like a good idea. Where were those waves of blackness when I really needed them? *My world doesn't exist anymore. Why should I go on breathing?*

I was vaguely aware that I was being lifted from the bed and carried.

Someone, probably Bill, was carrying me. Then my feet and my backside were cold. I realized I was sitting on the side of the tub at about the same instant the cold shower hit me. Caroline and Bill both steadied me so that I wouldn't fall.

They held me there until my teeth were chattering, then pulled my wet nightgown off and toweled me dry. I would've appreciated this if I had thought that either of them still loved me. Why were they paying so much attention to me? Caroline was the one having a baby—*their* baby.

Once I was back in bed, Caroline produced a steaming cup of chamomile tea. I guess that was her solution to everything. I really didn't care.

My teeth were still chattering when I sipped the tea. All of my strength was gone. I'd fight them tomorrow, if I lived long enough. Against my wishes, the tea had the effect of relaxing me, and I drifted off into a deep sleep.

The next morning, I got ready for work and left the apartment at the usual time. Bill and I weren't speaking, and Caroline was, thankfully, not around.

Outside, I started the car, drove to the bank, and emptied my account as soon as the bank opened. I called in sick and decided to take the next two days off as well; that would bring me up to the weekend.

I proceeded north with my camera on the front seat. It was a beautifully crisp fall day, and driving with the windows down cleared my head. An hour later, I was feeling better. In the next day or two, I would be able to think.

As the day progressed, I parked in a rest area and went for a hike into the surrounding forest. The chatter of birds and squirrels and the crunch of leaves underfoot brought me out of my mood, and I was reassured that the world was not such a bad place—the people in it were the problem.

I let the thought pass and didn't dwell on it. It was too nice a day. Caroline was right, damn her. I was going to get through this.

By mid-afternoon, I was feeling hungry, which was a good sign, since I'd had no breakfast. I decided to rent a motel room, have something to eat, and then I could scout around for pictures without worrying that I'd have nowhere to go when it got dark.

The man at the reception desk gave me my key and motioned to the dining room to my left. I kept my wedding ring on. I wasn't interested in being approached by any would-be admirers. I had enough troubles of my own already.

The lunch menu was relatively simple, and I opted for a BLT with iced tea. It was one of the rare times in my life when I have felt like having a drink, and I called the waitress back to change my order.

"Could you make that a double martini, very dry, on the rocks, with a twist?" I don't drink often, but I do know how to order.

She smiled and scribbled the change of order on her pad. At this hour, it was likely the waitress would have to make the drink herself. It was surprisingly good. The gin had been in the freezer, and she had chilled the glass before, so it arrived with the frosted coating around the outside.

Holding the first chilling sip in my mouth had the effect of straightening my spine and adding two inches to my height. Halfway through lunch, the backs of my legs tingled and went numb. I was glad I had reserved the room earlier. I wasn't here to do anything but think, and that could best be done after I had a little nap.

The next morning, rested and relaxed, I ate a hearty breakfast of two fried eggs, bacon, biscuits and gravy, toast and coffee. Then I asked for a sandwich I could take with me for lunch, along with a bottle of iced tea.

I dropped my small pad of paper into my jacket pocket, filled the other pocket with film and the sandwich, hung the camera on one shoulder, and carried the bottle of tea over the other. The motel room was too confining. I'd do my thinking much better in the woods.

I loved both Bill and Caroline, but all that had changed now. They were expecting a baby, and they belonged together to raise their child. I could be an aunt if I stayed in the picture, but nothing more.

My decision came down to divorcing Bill, so that he would be free to marry Caroline. It was a bleak and empty world I looked out upon from my seat on a fallen tree in the middle of the forest.

I ate my sandwich, which turned out to be a generous helping of rare roast beef and Swiss cheese with mayo and salt and pepper. I drank some of my now warm "iced" tea. The squirrels and chipmunks conned me out of the crusts from the bread.

Toward the end of the afternoon, I found a clear and beautiful mountain lake, nestled deep in the woods and no doubt teeming with fish. I walked halfway around the edge, waiting for the sun to sink low enough to add color to the sky and hopefully provide a perfect sunset photograph. Then, during the brief fall twilight, it would be a quick dash back to the motel before I ended up spending a night alone in the woods rather than risk a broken leg scrambling around out there in the dark.

My wait was worth it. The sunset was magnificent. Why couldn't I just stay out there, take beautiful pictures, and not have to go back and deal with people?

Unaccustomed to the outdoors, I was tired and ordered a pizza to be sent to my room when I returned. Then, comfortably wrapped in a quilt, with a roll of paper towels for a napkin, I started thinking again.

I wondered if Bill knew anything about Caroline and me. It was doubtful that she would have told him. It wasn't the kind of thing we'd share with anyone. Caroline had been my only female partner, though I wasn't sure about her past. Still, why would she jeopardize the chance to marry the father of her baby?

I was almost certain he didn't know. What difference would it make? Was I looking for there to be some future with these two? How? In a *ménage à trois*? I didn't think so. I doubted Bill was that open-minded. Caroline would be, though. I was as certain that she would as I was that Bill wouldn't.

Again, so what? Why would I *want* to remain with them? And how? As a visitor? Were we all going to live together, maybe on some little commune? We could all go on a talk show and announce to the world just how crazy and strange we were.

In reality, I knew I had to return and come to some common decision that we all could live with, including the unborn baby. I was in no hurry to return, so I spent Saturday driving around, exploring interesting-looking little shops and towns. The chill in the air sharpened my senses and helped me to focus my thoughts.

By that evening, I had the courage of my convictions to go back, dig my heels in, and face whatever lay ahead. Whatever happened next, life was never going to be the same.

After breakfast, I couldn't delay my return any longer. I had to see Bill and Caroline, preferably separately, to go over what their positions would be and find out what I was up against. I had realized by this time that they might not want the same things, and sorting this out could be a long and bumpy road ahead.

Bill had certainly taken all of our lives and turned them upside down. And I couldn't forget or minimize Caroline's part.

The trip back went much too quickly, and by eleven, I was hesitantly unlocking the door to our apartment. On the other side of this door was reality. I didn't know if I would walk in and find Bill and Caroline together, not anticipating my return until late evening.

I took a deep breath and let myself in quietly. The feelings of hurt and helplessness were gone, along with the shock of finding out. I would give Bill a quiet, uncontested divorce, to free him to carry on with his new life—unless of course I found them together in our apartment, in our bed.

Then I would find a lawyer to take him for everything he had. Let him figure out how to provide for his next wife and child. Guilt was a thing of the past; I was feeling very vindictive as I went through the rooms.

But I was alone. I looked through the closets to see if he might have taken his things and left me. Everything was still there.

The door opened, and Bill walked in carrying the Sunday paper. "Emily, you're back."

"We need to talk. And I want to talk to Caroline, too." My words came out cold and formal.

"I'll need the car. I'll be looking for a place to stay. That's why I was out buying the paper. I didn't know when to expect you. I'm glad you're back."

"You mean you're glad the *car* is back. I told you I need to see Caroline."

"Can't you call her?"

"This isn't something you do over the phone."

"Can you call her and ask her to come over? I'll be out, but you two can have your talk here."

"I'll call and see if that's acceptable to her." I tried to remain aloof and distant. It was hard not to run into Bill's waiting arms and take refuge from the world outside.

Bill separated the paper, taking only the classified section with apartments for rent, and left to read it in the car. I guess he didn't want to give me or Caroline a chance to change our minds.

I offered Caroline plain black tea. She'd have to get by without herbal today.

"Have you and Bill decided if you want to keep the baby?"

"Why wouldn't I? It may be the only chance I ever get to have a child, Emily."

It was very uncomfortable for both of us. In the past, in times of crisis, we would usually be in each other's arms, consoling one another.

"I'm willing to give Bill an uncontested divorce, if that's what he wants. It will free him to marry you and raise your child together," I offered.

"That's too easy." Caroline had seen right through me. "What is it you're not telling me, Emily?"

My strength and resolve evaporated. Tears glistened in my eyes. I could barely hold them back.

"I can't have a baby!" I blurted out. Then the tears came. Caroline was there for me as she always had been in the past, holding me and consoling me, offering assurance that I'd somehow get through this.

"I can't have any children, not even for Bill. I don't even want to explain why. I hate you because you gave him the one thing I can't. I thought that if I ignored it, it would just go away." I was babbling and sobbing, all at once.

"Have some tea, and I'll tell you something, Emily. You and Bill are in love. We were only in lust. You two belong together. Oh, Bill's a great guy, or we never would have been together in the first place.

"But what you don't know is that I've been married before. It didn't work out. You know me, so you can imagine why. I like girls more than I like guys. Anyway, I live very comfortably on the alimony from that misadventure, and I'm not about to give it up.

"Now my suggestion to you is, why don't you and Bill stay together and raise your child, the one that you both want so desperately? And after the child is born, I'll disappear. Okay? I really don't need my ex's lawyer to know that I've had a baby, either."

I didn't know what to say. There I was, a moment ago ready to give up my happy marriage to Bill and the relationship I had with Caroline, my dearest, closest friend—and now, this bombshell! I had to catch my breath. I finished my tea and kept hoping that Bill wouldn't come in just then.

I took another deep breath. "Are you sure that's what you want? I don't want you to disappear. I need you too much. I want you to be here, to see and raise your baby. We'll tell it, as soon as it's old enough, that you're the real mother. Don't go!" I sobbed.

"You're sure I won't be a grim reminder of something you'd sooner forget?"

"How could I ever forget you, or not miss you, especially when I'll be raising your child, a daily reminder of you?"

"I've done enough damage. I don't want to cause any more upset for the two of you, Emily."

"Whatever we're deciding, we have to consider how it will affect the baby, too."

"I still love you, Emily, whether you want to hear that or not. I want you to be happy, even if I have to leave you to accomplish that."

"This is a big decision to make. I think we should both think about what we're doing for a while and then discuss it again," I suggested.

"Okay. I'll call you." And then Caroline left.

Very cautiously, Bill and I climbed into our bed together that night. We stayed well apart, to the point of almost falling out of opposite sides of the bed.

"Bill," I said quietly, in the semi-darkness, knowing neither of us could sleep.

"Yes?" Bill was going through the same upset and had no close friend to talk to.

"How are you holding up?"

"I'm numb! I'm sorry, angry, frustrated, lonely, confused, but mostly I'm numb. I never meant, never expected anything. I mean you're on the Pill, so we never use anything. I didn't have any—it was irresponsible, I know. I don't know what you want me to say or do."

I could hear in his voice that Bill couldn't have been more guilt-ridden or remorseful. I actually felt sorry for him.

"I'm not on the Pill, Bill. I never was."

"What? But, you and I, we never used anything and—"

"I think we are going to have a baby, Bill."

"What are you talking about?" Bill sounded exasperated.

"Caroline and I had a long talk today, and we decided that, if it's all right with you, we should keep the baby. You see, I can't have children of my own. That's why I was never on the Pill. I didn't know how badly you wanted a baby, and I didn't dare bring up the subject. I dreaded the day you'd find out." There were more tears by the time I'd finished that little speech.

"I'm so sorry that you didn't tell me," he said. "It shouldn't have come out this way. I've hurt you more deeply than I'd expected, and I never wanted to do that."

Nothing more needed to be said. We met in the middle of the bed. I kind of melted into Bill's arms, and he held me as he always had. I never thought we'd make love again, not after what had happened, but we did. It just sort of happened, by mutual consent.

Afterward, instead of going to sleep as he usually did, Bill held me and whispered to me that he had always loved me and asked if I was going to go on seeing Caroline after the baby was born and we adopted it. I told him I wanted her to remain in her child's life and in ours.

"I know you don't run around, and Caroline's kind of special to the both of us. I think she should remain in the baby's life and yours, if it doesn't make you nervous," I said.

After that, Bill maintained what I guess was to him a "safe distance." I resumed seeing Caroline, and he asked about her daily but made no move to see her. If she called and he answered, he would immediately hand the phone to me. My own head was swimming for weeks as I tried to separate the roles each of us played in this puzzling extended family that we had created.

Being pregnant agreed with Caroline. She was radiant and glowing, her complexion fresh and healthy, her eyes sparkling with vitality, and her enthusiasm for affection at a new high. Without our having to discuss it, Caroline and I found ourselves drawn more closely together than we had ever been before.

We arranged to see an obstetrician, and I accompanied her on each visit. As she started to show in her fourth month, we went to department stores and boutiques to shop for baby things. Caroline was thrilled to be pregnant.

In her sixth month, Caroline was feeling pain in her abdomen. She began to experience morning sickness, which she had never had, and lost her rosy glow. Within weeks, the sparkle in her eyes was replaced with dark circles underneath, giving her an exhausted, hollow-eyed, pale look. Her once-beautiful hair became dry and brittle, and her strength ebbed.

Dr. Mason suggested bed rest, asking me if it would be possible for me to move in with her and care for her for the duration of the pregnancy. I agreed to do it. Bill was largely self-sufficient when he was forced to be, and I would visit him now, as I had visited Caroline, on a regular basis.

I waited until after dinner that evening to break the news at home. Concerned and asking for a diagnosis, Bill readily accepted the news and the changes in living arrangements.

We were on the sofa when I told him. He put his arms around me and put his head on my shoulder. I could feel the tremors in his chest and felt the warm wetness of his tears on my neck. It was possibly the only time I've ever seen Bill cry.

We made love there on the sofa, consoling one another with lingering hugs and kisses, not speaking a word. Half an hour later, I forced myself to get up and pull myself together. I took a cab with a small suitcase of the things I didn't already have over at Caroline's.

We had signed up for Lamaze classes, and Caroline insisted on attending, although her condition was deteriorating and she had little strength left. Luckily, the classes were held right in the hospital where she was registered to deliver. When she collapsed in class, she was rushed to the emergency room and from there into the operating room.

While I waited, I called Bill. He listened as I sobbed hysterically over the phone and said he'd be right over. A nurse's aide gave me a glass of water. Bill arrived, hugged me, and then we went on waiting.

While living at Caroline's, I had gone through her phone book to find her family's number, just in case. I'd called and spoken to her mother only the week before, an elderly woman who listened as I had described her daughter's condition with a cold, detached, almost uncaring attitude.

Caroline had never spoken of her family, and now I understood why. Unable or unwilling to understand her or her lifestyle, they had pulled away, perhaps disowned her, and could not offer any emotional support.

A cancerous ovarian tumor, one which could've gone undetected for years, had been diagnosed during Caroline's pregnancy and was growing at an alarming rate. This ultimately led to her untimely and unfortunate death.

It was nearly ten that night when a doctor finally came to bring us the news. We sat, dumbfounded, speechless. I couldn't believe it. How could this have happened?

Bill was finally able to form the words to ask, tentatively, about the baby's fate. Fearing the worst, there was nothing to do but pray as we listened.

"She's three pounds, three ounces, two months premature, and doing fine." The doctor smiled.

It took us a while to clear our eyes before we could speak again. Then we both asked if we could see the infant.

"The nurse will come and get you in a little while, as soon as she's brought down to the maternity ward. Give them about fifteen minutes."

Caroline had had the foresight to have a lawyer make out all the papers, as though sensing—or maybe knowing—something she had kept from us. We were to have her baby if anything went wrong with the delivery, or afterwards. She wanted us to be happy and she had given her life to achieve that.

Little Caroline is now three and has her mother's eyes, rebellious spirit, and a great sense of humor, which helps around our house. We sing her lullabies at bedtime, but her favorite song is the Rolling Stones'

"Satisfaction," which she seems to know every word of.

I thank God every day that Bill and I knew her mother, and I think every day of the joy her daughter has brought us. In the end, Bill, her mother, and I have produced quite a beautiful family. THE END

KISS, DON'T TELL
Keeping my affair from him was the right thing to do

A motorcycle accident changed our lives forever. Brad and I had grown up together, living only a block apart. We played together as children, and in high school, we discovered we were in love—a love that withstood separation as Brad attended law school and I went to business school at the other end of the state.

We married a week after his graduation, a sort of fairy-tale union, both of us attractive, successful, and destined to live happily ever after. Brad joined a big law firm, and I went to work as a computer analyst at a bank. We settled into the ideal life—a popular, savvy couple who had nowhere to go but up.

Within two years, Brad had become an associate in the firm, and I was promoted to assistant bank manager. Looking back now, I realize that I had become a little vain, accepting all the blessings that life offered as deserved and earned.

Still, success had never changed Brad. He was always the sensitive, caring person I had fallen in love with, a very decent man who never met a stranger. He treated everyone with the same compassion and fairness that caused him to make friends wherever he went, in every social strata. The only thing lacking in our marriage was a child, something we planned to rectify before I turned thirty.

We loved life and indulged in all our hobbies to our hearts' content. Brad's favorite was taking off on his motorcycle on weekends, entering races, attending bikers' conventions—in general, living life to the fullest. But the gods got jealous.

Brad's terrible accident occurred at a national biker convention. He was coming up the rear of a line of bikers. Not wanting to be separated from them, he raced after them when the traffic light was changing. A pickup truck sideswiped him, slamming him against the passenger side and throwing him under the front wheels.

Miraculously, he survived, but at a cost: A spinal injury left his legs paralyzed but the rest of his body intact. He had become a paraplegic.

Traumatized by the accident, I nevertheless vowed to do everything in my power to bring him out of the deep depression that enveloped him for three months while he was undergoing intensive physical therapy. With the help of counseling and the assurance of the law firm that his position was ensured, he gradually pulled out of his terrible despondency and got used to the wheelchair that would always be with him.

He became a familiar figure around the courthouse as he wheeled himself up the handicapped ramp. Strange as it sounds, his restricted physical state seemed to have sharpened his intellect. He recaptured his usual, cheerful self and delved into legal arguments his opponents had never heard of to win many difficult cases. His output at work became prodigious and he was being considered for partnership.

As far as our marriage was concerned, my love for Brad had reached new heights as we sought to find some kind of equilibrium in our personal relationship.

Despite his useless legs, we were able to resume conjugal relations. Brad would joke that if he had to make a choice, he would opt for his manhood being intact rather than his legs. Our lovemaking might not have been as exciting as it once was, but we were happy for the good fortune we still had.

Brad followed a solid regime of the kind of exercise he could manage, and by the end of the year, he had built up the muscles in his upper torso—his chest and arms— to the extent that his upper body looked like that of a wrestler.

Even though we had hired an aide to help Brad for a few months after the accident, I took a six-month leave from my job so that I could ensure that he had adequate care. When he did return to his firm, I resumed my own career with a vengeance, partially to make up for the time lost and partially because it offered me an opportunity to distance myself during the day from the nightmare our lives had become.

Since my research on improving banking techniques had caught the eye of the bank president, I was in line for a promotion when the opportunity arose. My success at work made me feel better about my family situation.

At home, there was an unspoken agreement between us to accentuate the positive as much as we could. We were both determined not to fall into long silences when I'm sure Brad's thoughts, like mine, centered on his handicap. Instead, we talked about our work. He would go into detail about clients, describing them vividly. The images were riveting.

I, in turn, related humorous incidents at work that I would embellish to get a laugh out of him. Humor was a great healer. When Brad was bungling or awkward in something he tried to do, I pretended not to notice and refused to allow him to apologize for the result.

As we clung to each other at night, we talked about the future, attempting to discard the past. But the heart remembers the good times and grieves when they come no more.

We began resuming our social life. When I gave our first dinner party after the accident, our friends were elated at the get-together. Brad, a wonderful conversationalist, was the life of the party, and our friends had missed his humor, his ability as a raconteur. It started a continuous flow of invitations to various events, and we attended as many as we could.

Although I constantly reminded myself of how fortunate we had been, I guess part of me resented the dramatic change in our lives, a feeling I managed to ignore—until the wedding of a young lawyer in Brad's firm.

At the hotel reception after the nuptials, I watched the bride and groom in all their youthful exuberance greet guests and then glide out to the dance floor for the first number. My spirits suddenly hit rock bottom. How I had loved to dance, swaying to the rhythm of our favorite tunes, feeling my entire being caught up in the music and lyrics, finding our own highway to the stars as we danced the night away.

A deep hunger to be part of the magic and glamour threatened to strangle me as couples joined the bride and groom on the dance floor. A cold anger seemed to envelop my soul. It was as though I were releasing all the feelings I had kept bottled up for months. I hated being different, being deprived of some of the joys normal people had, destined to live the rest of my life with a handicapped husband.

I looked at Brad, engaged in conversation with two acquaintances at the edge of the dance floor. Handsome in his tuxedo, his face nevertheless showed signs of discomfort, of sadness in repose. No one seemed to notice as I slipped away with drink in hand to an outside balcony.

Finishing my drink, I set it on a table and leaned on the railing, the star-covered heavens and crescent moon above a cruel tease to my heart. I was totally honest with myself: I could pretend from now to eternity that we were happy, content with our lives—but it was a big fat lie.

The storybook scenario I'd imagined wasn't holding up. I was tired of always having to make arrangements for Brad's comfort, tired of fears that he would have an accident, tired of walking beside him in a wheelchair, tired of what I knew were piteous glances from strangers and acquaintances.

My once handsome Brad was now an invalid, half a man, and I was his caretaker—not the devoted, loving wife, but a woman seething with resentment. I was angry at Brad for the accident, for the position in which it had placed me, and especially at being deprived of a normal marriage to a normal guy.

I was successful at my work. But what else did I have? I had been pretty smart, but now I was quickly going down the drain with a noose around my neck. I didn't deserve this. I'd never done anyone any harm.

Brad and his infantile need for adventure on a motorcycle has caused this. He'd brought it all on himself. I thought of the bride and groom again. Had Brad and I been like them such a short time ago?

The demon within me raged. Why should I have to suffer because of his stupid behavior?

I turned around and looked into the ballroom. Brad was keeping time to the music with his head, then greeting guests who were approaching him. He was acting as if life were a blast, that we were part of the action.

I turned back to the railing. I was tired of it, tired of our pretending, tired of his happy expression that was usually forced.

My eyes filled with angry tears. Damn it! Why should I have to put up with half a man the rest of my life? The cruel thought made me wince. I put my hand over my mouth. I felt crazy.

Brad was still a successful lawyer, a wonderful, caring, loving husband who wanted to spare me all the misery his accident had caused. Our lives were filled with our work and our feelings for one another. We were successful and had a comfortable life. We really loved each other. I couldn't love another man the way I loved him.

I stopped feeling sorry for myself, dried my face, and took out my compact to repair the damage.

Brad was my man. If only the adjustment to his useless legs wasn't so difficult. I straightened my gown and walked back into the ballroom provocatively, holding my chin high. My legs rustled the taffeta of my dress as I walked. I was suddenly aware of appreciative glances from men.

A few yards from Brad, I felt a tug on my arm and found myself gazing up into the handsome face of Max Witheridge, a member of the country-club set who had gone to law school with Brad.

Big and brawny, he was head of a law firm his wealthy in-laws had started. His marriage to their arrogant socialite daughter, Nancy, had assured him some of the biggest corporate accounts in the city. Smart, cagey, and wily enough to follow Nancy's social agenda—at the same time concealing from her the little affairs sometimes whispered about on the golf course—Max's firm was at the top of the heap.

"Where are you hurrying to, Jill?" he asked, his eyes raking my figure and coming to rest on my rather deep neckline. "How about a little whirl around the dance floor? Brad won't mind."

Before I could reply, he had taken my hand and firmly guided me out to join the other dancers. My heart pounded as he placed his arm around me and we flawlessly stepped in time to the music.

Max was an excellent dancer, amazingly light on his feet for a large man. God, how I loved to dance! Before Brad's accident, we'd hardly missed a club dinner-dance or community fund-raising affair. We enjoyed dancing so much that we even won a prize in a cruise-ship contest.

When the band broke into a rock number, Max and I threw discretion to the wind, gyrating and improvising all over the place. As he held me close, I could feel his rippling chest muscles, his strong athletic thighs. I marveled at the great shape he was in, with little excess poundage on his large form. We were so perfectly attuned and executing steps so flawlessly, other dancers stopped to watch.

"Where's Nancy?" I asked as we broke for intermission and headed for Brad's table, where he was sitting with friends.

"In Africa on safari," he said, shaking his head. "The poor animals there don't have a chance."

As we neared Brad, I murmured, "Enjoyed it."

Max squeezed my hand and looked into my eyes. "Must do it again sometime." He left for his own table.

I simply smiled and walked the rest of the way alone. Brad reached out a hand to take mine as I seated myself. I breathed deeply to calm my racing pulse and took my time opening my napkin.

"You and Max looked good out there." Brad smiled, kissing me on the cheek. "You stopped the show."

"It was fun," I told him, thankful that the waiter was approaching.

The other couples at the table were old acquaintances, and conversation flowed easily. Brad injected a little humor, as usual, when the conversation became too serious, and everyone appreciated him. All of this intensified the feeling of guilt that threatened to gag me.

Though I was trying to concentrate on the conversation, I found myself arguing with my conscience. Why shouldn't I enjoy myself? Brad was the one in the wheelchair, not me. Besides, I insisted to myself, as caring and insightful as he was, he surely wouldn't begrudge me a little fun, an opportunity to do for myself what we couldn't do together.

As a matter of fact, it certainly wouldn't hurt Brad if I started pleasing myself instead of always worrying about his welfare. I worked hard and had more responsibilities than most women at home.

I had pretended for too long that our lives were satisfactory. They weren't, and part of the trouble was my concentrating too much on Brad. I needed some time for myself.

After the festivities were over and we were ready to leave, Brad told me he was going to the restroom. I said that I would go outside the hotel to wait while the valet brought the car. As I waited, I was startled by a pair of hands around my waist and turned to find myself again staring into Max's magnetic green eyes.

"You're a great dancer," he whispered. "I'd love to see you again sometime."

My heart hammering at his words, I looked through the glass doors of the entrance to see Brad wheeling himself toward the exit. On reflex, I stepped backward, leaving more space between Max and me. Brad was almost at the door.

I gave Max a quick nod, then turned from him and walked up to greet Brad. I prayed he hadn't seen our encounter.

Brad was driving his specially designed car. I locked the wheelchair while he hoisted himself into the driver's seat and then folded it, placing it in the rear. When I had seated myself, he started the engine, then leaned over to kiss me.

"Jill, you were the prettiest girl there. It made me feel good just to watch you."

I quickly returned the kiss, suddenly wanting to cry. Why did he have to be so understanding?

My husband went to bed before I did. After I showered and lay down beside him, he gathered me into his arms.

"God, I love you so much," he told me, his chin resting on my head.

As our bodies came afire with the movements of lovemaking, somehow the handsome face of Max Witheridge inserted itself into my consciousness. What would it be like to love a whole man again? What would it be like to feel again the demands of a vigorous, handsome stud, to feel that sturdy body against my own?

Long after Brad was asleep, I lay silently weeping at my own duplicity. Why did I find Max so intriguing?

It didn't take Max long to act on what he considered my encouragement. The next day, as I was emerging from the bank for lunch, he was walking toward me, handsomer than ever in a gray suit with a blue tie, a nice complement to his roguish green eyes. He was holding one long-stemmed red rose in his hand.

"An American Beauty for an American beauty," he murmured, handing it to me, his white, even teeth gleaming, his golfer's tan unblemished.

"Thank you," I said. "Very pretty."

His eyes quickly appraised my body and then settled on my lips. "How about lunch with a lonely admirer?"

My thoughts raced maddeningly, my heart pounding. What would be wrong with having lunch? I often had lunch with clients.

I looked at the rose. "Okay, let me put this inside."

When I returned, Max, car keys in hand, again brazenly scanned my figure, my face, my hair. Then he led me to the parking lot, where his car was parked. The Mercedes he drove was like him—sleek, polished, a status symbol.

I thought about his appearance. He apparently made quite an impression on jurors, rarely losing a case, and the papers reported his branching out into international law.

He kept the conversation light and amusing, but clever enough to insert suggestive innuendoes when he had the opportunity. I wondered if his wife was also playing around. She was so involved in the Junior League and club activities that I doubted if she had the time. Was it one of those modern marriages where each spouse did their own thing?

"I know a nice Chinese place at the other side of the highway that just opened," he said. "What do you think?"

I cleared my throat before replying. "I love Chinese."

He drove with one hand on the wheel and the other on the back of my seat. On the way to the restaurant, he did most of the talking.

The place was housed in what seemed to be an imitation Chinese castle, with a Mandarin roof, reflective pool, and bright orange décor. The waiter led us to a table in a little alcove overlooking an enclosed atrium filled with exotic birds.

Though we ordered only garlic chicken and egg rolls, several side dishes appeared as well. The red wine Max ordered was delicious. After filling our glasses, Max toasted me over the rim.

"Here's to an intimate friendship." His eyes were teasing.

I felt my cheeks redden. Were my erotic thoughts that transparent? I returned his smile and sipped my wine. Max, like Brad, was a good storyteller. He talked about a current case, defending Native Americans against charges of illegal casino gambling.

"They always get the short end of the stick," he complained.

"They're finally asserting themselves," I offered.

He nodded. "You got it. Like women, they're second-class citizens. Case in point: Society scorns women courageous enough to indulge in things men take for granted." He sipped more wine. "Like extramarital affairs."

I flinched and changed the subject, rambling on about one of Brad's cases.

Max ate an egg roll while I talked. "Brad is a great guy. But it must be tough being married to a paraplegic."

His comment caught me off guard, and I felt an overwhelming anger welling in my throat. "I'm the luckiest woman in the world. Brad is a wonderful man, a wonderful husband, with no peer in his work," I found myself sputtering, stopping to try to collect myself. My eyes filled with tears.

"Even in the sex department?" Max asked innocently.

I swallowed my tears, bitter anger surpassing shock at his words. I put down my fork and picked up my napkin, wiping my face.

"I've got to be getting back," I told him. "The lunch was very good."

The waiter appeared with the check, and I waited while Max produced his credit card and signed the receipt. Still, his hand on mine kept me from rising.

"Ever miss having sex with a passionate, full-bodied man?"

I picked up my purse with my free hand, but he clutched my wrist. The smile he gave me was slightly off-center.

"Look, Jill, I'm sorry if you take offense. I'm as sorry for what happened to Brad as I can be. He's incredible before a jury. But none of that character reference changes the price you've had to pay for standing by him. You deserve more. You've suffered along with Brad. I know that. But it's a pretty bleak future if you put your life on hold forever, depriving yourself of some real fun."

I shook loose of his hand and rose. He stood beside me. We walked silently to the car. He turned to me before starting the engine, giving me a beguiling smile.

"No hard feelings?" he asked, extending his hand.

As I extended mine, he took it to draw me into his arms, suddenly sliding his tongue between my lips and sending sparks and tremors into every nerve ending, every part of my being. When I pulled away, my heart was doing somersaults, my breath coming in tiny gasps. His eyes seemed darker, locking with mine.

"Honey, we could make beautiful music together," he whispered.

I turned away from him, staring straight ahead. "I've got to get back to the office," I said as firmly as I could.

We drove back to the bank silently, and he parked in front of the entrance. As I started to open the door, he placed his hand on my arm.

"Jill." His voice was husky. "I'll be up front: I'm attracted to you. Think it over. What do you have to lose? Just think about it. If you're curious, take a nice, long lunch break Friday about twelve-thirty. I'll be at the Grand Street Motel, right off the interstate at Main, registered under the name of Glen Wells. Room two-forty. You won't regret it."

I stared at him. I could think of nothing else to say, so I walked into the entrance, taking the stairway to my third-floor office instead of the elevator, in order to give myself time to think.

Max was so incredibly attractive and such a hunk of masculinity—vibrant, energetic, magnetic. And obviously I was giving off signals that I was interested. I berated myself. A little flirtation was all I intended. What he was suggesting was an affair.

That afternoon, as I advised clients about a variety of services, my mind kept wandering to Max. He had so much sex appeal. He had it all and was egotistical enough to use it for any urge that came to mind.

He couldn't hold a candle to Brad in the character department. Brad had compassion, a real concern for all mankind. What Max had was mesmerizing, though. As I watched a client sign a request for a loan, the idea of the Grand Street Motel kept swirling in my brain.

A long lunch hour would be no problem. I'd put in enough overtime for a month of days off. By the end of the day, the idea didn't seem so outrageous.

He must be something in bed, and I had a feeling he would do everything he could to satisfy himself. Even before the accident, Brad was always so eager to please me, coddle me, always placing my needs above his own. Max, I was certain, was the exact antithesis. He was probably always taking—giving would be an afterthought. What would it be like to be used, totally dominated?

That night, Brad was late getting home, giving me time to whip up a salad and presentable chicken stir-fry. I greeted him more warmly than usual, meeting him at the door and seating myself in his lap as he manipulated the chair. He caught his breath as I crushed my lips to his, then smiled as I stood beside the wheelchair.

"What did I do to deserve this?" he asked, kissing my hand.

"Just being you," I told him. "I love you, Brad."

As we ate dinner and I listened to his account of winning a big drug case, guilt overcame me to the point that I wanted to cry. I loved this man with all my heart—his decency, his courage, his goodness. And I was considering doing something that would hurt him more than anything, succumbing to an adolescent's daydreams.

Still, I couldn't get Max Witheridge off my mind. As Brad and I made love that night, images of Max kept intruding themselves—handsome, overbearing, egotistical. I seemed to be mesmerized with him. Brad, always considerate, moved with me gently, always attempting to satisfy me before he allowed himself to reach climax. Why did he have to be so considerate?

Friday was two days away. Thursday morning, I was sitting around in my boss' office, reviewing measures to take because an account had gone bad.

As I rose to go, I found myself asking, "Would it be all right if I take a couple of hours for lunch tomorrow? I have some personal business to take care of."

He laughed, "Need you ask? With the time you've put in, you probably have six months of compensatory time."

That evening, Brad and I ate out with friends. I felt like I had a totally split personality. One part of me was listening curiously to the good-natured banter of our friends, to my husband's anecdotes, even to my own lighthearted asides. But another part of my brain focused on how much I really loved Brad, admired him, even idealized him, would die if I ever lost him.

Why couldn't I be satisfied with a good man, a wonderful husband, capable of being an incredible father to a child? I grew almost panicky trying to understand my duplicity.

I only knew that I was hopelessly intrigued by a scoundrel who cheated on his wife and used people as pawns as part of his selfish pursuits. He could attract any woman he wanted, and gossip said he did exactly that, discarding them when his interest waned, as easily as brushing off a crumb.

Born poor, Max had gone for the gold after law school, using his good mind and charm to follow a lifestyle that was the envy of many of his colleagues. Lawyers joked about his readiness to console willing matrons seeking divorce by sleeping with them as part of big alimony awards. I knew all this, but the stories made him even more interesting.

On Friday, there was no doubt in my mind that I would accept Max's invitation. I left the office in time to get me to the motel by twelve-thirty. It was a surprisingly modest structure. I almost turned back in the parking lot, and then I spotted Max's Mercedes.

I talked to myself for a couple of minutes. What harm could there be in doing something for me once in a while? Brad would never know, and it certainly wouldn't change my affection for him, my devotion.

I walked slowly toward the entrance and went through revolving doors to the elevator, which I took to the second floor. The room door was ajar and as I approached it opened wide, revealing Max dressed in shorts, his athletic legs husky and tanned, his muscular form like a health-club ad. His smile revealed white teeth, a striking contrast to his appealing tan.

"Come in, Jill," he greeted me, taking both my hands in his.

"You're right on time."

I was suddenly tongue-tied. This was crazy, a surreal scene from a cheap novel. He pulled me into the room and closed the door, then handed me a drink from the minibar. I sipped it more quickly than was my habit, trying to slow my racing pulse.

He finished his own drink and then set down both our glasses, drawing me forcefully into his arms, crushing his mouth against my own, kissing my cheeks, my eyelids, the secret pulse in my neck.

My heart was beating furiously under his caresses as I tried to catch my breath. He held me at arm's length and then, with a crinkled smile, began undressing me slowly, sensually, his eyes not roving from my face.

"You're so pretty, Jill," he uttered, "an earthly goddess, one of God's better creations." His eyes probed into mine as he unbuttoned my blouse and removed it, then my skirt, my bra, my stockings—almost effortlessly. I didn't resist as he began massaging my breasts.

He stopped for a moment, studying my face. "If I weren't so strapped for cash after law school, I might have married you myself."

Suddenly drawing me closer, he thrust himself between my thighs. His tongue forced open my lips and followed a rhythm of its own, moving in and out, at times playful, then possessive as he sent sparks and trembling through every nerve ending.

I delighted in my aroused passion and felt myself coming alive under his powerful probing. Pulling off his shorts, he picked me up and carried me to the bed. Without hesitation, he lowered himself on top of me. His hands on my shoulders felt heavy, draining.

I tried to shift position, but he ignored my efforts, nibbling and teasing me with abandon. When his nibbles became sharp bites, I cried out in pain. But concerned with his rising need, he ignored my cries. He began moving faster and faster, his body heavy and perspiring on my own.

Like a raging bull, he pushed deeper and deeper, until I was uncomfortable and suddenly frightened. Brad was always so gentle, so tender, letting both our moods set the pace, always cognizant of my comfort. But Max seemed to operate with a fury and strength all-engulfing, overpowering, almost consuming.

I suddenly found myself bereft of desire under his unremitting grasp, eager to end this crazy encounter. My little extracurricular dalliance was turning into a wild, frenzied ordeal. As he rotated above me, I prayed he would finish quickly, but apparently he was determined to extract every bit of pleasure from this escapade.

When he finally rolled off me, he lay back perspiring and smiling with satisfaction. He brushed a strand of hair from my face, then bent over to force his lips over mine, his hand clutching my chin. My lips felt sore, bruised. When he released me, he patted me playfully on the bottom.

"Now, how's that?" he asked. I could hear the pride in his voice.

Wanting only to escape from this wild, threatening encounter, I managed to crawl out of bed, find my clothes, and hurry to the bathroom.. When I got out, he was already dressed, resplendent in a well-tailored suit and matching tie, his dark hair wet with perspiration. His smile was wide.

"Hey, we're not bad together." He approached me. As I stepped back, he caught me in his arms. "Care to make it a weekly event? It can only get better."

Sick to my stomach and trying hard to control a crazy trembling that made me feel cold, I was a little fearful about my state of mind. I had actually encouraged this insane predator, actually believed that I was missing something in my marriage to Brad.

I was afraid of not only what I had done to my marriage but a more imminent danger: How could I pretend that I was still a faithful, contented wife? How could I live with what I had done?

I broke out of his arms and picked up my purse. "I've got to be getting back to the office."

His hand shot out and clutched my wrist. "You didn't answer my question." The smile had vanished. "Next week? Same time?"

I tried to keep revulsion out of my voice as I looked directly at him. "No thanks. I won't be able to."

A scowl darkened his features as he shook his head. "You know, Jill, I'm the one who usually calls the shots." His eyes were piercing as they bore into mine. "Next week, same time." This was a statement, not a question. His tone was a little ominous.

I hurried out the door and didn't look back as I took the stairs to the lobby. Dear God, what had I gotten into? His words sounded like an implied threat. Would he go to Brad? To my boss? Could this monster blackmail me into a permanent affair?

After work, I hurried home to fix Brad his favorite dinner—London broil, baked potatoes, spinach casserole, and a salad. But he was held up in court and didn't get home until late. I tried to keep everything warm.

When I heard his key in the lock, my eyes filled with tears. My loving, wonderful Brad. How could I ever have imagined I could be easy prey for an animal like Max? Brad was caring, giving, and understanding. Brad was my hero, my love. How could I have ever doubted I was married to such an extraordinary human being who loved me and whom I loved with all my heart?

I rushed to the door, flung it open, and embraced him almost frantically, covering his face with kisses. He wheeled himself into the entrance holding my hand and kissing it tenderly.

"I wonder how many men are so fortunate," he whispered, pulling my face down to his, pressing his lips against my own.

"I love you, Brad," I said quietly when he released me. "You're a wonderful person," I added.

"Ditto, sweetheart." He smiled.

He raved about the dinner and ate with relish, telling me proudly about being given a large new office and now being certain of becoming a partner. My heart was bursting with pride at the news.

"I hope you know you're married to a top-notch lawyer," he said teasingly.

As we lay in bed that night wrapped in each other's arms, I wondered if he could ever forgive me for my betrayal if he knew. Even the thought of Max was becoming as frightening as a nightmare. I felt my insides sicken. *God, forgive me!* But would I ever be able to forgive myself? Could I ever erase my sinful actions from my memory?

But that was not in the cards. All through the week, devilish images of Max and our encounter plagued me at work, at home, and especially through the sleepless nights. Would he leave me alone? I got my answer

Thursday afternoon as I was leaving the building after work.

After I opened the exit doors, I saw Max standing on the sidewalk, waiting. He approached me quickly as I emerged through the massive doors. In a crazy daze, I continued walking with him at my side. After a block, he stopped me with a tug on my arm.

"Why don't we sit in one of those kiosks in that park across the street?" he suggested. Not waiting for my reply, he firmly ushered me over to the small city park. We sat down in a shaded kiosk, and he unbuttoned his jacket, appraising me from top to toe.

"You're looking very beautiful today, Jill," he said. "Pink looks good on you."

I felt my body tense at his words and moved away from him a little. "I can't meet you tomorrow," I told him as firmly as I could manage. "As a matter of fact, I don't want to meet you ever again." I forced myself to look directly into those aquamarine eyes as I spoke.

His smile slowly turned into a frown as he stared at me. When he spoke, his words came with biting enunciation. "Listen to me, girl. I told you last week that I'm the one to break off these little trysts and I'm not ready yet."

He placed an arm around my shoulders and squeezed tightly, his face red beneath the tan. "Tomorrow at noon."

When I didn't reply, he continued, "Do you think Brad might be interested in how his lovely, successful wife spends her lunch hour?"

I'm not sure why, but I was finally immune to his threat. Perhaps I was seeing him fully for the egotistical cad he was. Whatever the reason, my gut-wrenching fear was suddenly gone. As I gazed at him, he might have surmised the revulsion I felt, but his threat had lost its power.

I saw the sleaze for what he was—a browbeating, immoral, one-dimensional overgrown bully with the principles of an alley cat, taking everything he wanted, interested primarily in realizing his own animal impulses with the phony status that money had brought him.

Instinctively, I somehow knew that the only way to deal with a bully was to stand up to him, to use his own tactics.

My voice was calm, and my eyes didn't waver from his face as I spoke.

"You do that if you want. But listen carefully to me, Max. If you breathe one word of our tryst to Brad or anyone else, it might destroy me, but I'll have some juicy revelations of my own. One word, and I'm filing sexual assault charges against you with the district attorney's office. One word, and I'll pay your wife a visit and describe our encounter in full detail."

I settled back on the bench, my voice rising in confidence. "Now, those two little efforts on my part ought to make you the laughing stock of the local bar and country club for some time to come, let alone taking away your rich wife."

His expression shifted from anger and disbelief to unmistakable fear, vulnerability. He gaped at me with his mouth open, the haughty eyes filled with mounting consternation. He licked his lips, took a handkerchief from his jacket, and wiped his face. He seemed to have difficulty speaking for a moment. Then he rose from the bench and began to talk, almost spitting out the words as he leaned close.

"Why, you little bitch," he seethed. "Who do you think you are? Your kind are a dime a dozen. I can pick up sex-hungry sluts like you anyplace in this city." His face was inches from mine. "How dare you threaten me? Let me tell you one thing—"

His finger wagged in front of my nose. "If you start that crap with the district attorney or my wife, I'll not only have your hide, but I'll take care of your sanctimonious husband as well."

I leaned back on the bench, feeling strangely relaxed. I nodded. "Okay, it's a deal. We'll both forget that last week ever happened."

He wiped his face again and spoke through gritted teeth. "I hope I never see you again. And let me tell you, you're not such a hot lay. I feel sorry for what Brad has to put up with."

With that, he stumbled from the kiosk like a man possessed. After he strode away, I remained where I was for a few minutes. At least we understood each other. We both knew that he had more to lose than I did. I knew I had silenced him permanently.

I returned to the office in leisurely fashion, relieved and almost proud of myself. But after sitting at my desk for a moment, depression overcame me like a dark cloud. I had gotten rid of Max, but the overpowering guilt toward Brad grew stronger.

How could I survive my guilty conscience? I had betrayed the person I loved most in the world. That was a fact of life. How could I survive the betrayal?

As I drove home after work trying to calm myself, the guilt only grew stronger and bitter bile made me want to retch. I'd cheated on Brad with a zero like Max, selling out a vital part of me—my morals, my standards. How could I ever regain them?

As Brad and I sat on the sofa after dinner watching the evening news, I held him tight. I was sure he was puzzled by my impulses, but he said nothing, only accepting my overtures with embraces of his own.

Sleepless nights began to give me a haunted look, and Brad became concerned. He insisted that we take weekend trips to the lake to relax. We'd sit on the beach enjoying the early springtime, listening to bird cries and especially to each other. Touching, loving, sharing—we reveled in each other's company.

I'd watch him while he slept. He had everything women looked for in men, and the miracle of miracles was that he loved me so completely. I'd close my eyes against the pain. How could he love me—a lying, immoral double-crossing excuse for a wife? We had had such a good life. And now I was tainted, damaged goods, undeserving.

Spring turned into summer, and I began fearing for my state of mind. On the surface, I guess I appeared normal, carrying on my usual routine. But it was in the evening that the doubts would explode, the fear of the future almost overwhelming.

One night after we had made tender love, I found myself shaking with sobs. I couldn't go on like this. I had to tell him.

Brad sat up in bed holding me, soothing me as one would a child. When my sobs had subsided, I decided I was going to tell him. I had to for my sanity. I snuggled onto his chest.

"Darling," I began, "do you ever feel guilty about things, about thoughts, about stuff you would have done differently with hindsight?"

He rested his chin on my head. "Of course—everyone does. We've all done things we've regretted, used words we wish we could retract." He was a silent a moment and then asked. "Is it something at work?"

I steeled myself. "At home, at work—not being good enough, loyal enough to people who mean the world to you, who've helped you. It's like . . . like a terrible betrayal."

He held me tighter. "I wish I had a nickel for every time I've done that." He reflected for a moment. "We get rushed or aren't thinking, and suddenly we've done or said things we'd bite off our tongues to take back."

He kissed my forehead. "The good people in the world try to make amends in some way. It's the good guys who have the overdeveloped self-censors. The others don't give a damn and are hardly aware of their shortcomings."

I concentrated hard on his words. "How do you get rid of the guilt?"

He thought for a moment. "I don't know. Everyone has his own way. I try to do things for the people I feel I've wronged. Or as my mother used to say, when people tried to thank her for something she'd done for them, when they asked how they could repay her, it was always the same: 'Do something for somebody else. Pass it around.'

"I guess that's about it. As you know, sweetheart, doing something for others is the best way of getting over it." He paused. "You ought to know, being the most giving person I know."

I hardly had time to digest what he was saying when he continued. "When I first started practicing and the firm expected me to bring in new cases, I did something I've always hated. I stole a client from a guy also starting out who I really liked; he was my friend. I won't go into details, but it was horrible when I fully realized what I had done."

He paused before continuing. "I never apologized, but I sent him as many clients as I could when we were overloaded. And through the years, the guilty feelings have mostly passed."

He paused for a moment. "But not completely. I still suffer occasional pangs of guilt. You know the guy—Josh Simonsen. I backed him for county judge last year, contributed to his campaign. And he won."

I reached up and kissed him. "You're a good man, Brad McDonnell, a very good man."

He kissed me back. "We've just got to learn not to be consumed by our less-than-virtuous actions. Once a deed is done, all we can do is forgive ourselves and vow never to repeat the mistakes. It works."

He tousled my hair. "Let's get some sleep, okay, Jill? I've got a heavy workload tomorrow."

His words began to soothe me like a warm blanket. He was so right. Everyone committed sins—some big, some small. But he had the right formula: never repeating the mistakes, doing what we can for the aggrieved people, and most of all, forgiving ourselves.

It was with the last part that I wasn't making any progress. The fact remained: I hadn't told him. What would have his reaction been then?

We attended a small neighborhood church, and I had always felt comfortable with the minister, an earnest, kindly man. He had been a counselor before entering the ministry. I decided to seek him out the next Friday afternoon.

When he invited me into his study, words spilled out of me in a flood. I told him everything, holding back no details of my humiliating experience as I bared my soul.

I finished my revelation, commenting, "I can never forgive myself. I've been considering telling Brad everything. I think I could live with the sin a little better."

He paused for a long time and then shook his head. "That's probably not a wise idea—not that he wouldn't forgive you. But Brad has withstood so much pain in the last year that telling him would only inflict more emotional pain.

"Ask yourself: What good would it do? It's over, done with, and you'll never repeat the experience. No, I think you've followed the right course. Don't burden Brad with it."

He stood by the window of his study. "The hardest element of our wrong doings is forgiving ourselves. We can forgive others more easily than we can ourselves. And how do you do that?

"As you've told me, Brad said that the easiest way is through good deeds, making amends as best we can. And then, positive thinking gets rid of the little demons that possess us."

He turned to smile at me. "As a philosopher once said, 'Thoughts cause feelings.' We can control our thoughts. Therefore we can control our feelings."

He walked over and stood beside me. "You can forgive yourself, Jill. You have a solid marriage. You two love each other very much. It'll just take time. You're already on the right track—doing more for Brad to show him your love. And helping as many people as you can."

He removed his glasses. "Say, there's a little program in our church we've just started for helping young women who are in trouble for one reason or another. Maybe donating a little time to them would help you put all this in perspective. Why don't you try it?"

I did and it worked. Sometimes Brad comes with me to the self-help session for troubled young girls. I've begun to understand what the minister told me on a gut level. If I spent enough time doing for others, the horrible escapade with Max would fade in time and I would forgive myself eventually.

I knew I had succeeded when one day, about six months later, Brad told me how radiant I looked, how proud he was of my efforts to help one of the girls.

I realized I had arrived at a kind of peace with myself. I felt more confident and accepting. I wasn't a bad person. I was a devoted wife, a person who had learned from her mistake, who appreciated totally the life I had and the man I loved. I had indeed forgiven myself!
THE END

MOM'S BOYFRIEND TOOK MY VIRGINITY
I dangled my goods in his face so he'd make me feel like a woman

I knew what was up the minute I laid eyes on Turk Raiford. I knew by the cocky way he hooked his thumbs in the front pockets of his tight jeans and stood with his hips cocked forward, there in the doorway just behind my mother.

Marla, my mom, was laughing her coy, girlish laugh and cutting her eyes around in Turk's direction as she introduced him to my Aunt Barb and me.

"His name's Thomas, but everyone calls him Turk," she giggled, rolling her violet-blue eyes.

"Gee, I wonder how he got that name," I muttered under my breath.

Just as Marla said: ". . . .and this is my other sister, Britney. . . ." gesturing toward me and smiling her devilish grin. I felt my mouth twist into something that I tried to make into a smile, but I suspected it was more of a grimace.

There she goes again, I thought. *Testing to see what she can get away with*.

As I watched Turk coolly, his chocolate-brown eyes swept over me from head to foot in what was very obviously an appraisal. I sensed that he liked what he saw, as his mouth quirked up at one corner in a grin that was a perfect imitation of Elvis's trademark look. His level gaze held mine just a heartbeat longer than it should have.

"Well, beauty sure runs in the family," his rich, baritone voice rumbled out in a deep Texas accent.

As Aunt Barb and I exchanged looks, I saw the color blooming in her cheeks. I couldn't tell if she was embarrassed, or just flustered by this tall, muscular hunk my mom had dragged in on us unexpectedly. But Aunt Barb's whole face obviously said: *Here she goes again.* Mom—or Marla, as she preferred I call her—was "at it again."

My mother was, at thirty-five, still a good-looking woman. She could, and did, pass for ten years younger than she really was. She took great delight in astonishing people with the fact that she had a seventeen-year-old daughter . . . when she admitted to it. Most often, however, her relationship to me was left ambiguous. It was obvious that I was *some* sort of kin—the resemblance was too strong—but Marla liked to leave people guessing. And the men she attracted tended to be years younger than she was, a lot of them closer to my age. Turk appeared to be no exception. I guessed his age at somewhere in his late twenties.

A well-kept twenties! The slim fit of his crisp, white, western-cut shirt tucked into his tight jeans, revealed a trim, well-muscled body that tapered from broad, squared shoulders. His golden-brown skin and jet-black hair indicated to me that he had a good bit of Native American blood. His straight nose, full, lush lips, and almond-shaped eyes confirmed it.

A bittersweet twinge went through me. My father was Native American. Turk bore a striking resemblance to him. At least, from what I could remember of him. He'd been out of the picture for years now; I'd seen him only once in the decade, and he was not in touch.

So when Turk set those impenetrable, dark pools of his eyes on me, I felt a tug at my heart. God only knows what my mother felt. Something had always been there in her for my father.

"She could never say no to him." Aunt Barb had told me that much.

And now it looked like she might have found a close substitute . . . a younger substitute—about the same age my father would've been when he left us.

Substitute or not, who could blame her for picking up on Turk? He was something to look at—that much was all too obvious—and he had a lazy, casual way about him that made me think of something lying, soaking up the warm sun, but still coiled and ready to strike. There was a hint of danger to him, all right, but I could have no idea just how much danger.

And I had no way of knowing that I would find out all about it.

I remember Marla coming into my bedroom one evening in spring, shortly after she met Turk, to borrow a sweater from me to wear on a date. I was lying across my bed, reading an English assignment.

"Brit, honey, where's that powder-blue angora sweater?" she asked as she began to rummage through my chest-of-drawers.

I glanced at her. She had her long, auburn hair all curled and fluffed—great, sweeping waves and curls that tumbled and cascaded down her shoulders. Her makeup was perfect, as it always was, and the violet-blueness of her eyes seemed to burn its way out through the heavy fringe of her black lashes. She was still a perfect size eight, making it very convenient for the both of us, as wearing the same size virtually doubled our wardrobes. Although, sometimes, Aunt Barb would make comments about some of my clothes looking just way too young and inappropriate on a thirty-something mother. Still, it didn't seem to bother Marla in the least. She just went right on, looking a lot less than thirty-something—and acting it, too.

Later, around one o'clock in the morning, I was awakened when I heard Marla letting herself in, then some muffled giggling and shushing. Obviously, she'd brought her date home with her. Then I heard the door to her bedroom close softly.

I tried to go right back to sleep, but it was really hard, as through the wall that separated our rooms, I could hear muffled voices, then silence, then a throaty moan, then the headboard bumping and clunking against the wall in a telltale rhythm. I made a mental note right then and there to pull her bed out from the wall a bit the next day, because I had a feeling this was going to be happening from now on on a regular basis. When I finally fell back to sleep, I had disturbing dreams . . . of smooth, brown skin covering hardworking muscles . . . strong arms that reached out and enfolded me. I could never see the face on that body; it was too hazy to make out. But in those dreams, I could feel the strength in those arms as they cradled me and held me tight, pressing me close against a smooth, brown, warm chest.

Two weeks had barely passed when I woke up one Sunday morning and on my way to the kitchen, spotted Turk's fancy-tooled cowboy boots sitting on the floor beside the sofa. His shirt was draped across one of the chairs, where it seemed to have been dropped heedlessly, as though the owner had shed it in a hurry.

He'd finally gotten around to staying over.

I'd wondered how long it would take.

For the past week, Marla had had me answering the phone every time it rang, intercepting calls from her regular "boyfriend"—anyway, I guess that's what you'd call him, Larry—telling him she wasn't home, or in the tub, or whatever she could dream up. I felt kind of bad about it, but it wasn't the first time Marla had handled things this way.

As it was, my mother was never without a man in her life. She never broke up with one until she had another one waiting in line. And even then, she never seemed to make a clean break; she just sort of slid out the back door, stopped taking their calls.

Apparently, she'd now opened the door to Turk.

I was sitting at the kitchen table, eating my breakfast cereal and reading the Sunday funny papers, when Marla waltzed into the kitchen, wrapped in her silk kimono and towing a tousled and sleepy-looking Turk behind her. She had him sit in a chair across from me at the table and turned to get the coffeemaker started.

"Here you go, sweetie," she chirped to him, flashing a coy smile. "I'll have us some coffee ready in two shakes of a lamb's tail!"

I glanced up as Turk sat down.

"Morning," was all he got out, as what I can only characterize as a shit-eating grin spread over his face. He cocked his head sideways, squinted one eye closed, and peered at me.

"Britney, right?" he asked.

I nodded.

He'd put his rumpled shirt on, but hadn't buttoned it; it hung open just enough to reveal his smooth, well-muscled chest. I had a hard time taking my eyes off it.

He caught me looking, and seemed to enjoy it. His grin broadened.

Catching myself, I jerked my eyes up to meet his, deeply embarrassed. His eyes locked on mine in a sly, smiling kind of way that made me catch my breath.

Turk looked like he could read my mind. I felt almost naked under his gaze.

I dropped the comics to the table and jumped up, grabbing my cereal bowl and plopping it in the sink.

"You finished?" Marla asked as she glanced in my direction.

I didn't want her to see the look on my face. I was afraid she'd read my mind, too. "Yeah," I muttered, head down, and left the kitchen.

As I crossed the living room, I could hear Turk saying to her, "I hope I didn't make her too uncomfortable, Marla. Maybe I should've left last night."

"Oh, don't be silly," Marla answered. "She's a big girl."

Turk began staying over every weekend after that, and some weeknights. too. Marla hadn't let anyone come this close to moving in before that I could remember. Turk's razor and aftershave took up permanent residence on the shelf above the bathroom sink. His laundry began to show up in our dirty clothes hamper, mingled with Marla's and mine. And thick, juicy T-bone steaks, a previously very rare treat in our household, started appearing in the fridge on a regular basis, along with a steady supply of Dos Equis beer.

When two stout beer mugs turned up chilling in our freezer, I knew Marla was really putting on the dog for this guy. And from the sounds I heard coming from her bedroom and the smile on her face, I had to assume that Turk Raiford was well worth it. Maybe that's not the sort of thing you'd expect to hear from someone's seventeen-year-old daughter, but you have to remember: Ours was hardly your average mother/daughter relationship.

Turk was kind of quiet, but he teased me a good bit when I was around him. He'd give me these "looks" on the sly, or put his arm around me and squeeze me, asking if I had any idea what a beauty I was turning into, and saying that I might be even prettier than Marla one day. Sometimes, he'd wrap his hand in my long, black hair and tell me that he thought the gold flecks in my hazel eyes were fascinating.

But I noticed that he never said any of that when Marla was around. It was like our little secret, something just between Turk and me. It made me feel kind of special. At least, special to Turk.

Then, one Friday night, I came home from a date to find Marla sitting in the dark living room alone, smoking pot and sipping on a toddy. I knew right away that something big was wrong because Marla only smoked pot when she was really upset.

"What's going on?" I asked, turning on the lamp by the sofa.

She cringed and shielded her eyes from the sudden light. Her eye makeup was all smeared and streaked from obvious tears, though she wasn't crying anymore.

"Marla? Are you okay?" I asked.

"Ha!" she replied. "I'm not okay right now, but I soon will be," was all she offered.

Her voice had a bitter ring to it, so I figured nothing terrible had happened to anybody in the family, but then again, I had no idea what *had* happened. Anyway, I supposed that if she wanted to talk about it, she would. And, sure enough, after a brief silence, she began to open up.

"That son of a bitch," she muttered. "Here I've opened my heart and my home to him, and what does he do? One minute he's telling me he's in love with me—that I'm the best thing that's ever happened to him—and the next, he's out making time with any cheap whore he can pick up! The bastard!"

"What are you talking about?" I asked.

"That damned Turk Raiford! He was out with Heather James tonight!" she practically yelled at me.

"How do you know?"

"Oh, I know, all right! When he didn't show up or even call tonight, I got this gut feeling. I went over to the Creedmore Lounge, just to see. Well, I saw, okay! I saw that son of a bitch, drunk as a skunk, come out the door with his arm around that bitch. Then he got in her car and drove off with her!"

Marla was silent for a minute, the wheels obviously turning in her head. "Well, we'll see about that! We'll see, all right!"

"Uh . . .you wanna watch some TV?" I asked lamely. I didn't have a clue as to what to do or say. This was a new one for me; I couldn't even remember Marla ever getting dumped on by a guy before. It was usually the other way around. Marla was not one to let a guy get the upper hand on her.

"No," she replied. "No . . . but come with me!" She jumped up suddenly, nearly spilling her drink.

"Where?" I asked.

"To the Creedmore. I wanna see if he comes back there—or if he stays with that filthy whore!"

She grabbed my arm and steered me toward the door. Then: "Wait a minute! Let me fix my makeup!"

I tried to act as nonchalant as possible as we walked into the Creedmore. We got carded at the door, and Marla was somewhere between pleased and irritated when it became hard to convince the bouncer that she truly was my mother. Anyway, she got through to him and he let us in.

This wasn't the first time I'd been in a bar with her, but I was a little worried about what would happen if we did, indeed, catch Turk up to "studly" pursuits. Marla acted all feminine and girlish, but, boy—did she have a temper when she was crossed! And if she caught Turk in what she considered a double cross, I knew there might be quite a scene.

After cruising the room a bit, checking to see if he was there, we sat at a table that gave us a good view of the door. If he came in, he probably wouldn't see us, but there was no way we could miss him.

Marla sat there in stony silence, sipping a margarita while I nursed a Coke. About thirty minutes had passed when the door opened and Heather appeared, followed closely behind by Turk. As they moved into the room, I could clearly see his hand rubbing around on her back in a very familiar way. Glancing at Marla, I saw her watching them. She was completely calm. I, on the other hand, was astonished by the jolt of jealousy that shot through me when I saw Turk touching that woman like that.

We sat there for what seemed like hours, but must've been no more than twenty minutes. You'd have thought Turk's head would have exploded from the heat of our stares boring into him. Neither one of us took our eyes off him until Marla suddenly nudged my arm and jumped up, muttering, "Let's get out of here."

The silence in the car on the way home was palpable. I don't know what Marla was thinking, but I was wrestling with some very confusing emotions. I hadn't thought that I cared one way or the other about Turk; I'd figured he was just another one of Marla's boyfriends—nothing to me. But the burning in my gut was telling me something entirely different all of a sudden.

The next afternoon, good old Larry was sitting in our living room, waiting for Marla to finish getting ready so they could go out. It never ceased to amaze me the way Marla could just twitch her little finger and some guy would jump right to attention. Then they were off to the races. Literally. It seemed Marla had a sudden yen to make a little trip down to the track to watch the horse races. This would involve an overnight trip. Larry was summoned and they were gone, almost before you could shake a stick.

I didn't have a date for that night, but rather, decided to stay home and watch a movie, rather than go and stay with Aunt Barb and Uncle John. I wasn't too crazy about Uncle John; I'd caught him over at our house quite a few times without Aunt Barb . . . sniffing around Marla. Marla was twinkling back at him, just as if he wasn't married to her very own sister. Needless to say, I could do without "Uncle" John.

I ordered a pizza, stripped down, pulled on my "lounging around" outfit, which amounted to an ankle-length T-shirt, put *Legends of the Fall* in the VCR and proceeded to veg out. I was appreciating Brad Pitt's fine body in a love scene when there came a knock at the door.

Before I could get up, the door opened and Turk walked in, finding me sprawled out on a blanket in front of the TV. I upset the bowl of popcorn as I rolled over onto my back and propped up on my elbows, caught completely off guard. He grinned his sly, secret grin as his eyes roved over me.

"Hi, beauty. What's up?" he asked.

"Turk!" I exclaimed in my surprise. I hadn't even realized that the door was unlocked, much less expected him to walk in.

"Where's Marla?" he asked, still not taking his eyes off me.

"Ah, um, well—Marla went to the races," I said, trying not to give too much away.

"Oh yeah?"

"Yeah."

"By herself?"

"Well . . . uh, no."

"Well?"

"Well . . . what?"

"Well . . . who's she with?"

"Uh, an old friend."

"Well, how about I wait for her here, then?"

"She won't be back until tomorrow evening."

"Cool," he replied. "Hey, it wouldn't bother you if I stayed the night, would it? I mean, it's not like I haven't spent the night here before, right? My apartment's being fumigated."

"Well, I . . . guess it would be okay," I conceded awkwardly.

"Great, thanks!" he said, and plopped down on the sofa. "Whatcha watching? Looks good. Say, how about a beer?"

I got up and went to the kitchen to get his beer. I was standing at the counter by the fridge, carefully pouring the golden liquid into one of the frosted mugs, when I felt Turk behind me.

As he pressed against me, I nearly melted. His firm body was so warm against mine, I was almost burning up. Then he slid his arms around me and, with a sudden movement, jerked me back hard against him. I felt light-headed; I couldn't help swaying slightly in his arms. The beer ran over, white foam sliding down the sides of the mug and onto the countertop. Turk's hands reached around to cup my breasts, naked beneath my T-shirt; my hand went limp and I dropped the bottle.

He held both my breasts in his big, warm palms, teasing the nipples till they were rock hard; then one hand slid down my belly, searching. He turned me around to face him and bent to kiss my neck. He nibbled and kissed all the way up my throat and chin to my mouth, then back down again. He stretched the neck of my T-shirt and pulled it down below my breasts, baring them in the harsh, overhead light. I closed my eyes as I felt his hot mouth on me, sucking hard at my stiffened nipples.

It wasn't my first time, but it was the first time I had it done right. I was almost out of my head with passion when he lifted me onto the kitchen table and thrust himself into me.

Much later, we lay side by side on my bed, exhausted, satiated. I hadn't known that lovemaking could be so good. No silly teenage boy could hold a candle to this man. Now I knew why I heard those moans coming from Marla's room in the night. I rolled over and gazed into his face. Turk opened one eye, and my heart fell into its chocolate depths.

"Penny for your thoughts," he murmured, smiling smugly.

He wrapped his strong arms around me and I laid my head against his smooth, brown chest and drifted off into the deepest sleep I'd ever known.

Sunlight streaming in through my bedroom window onto my face woke me. Turk was still sound asleep as I stretched and kissed him tenderly. He woke suddenly.

"What time is it?"

He jumped up, grabbed his clothes off the floor, and headed for the shower. It was still early, and I didn't see what his hurry was. I didn't remember him bounding out in such a hurry all the other mornings he'd spent here before.

When he got out of the shower, he hardly took time to drink a cup of the coffee I'd made him before setting out to get rid of any evidence of our wild night together. He said he didn't want anything that would give us away lying around when Marla got home.

"And why is that?" I challenged, suddenly feeling a burning, roiling sensation in the pit of my stomach.

"Are you serious?" He looked at me like I'd just come from Mars.

"Well . . . yeah. I mean, what does it matter? She's with old Larry."

"Britney." He stood stock-still, his hands on his hips and an incredulous look on his face. "You're not even eighteen yet! You're still underage! And I don't think your mother's gonna be too understanding if she ever finds out about us."

"Screw Marla!" I spat. I wanted Turk. And I didn't care who liked or didn't like it.

"No, Britney—it doesn't work that way. We have to keep this quiet until you're eighteen. You don't get it, do you? I could go to jail, and Marla could have you sent away!" he exclaimed.

I didn't want to hear it. I didn't care. But, to keep him happy, I'd have to go along with him . . . for now.

Turk was sitting on the sofa, drinking and watching TV, and I was in my room, pouting, when Marla came home that evening. Earlier in the evening, I'd tried to get Turk all heated up again, as I could barely stand to be in the same room with him without wanting his hands all over me. But he wouldn't go for it. He said we'd just have to be good for a while. I yelled at him to go home then, but he said it would be better if he were here waiting when old Larry brought Marla home.

So, there we were when Marla opened the front door and took her bags from Larry. She wouldn't even let him set a foot inside. In fact, she almost shut the door in his face.

Do you suppose he had even an inkling of how he'd been used?

Turk just sat there, cool as a breeze, watching her levelly, and looking for all the world like the injured party. And it worked; Marla was really flustered. Turk played his cards close to his vest and kept her guessing. She tried to bluff him, but failed. And I just sat in my room feeling jealous and angry.

During the next week, Marla and Turk engaged in something of a hit-and-run battle. That first night she was back, she didn't have much to say to him, nor he to her. He went home about an hour later. I stayed in my room, waiting to see if he'd come to tell me good-bye.

He didn't.

It hurt and made me mad. If he knew what was good for him, he'd do better than that in the future. It wasn't that long until my eighteenth birthday, after all, but I wasn't sure I could stand to wait before coming out in the open about us. So if he wanted me to keep quiet, he'd better pay more attention to me and not try to shove me on the back burner.

Then that Thursday morning, I got up late and was rushing around getting ready for school when I saw it—Turk's hand-tooled leather belt—on the floor beside the sofa. My eyes darted from it to Marla's bedroom door, which was shut tight. My stomach churned as I realized what was going on; Turk had evidently come in the middle of the night, and tried to hide all evidence of himself until I was safely on my way to school.

But he'd missed the belt.

I stood there, steaming. Well, there was nothing I could really do right then, short of bursting into the bedroom and confronting him. But even in my state, I realized that probably wouldn't be a good move. So, I swallowed my anger and went off to school. I would have to think about the situation later.

Still, despite my good intentions, all day long, images of Turk and Marla rolling around naked on her bed together kept ricocheting around in my head. It went on like that all weekend, too, though I tried to spend all my free time with my friends, away from the house. Finally, Monday night, I told Marla that I needed to go to the library and study, and that I'd pick up a hamburger on the way. I already knew Turk wasn't coming over that evening, because I'd come right out and asked her.

When she answered, "No," a plan had formed almost instantaneously in my besotted brain.

Well, sort of a plan, anyway.

What I did was go directly to Turk's apartment and bang on the door, yelling for him to let me in. He jerked the door open after a few minutes and grabbed me by the arm, pulling me in as he leaned out into the hallway and looked around to see whether or not I'd drawn a crowd yet. He pulled me into his living room and slammed the door.

"What the hell are you trying to do?" he yelled at me.

"Nothing! I just wanted to see you!" I cried.

"Britney, we can't do this—not right now, anyway. Don't you understand?"

Turk almost seemed to be pleading with me. I sensed his control slipping. I grasped his hand and thrust it under my sweater to cup my bare breast, then pressed against him tightly, swaying gently into his hard, lean body.

"Oh, please, Turk—*please*! You know it's special with us—you know it's the best!" I gasped, my breathing becoming ragged as his fingertips stroked my stiffening nipple.

I pulled him forward to my waiting lips. As I kissed him passionately, I moved my other hand from his and let it roam downward, feeling for a hint of my effect on him through his jeans.

Oh, my—*yes*! He wanted me. He was ready for me.

He removed his hand from my breast and reached to slip my sweater off over my head, dropping it to the floor. We unfastened each other's jeans, fumbling in our haste. He pulled at his shirt, popping all the snaps open; it was off his body in one motion.

We sank to the floor, groping and kissing, consumed by our passion. Turk pushed himself deep inside of me, all the way in, and thrust wildly, stroking hard till we were both swept up into that moment of absolute Nirvana.

Then, as he arched his back in a great, final thrust, he called out, "Marla, oh—*ohhhhhhhhhhhhh*!"

"What?" I yelled at him.

"I mean—Britney—"

"What?" I yelled at him. "What did you call me?"

"Britney—I called you Britney. . . ." he panted, falling limply beside me.

"No, you didn't—you called me Marla! You bastard! You called my mother's name!" I screamed. I reached over and slapped him as hard as I could. He grabbed my wrist and held me tightly.

"No—I didn't, baby," he crooned, "you're imagining things." He pulled my head down onto his warm chest and stroked my hair. "Shush, now."

The anger slowly melted from me as the spicy smell of his skin filled me. Perhaps he was right; perhaps I *had* imagined it. I lay there in his arms, soaking up the tenderness.

Turk was at our house the next night . . . and every night thereafter for a week. He always slept behind Marla's closed bedroom door, though he would send secret signals to me with those velvet-brown eyes of his. We finally had a few minutes alone one afternoon when Marla had to run to the grocery store for some last-minute stuff. I flung my arms around him and reached for a kiss. His arms enfolded me gently, but he avoided my lips.

"We can't, baby," he said with a catch in his voice.

"Sure we can. She'll be gone for at least an hour, trust me."

"No, Brit—you don't understand," he went on.

"Don't understand what?"

"About us . . . your mother and me."

"What about you?"

"We—we're going to get married, Brit," he said.

The words didn't register for a minute, but when they did, I thought I'd faint.

"What did you say?" I asked incredulously.

"Marla and I are going to get married, Brit . . . we have to. She's— Marla's pregnant."

The words spilled out with electric effect. I could hardly believe my ears. Then, all of a sudden, hurt and anger flooded through me.

"Pregnant? You son of a bitch! How could that happen? She's been screwing around all these years and she never got pregnant before! How did it happen?"

Then it dawned on me. She'd been asking little questions of Turk— like how I felt about him. Feeling me out. I figured she'd guessed something was afoot, and taken steps to nail him down for herself. That would sound about right for Marla.

"You idiot!" I screamed at him, pounding his chest with my fists. "You poor, stupid idiot! She did it on purpose!"

The look on Turk's face told me he'd had his own suspicions about that.

"Well, it's done, now," he said quietly, tiredly. "And she won't even *consider* an abortion. So I guess there's only one thing to do."

"No, there's not just one thing to do!" I yelled. "Let her have her baby! Let her take the responsibility! She did it—so let *her* take care of it! You can't let this come between us, Turk!"

"Britney, I want you more than you can know, and I always will. But, I can't do that. I grew up without a father and so did you, so you know how hard that is. I'm not going to do that to my kid."

"Oh, Turk!" I started sobbing as I melted into his strong embrace.

"Britney, I'll always be here for you, no matter what," he said gently.

"Oh, sure!" I wailed.

"I will, I promise," he whispered as he stroked my hair and held me against him.

Then I heard a car door close outside; I realized Marla was home. I ran to the bathroom, splashed cold water on my face, and grabbed a wet washcloth. I holed up for the rest of the night in my room on my bed with the washcloth on my forehead. I wasn't faking; I had a splitting headache.

To say the atmosphere around that house was strained afterward would be putting it mildly. Marla and Turk were married three weeks later, and he moved in for good. Marla was either throwing up or nauseated beyond belief for the next three months straight. She couldn't stand cooking smells, and when she ate, right back up it would come.

I don't see how she managed to gain any weight, but she ballooned. By her fifth month, the doctor told her that she'd gained all she needed to for the whole pregnancy. But there was no way to avoid it. I mean, she couldn't exactly go on a diet. Then her face broke out. She'd never even had acne when she was a teenager, so she was beside herself with the problem. For a woman who'd looked good all her life, even through her first pregnancy, Marla was a sad sight.

With that, and what with feeling so sick, she developed the disposition of a wounded animal. The voices I heard through the bedroom wall at night were now yelling, not making love. And each time I'd catch Turk looking at me, an aching pain would shoot through my heart. We were trying so hard to be good.

In her eighth month, Marla decided to go on a short trip with Aunt Barb to Kansas City to do some baby shopping. We all agreed that the break would probably do her a lot of good. The night after they left, I was holed up in my bedroom, studying, when my stomach told me it was time to investigate the aromas coming from the kitchen.

There stood Turk, an apron around his waist, slicing and dicing away at a pile of tomatoes, onions, and garlic. He would get some all chopped up, then dump them into the big skillet that was sizzling on the stove. It smelled heavenly. This was a side of Turk Raiford that I hadn't seen before. I could smell garlic toast in the oven, and spaghetti was boiling in a large pot on the front burner. He glanced up as I entered the kitchen.

"Hi, beautiful! How about grabbing that strainer and putting it in the sink? I need to drain the spaghetti. Then, just a few finishing touches and we'll be ready to feast! You do like Italian, don't you?"

It was unbelievable. He'd cooked the best pasta dish I'd ever tasted. We even had a nice bottle of wine to go with it. First class, all the way.

We were sitting at the table, finishing the last of the wine, when my leg accidentally brushed up against his. I don't know what happened, but I was paralyzed; I couldn't move my leg away. It just kept pressing against his as the heat of his flesh burned through the denim of his jeans. His eyes met mine and we both stopped breathing. It seemed like time had come to a standstill, and there was only the two of us in the world.

"Oh. . . ." escaped from my lips as he reached out and brushed his fingertips across them.

In minutes, we were on my bed. I don't remember going there; we just seemed to end up in my room. We were naked together. The warm, dark smoothness of his belly rubbed against mine. His mouth was hot on my skin. The manly strength of him held me fast. Wave after wave of passion rolled through us until we lay, exhausted, in each other's arms.

Then we heard it—

Marla's voice calling: "Anybody home?"

She and Aunt Barb hadn't gotten all the way to Kansas City before Marla started feeling too sick to continue on. They'd turned around and come back.

Then she must've seen our clothes strewn across the living room floor.

"Turk? Where are you? What's going on?"

The words had barely left her lips when she followed the trail to my bedroom door. Turk was leaping out of the bed and I was grabbing for the sheet to cover myself.

Marla froze in the doorway, a look of disbelief, hurt, and outrage all rolled into one on her face.

"You bastard!" she screamed as Turk stood there, naked, his mouth hanging open.

Marla lunged at him, fists flying, screaming, "You filthy bastard! You worthless son of a bitch! How *could* you?"

Turk was trying to fend off her blows and catch her arms when she kneed him in the groin as hard as she could. He crumpled to the floor with a yelp of pain. She landed a kick in his back as she headed for me. I was trying to wrap the sheet around me and climb out of the bed all at once. Marla made it around the bed before I could get away. She wrapped my hair in her fist and jerked my head back, then slapped me so hard that I saw stars.

"Mama!" I sobbed.

"Don't you 'Mama' me, you little tramp! I'm not your 'Mama' anymore! How could you *do* this? You little bitch!" she screamed as she pummeled me with slaps.

I was curled up in a corner trying to ward off her blows when she finally quit in exhaustion. Turk still lay on the floor, all doubled over, clutching his privates with both hands.

Marla lurched to the doorway, then turned back toward us as she leaned, staggering, against the doorjamb.

"Get out of my house! Both of you! Get out right now and don't ever try to come back!"

Turk was beginning to recover. He tried to stand and follow her out of the room. She picked up his jeans and flung them in his face.

"Get out, you bastard!"

"Marla, wait a minute! Let me talk to you! Don't make me leave—I want to be with you and the baby! I don't know how this happened—

I'm sorry! Marla, please!"

He was begging. I couldn't believe my ears.

Then I could hear Marla crying, and Turk talking in that, "Aw, baby" tone they all use when they've been caught with their pants down and are trying to wheedle their way out. I peeked out the door to see them standing in the middle of the living room, Marla's face buried in Turk's chest, his arms around her and his face bent down to hers. His voice was soothing, placating. Marla was hysterical to the point of hiccups.

It broke my heart. I closed the door to my room, got dressed, and straightened up the bed. I was just sitting there in the dark when Marla opened my door and, in an icy tone, told me to get some things together; Aunt Barb was coming for me.

I didn't say a word, just got my duffel bag out of the closet and started putting clothes into it. I just felt sort of numb.

After awhile, Aunt Barb came into my room.

"Where's your stuff?" she asked bluntly.

I motioned to my bag.

"Then come on," she said, "we need to get out of here now." She grabbed my bag and motioned with her head for me to come on, then headed through the living room to the front door.

I couldn't seem to raise my head as I left, but out of the corner of my eye, I saw Turk sitting at the kitchen table, his head hanging, and Marla sitting like a stone on the sofa, her arms crossed over her swollen belly, glaring at me.

Well, I was to stay with Aunt Barb for an indefinite period. Turk got thrown out, too, but I didn't know where he was staying. Marla refused to take his calls, from what I overheard Aunt Barb telling Uncle John.

Then, about three weeks later, I missed my period. Talk about mixed emotions! I was upset, but also glad. Ashamed, but proud. I had to get hold of Turk. This would do it. This would make him mine for good!

As soon as I could, I went to a pay phone and called his work. When the receptionist asked who was calling, I told her it was a family emergency. That did it. When I heard his voice, my heart melted into my shoes. I could barely speak.

Finally, I managed, "Turk, this is Britney. I've got to talk to you! Meet me at the Sandwich Shoppe as soon as you get off work."

"Britney, I don't think that would be a good idea," he said uneasily.

"But, you've got to! It's really important! Please!" I cried.

There was a long silence on the other end of the line. Then: "Okay. Just this time," he said resignedly.

"As soon as you get off!"

"Okay."

Then he hung up.

I sat in the Sandwich Shoppe waiting, hugging my secret to myself. It wouldn't be long; soon, everything would work out right. Turk and I would be together. Marla wasn't going to take him back, anyway. She wouldn't even talk to him! And I wanted him more than I'd ever known it was possible to want someone.

When he walked in the door, my heart lurched. I was so excited and happy, I knew he would be, too. I could hardly wait until he sat down before I grabbed his hand and held it tightly in both of mine, wanting, actually to pull him across the table into my arms.

"Turk! I've got the best news!" I gushed.

He looked at me, puzzled, confused.

"I'm pregnant!"

The look that came over his face froze my heart in mid-beat. He didn't look happy at all. He looked like he'd just witnessed a train wreck.

"Oh, God," was all he said, as his head rolled back and he closed his eyes and pulled his hand away from mine.

"Turk! Aren't you happy?" I was dismayed.

"Happy? Are you sure? You're not sure, are you?" he asked anxiously.

"Well, my period's eight days late. That's never happened before. Turk, aren't you pleased?"

"God, Britney! I never meant for anything like this to happen. I'm so sorry." He inhaled deeply and looked toward the heavens. "What do I do now?"

It was a rhetorical question. He didn't want to hear my answer, that was for sure.

"Don't you want me?" My voice came out quiet and small. At first, I didn't even realize it was mine; I thought some little girl was behind me, talking.

"Oh, Brit, baby—I love you! But it can't be like that for us—not with your mother and the baby. . . ." He didn't finish the sentence. "It would just never—work out!"

"But, we'll have our *own* baby! You and me! It'll be wonderful, Turk—you'll see!" I was beginning to break down, but I didn't care who saw.

"Brit . . . Brit, don't. . . ."

He tried to stop me. Then he got up and reached for me, lifting me to my feet, putting his arm around me and holding me close as he took me outside to his pickup. He opened the door and helped me in. As he slid in behind the wheel, I scooted over and wrapped my arms around him, tears streaming down my cheeks. I reached to unbutton his shirt and slide my hand inside. He grabbed my hand and stopped me.

"Britney, no. We can't do that anymore. Stop."

He wasn't having any of it. He wasn't going to give an inch. I jerked my hand back and slid over against my door, where I huddled, miserable and angry.

He would be sorry! I *would* get my way! He was mine now, and the sooner he realized it, the better for all concerned.

Without another word, he drove me to Aunt Barb's and parked out front. He reached across me then and opened my door.

He wouldn't even look at me!

"Get out, Brit. I'll call you when I figure out something," was all he said.

I opened my mouth to tell him what a fool he was being, but nothing came out. I just got out of the truck and went inside.

That night, about eleven o'clock, Aunt Barb got a call. Marla was in labor. Aunt Barb left to take her to the hospital, but not before she dialed another number.

"Marla just called. It's time," I heard her say. Then she hung up.

I was pretty sure who was on the other end of the line.

I couldn't help myself. The next day, I walked quietly into the maternity wing of the hospital. There were a couple of newborns in the nursery, but none with the name *Raiford* on the crib.

I asked which room Marla was in, then crept down the hall to it. The door was ajar, and through it, I could see Marla sitting up in bed, cradling a tiny bundle in her arms with a head full of coal-black hair. Turk sat on the edge of the bed, and they were both making eyes over the baby.

Then, as I watched, they looked into each other's eyes, leaned across the baby, and kissed. A long and tender kiss. Then tears began to roll down Marla's face, and I knew.

It was like an icy knife run through my heart.

I left as quietly as I'd come, and didn't look back.

I was like a robot the next few days; I just went through the motions of living. I couldn't think; I couldn't feel. I felt absolutely nothing when Aunt Barb told me that I had a little brother. And the only thing I felt when my period started, two weeks late, was relief.

When school is out, and I've graduated, I'm moving to Topeka. I have a friend who lives there, someone who graduated last year. She says she can get me a job at the restaurant where she works. It's a real nice place. And I can share her apartment for half the rent. I think it'll be good for me to get out of town. For a while, at least.

Yesterday, I bought the cutest little blue-and-yellow jumper suit, in a zero-to-six-month size. I wrapped it nicely and gave it to Aunt Barb to take over there.

Maybe someday I'll see him. THE END